den. And of course tl
made yesterday morr

As always, Sophie
was like her Tante Isabelle in that way—a girl who couldn't hold her tongue.

When at last they came to dessert—*île flottante,* islands of toasted meringue floating in a rich crème anglaise—there was a satisfied silence around the table.

"Well," Viann said at last, pushing her half empty dessert plate away, "It's time to do the dishes."

"Ahh, Maman," Sophie whined.

"No whining," Antoine said. "Not at your age."

Viann and Sophie went into the kitchen, as they did each night, to their stations—Viann at the deep copper sink, Sophie at the stone counter—and began washing and drying the dishes. Viann could smell the sweet, sharp scent of Antoine's after-supper cigarette wafting through the house.

"Papa didn't laugh at a single one of my stories today," Sophie said as Viann placed the dishes back in the rough wooden racks that hung on the wall. "Something is wrong with him."

"No laughter? Well, certainly that *is* cause for alarm."

"He's worried about the war."

The war. Again.

Viann shooed her daughter out of the kitchen. Upstairs, in Sophie's bedroom, Viann sat on the double bed, listening to her daughter chatter as she put on her pajamas and brushed her teeth and got into bed.

Viann leaned down to kiss her good night.

"I'm scared," Sophie said quietly. "Is war coming?"

"Don't be afraid," Viann said. "Papa will protect us," but even as she said it, she remembered another time, when her maman had said to her, *Don't be afraid*.

It was when her own father had gone off to war.

Sophie looked unconvinced. "But—"

"But nothing. There is nothing to worry about. Now go to sleep."

She kissed her daughter again, letting her lips linger on the little girl's cheek.

Viann went down the stairs and headed for the backyard. Outside, the night was sultry; the air smelled of jasmine. She found Antoine sitting in one of the iron café chairs out on the grass, his legs stretched out, his body slumped uncomfortably to one side.

She came up beside him, put a hand on his shoulder. He exhaled smoke and took another long drag on the cigarette. Then he looked up at her. In the moonlight, his face appeared pale and shadowed. Almost unfamiliar. He reached into the pocket of his vest and pulled out a piece of paper. "I have been mobilized, Viann. Along with most men between eighteen and thirty-five."

"Mobilized? But . . . we are not at war. I don't—"

"I am to report for duty on Tuesday."

"But . . . but . . . you're a postman."

He held her gaze and suddenly she couldn't breathe. "I am a soldier now, it seems."

ABOUT THE AUTHOR

KRISTIN HANNAH is the #1 *New York Times* bestselling author of many acclaimed novels, including *The Great Alone*, *The Nightingale*, and *Magic Hour*. She and her husband live in the Pacific Northwest.

KristinHannah.com
Facebook.com/AuthorKristinHannah
Instagram: @kristinhannahauthor

Echoes of Sin

Touch of Evil - Book Eight

Kennedy Layne

Kennedy Layne Publishing, Inc.

Cover Designer: Sweet 'N Spicy Designs

Dedication

Jeffrey & Cole — I love you both so much!

Contents

Chapter One

Brooklyn Sloane

August 2010

Wednesday — 7:52am

College.

Senior year.

The campus hummed with a myriad of emotions as students and teachers rushed by one another to reach their first class of the day. It was the start of a new year, and the differences between freshmen and seniors were easily discernable.

Excitement versus relief.

Uncertainty versus pride.

Those experiencing their first day of college were no doubt filled with nervous anticipation. Everything was fresh and unfamiliar. They were embarking on a new chapter in their lives, about to pursue their dreams. Perhaps their palms grew sweaty and their stomachs churned with anxiety. Or maybe questions swirled in their minds, chipping away at their confidences until nothing was left but doubts and fears.

Would they fit into their new roles?

What if they couldn't handle their coursework?

Then there were the seniors, reflecting on the past three years. This final chapter of their lives was coming to an end. While it was normal for them to experience nostalgia, they conceivably held a sense of pride for their accomplishments. There was a sense of serenity in their movements as their familiar routines washed over them. Yet their apprehension for the future would only continue to mount as graduation grew closer.

What did the future hold for them?

Had they been given enough knowledge to survive the world that existed outside of the classroom?

"Hey, Sloane. What do you think about this outfit?"

Brook should have gotten used to hearing her new surname by now. After all, she'd changed it from Walsh to Sloane back in 2007. She'd driven to the courthouse alone, chosen a name at random that had been scribbled on a clipboard, and had legally become someone else three years ago.

Unfortunately, not even a name change could erase her true identity—the sister of a serial killer.

"That's my t-shirt," Brook said wryly after she'd turned away from the one and only window in their dorm room. "And it has a hole in the hem."

"I know," Cara Jordan replied with a smile before pointing toward the small knot that she'd fastened right underneath her left breast. "That's why I made a thot knot. I didn't get the most amazing tan over the summer to hide it. It's perfect, don't you think?"

Brook winced at the adjective Cara had used to describe her sun-kissed skin. Nothing was perfect in this world. Brook turned back to the window so her roommate wouldn't notice her reaction. There were moments when Cara reminded Brook so much of her best friend in high school, but she always did her best to push the comparisons aside. The last time Brook had seen Sally Pearson was the day that she'd bled out in an Illinois cornfield.

"A thot knot?" Brook asked after she was able to find her voice. There had been some very dark days in her past as she'd tried to come to terms with her role in Sally's death. Only there was no coming to terms with anything. Brook had been a bystander in her brother's crimes, and her lack of action meant that she was just as guilty as her brother. "Did you make up that term?"

"No," Cara replied as she walked over to her jewelry box. Brook could faintly make out her friend in the reflection of the window as she tilted her head to the side to study her choices. "I heard Misty call it that yesterday. I never even knew tying a knot in a t-shirt had a name. Go figure."

"Wear the blue feathered earrings," Brook advised before Cara could ask for another opinion. She tended to always ask which earrings looked better with each outfit. "The color of the feathers goes better with the lettering on the t-shirt."

Brook refocused her gaze before scanning the heart of campus one more time.

She'd been uneasy lately, but she hadn't been able to figure out why. Maybe it was because she'd gone back home for a visit. Spending time with her parents after what had happened with Sally three years ago was always hard. It hadn't helped that Brook thought she'd seen someone watching her while placing flowers on Sally's grave. Whoever it was had been too far away to make an identification. She'd even mentioned it to Chief Conway when she'd stopped by the police station to see if there had been any updates on her brother.

Jacob Matthew Walsh.

Her own personal brush with evil, and one that had stained her soul. She fought every day not to buckle underneath the weight of her guilt.

Brook had only been ten years old when she'd noticed there was something wrong with Jacob. He'd somehow changed without anyone noticing but her. It wasn't that she hadn't tried to bring up her concerns with her parents. Each and every comment had been brushed off with an excuse.

After all, who wanted to admit that their brother, son, or friend was a psychopath?

She'd often wondered how two siblings could grow up in the same household with the same parents in the same town...and yet turn out so differently. Her unanswered questions were the main reason that she'd chosen psychology as a major. She wasn't so sure she would find her answers by the end of her senior year, though.

"We have less than five minutes to get to class," Cara called out from across the room. She was standing by the door with a thick textbook and a red notebook in hand. "You've been standing next to that window for the past half hour. Did you hook up with someone over the summer? Are you holding out on me?"

"No," Brook replied as she let the curtain drop. She managed a smile, not wanting Cara to think anything was wrong. "I just wanted to see what everyone was wearing. Looks like your thot knot is the new trend, by the way."

It would serve no purpose to anyone if her roommate and classmates knew about Jacob. He'd left their hometown before the police could apprehend him, and Chief Conway had alleged that her brother would never show his face again for fear of being arrested.

Brook wasn't so sure about his assumption.

Once the truth had come out, she'd shared with her parents and the police her thoughts about Jacob. She'd even told them of the disturbing drawings that she'd discovered one day in her brother's bedroom of Pamela Murray, the female student whose body had eventually been found about a year after she'd gone missing. Everyone seemed to believe that Jacob was merely a sick individual who would eventually get caught, but she knew differently.

Her brother was a monster.

Jacob was extremely intelligent, and there was no telling where he was or what he might be doing. He'd warned her that he wouldn't allow her to be the normal one, which she took to mean that he would eventually come after her. She'd relayed the intent to Chief Conway and her parents, but they didn't seem concerned that her brother would follow through with his promise.

"Sloane, are you coming or not?"

"Yes," Brook replied as she walked over to her side of the room. She picked up the textbook for her morning class and then randomly chose one of the numerous notebooks that she'd picked up at an office supply store. "Let me grab a few pencils."

Once she had everything in hand, she picked up the travel mug of coffee that she'd poured around fifteen minutes ago. The caffeinated beverage kept her sharp, and she needed every possible edge imaginable. She should have trusted her instincts when she was younger, and she wouldn't make the same mistake twice.

Something told her that Jacob was nearby...watching her from afar.

Brook couldn't give a reasonable explanation as to why she was more restless than usual. Her mother thought it was due to Brook's inability to get more than three or four hours of sleep on any given night. Her father mentioned that it was because she spent more time studying than socializing with friends. Neither one of them seemed to grasp that she no longer had a normal life.

Was that why Jacob had returned to check on her?

Had he wanted to make sure his last wish had been granted?

There was no denying that Jacob had succeeded in making sure that there was nothing normal about her life. She could only hope that once he'd seen his accomplishment for himself, he would either leave for good or get caught by the police.

"Let's go," Brook said as she pasted another smile on her face. She could manage to keep up appearances for their senior year. "Remember, I'll be in the library most of the evening. I want to get a head start on this semester's course material."

As Brook closed the door and made sure that it was locked, a group of girls passed them as they walked down the hallway. They were laughing and debating about which sorority party to hit later this evening, with one of the sororities being a little higher on the list. One of the girls asked Cara if she would be there, and her roommate responded that she'd be too busy hopping some of the frat parties instead.

"This is it, Sloane," Cara said as she hooked her hand through Brook's arm. "Our senior year. Life can't get more perfect than this!"

Brook once again winced upon hearing Cara's chosen word for the day.

Jacob had killed Pamela, Sally, and who knows how many other young women due to their belief that their lives were perfect. While he wasn't around to hear Cara say something similar, Brook couldn't help but be affected by her brother's twisted logic.

She wanted to warn Cara not to take her youth, beauty, and blessings for granted, because it could all be taken away in the blink of an eye. Unfortunately, she couldn't do so without revealing the graphic details of her past. Seeing as there was no reason that Cara should walk around her daily life being afraid of every moving shadow, Brook kept to herself what she knew to be the truth—evil touched their lives every single day.

Chapter Two

Brooklyn Sloane

October 2023

Thursday — 4:11pm

A musty, stale scent of age and neglect hung in the air of the isolated cabin. Dust particles floated inside the beams of sunlight that were streaming through the sole window where there had once been a white curtain. The few remaining fibers clung to the rusted rod by the merest whispers of life. Where they had once adorned the window in its entirety to prevent intruders from seeing its occupants, they were now as grey and lifeless as ghosts.

The front room was cramped and claustrophobic, barely large enough to accommodate a couch and two chairs. A solid stone fireplace filled up most of the wall to the left of the entrance. The bookshelves on either side were devoid of everything but cobwebs that had been abandoned by their makers long ago. Toward the back of the cabin was a small kitchen space with a six-foot-long counter that had been smothered in a thick layer of dust that had hardened like concrete over time.

"...brought in as a consultant. The federal agents in Charlotte are stretched thin with the domestic terrorism case that's been in the headlines lately, and..."

The one-room cabin had been crafted from Eastern White Pine. The log walls were milky in color, and there were wisps of gossamers that moved in time with the cool breeze that flowed through the open door. Unfortunately, not even the refreshing mountain air could mask the overwhelming stench of death and decay that permeated the room.

"...sunset occurs in three hours. Riggs met the forensics team in town about forty-five minutes ago, but only two of them are able to make the hike. They should be here in..."

Brooklyn Sloane tuned out the numerous conversations that were taking place outside the cabin. She'd wanted a moment alone to cavass the crime scene. From her understanding, an organized search party had discovered the body of a hiker who had gone missing last week.

The woman's remains were already in an advanced state of decay. The only reason that she'd remained upright in the chair were due to the ropes binding her wrists to the spindles behind her. The same had been done with her ankles against the legs of the wooden seat.

The victim's skin was bloated with a purplish tint that only magnified the maggots writhing inside the open wounds. She'd been cut at least a hundred times by the sharp, smooth blade of a knife all over her body. They were clean cuts that had gone right through the fabric of her blood-soaked jeans and shirt. There wasn't one part of her body that hadn't been mutilated by the killer's choice of weapon. His blade hadn't been serrated, and he hadn't shown any hesitancy during the applications.

The hiker's death had been painful, prolonged, violent, and brutal.

Had the unsub chosen a knife due to his ease with such a weapon?

Brook's attention wasn't exclusively focused on the victim. She'd wanted the ability to profile the unsub, aka unknown subject. To do that successfully, she needed to examine every inch of the cabin. Nothing lacked importance, and the slightest disruption could give special insight to the killer.

The hiker's backpack lay a few feet away from her. The zipper remained closed, a canteen hung from a hook on the side, and the contents looked to be intact. Her jacket had been placed between her backpack and the wall. The victim's belongings had been close enough for her to see, yet far enough away that she couldn't reach them.

Had such a strategy been by design or happenstance?

The victim's hiking boots had been removed, presumably to give the killer access to that part of her body. Her blood-soaked socks made it difficult to tell the original color of the fabric. The hardwood floor had absorbed most of the woman's life source as if it had wanted one of its own.

Brook bent down to get a better look at the section of hardwood floor that hadn't been saturated with blood. The floor was scuffed and there was an obvious circular pattern around the victim. The closest place to sit was the couch near the front door, though one of the cushions was missing. Brook got the impression that the unsub hadn't taken advantage of such luxury.

The killer had walked continuously around his victim for hours.

Had he done so to keep his prey guessing as to when and where he would slice into her skin? Or was his reasoning for such incessant motion more personal? Did such repetitiveness sooth him as he worked?

Brook pushed on her knees to stand before she slowly followed the unsub's path, mindful not to disturb anything before the two forensic techs arrived on the scene. The thick blanket of dust on the countertop hadn't been disturbed, the cobwebs displayed on the single cabinet above the counter exhibited no sign of tampering, and there were no marks on the grime of the two remaining couch cushions. The lack of disruption to anything inside the cabin other than the victim indicated that the unsub was methodical and patient.

The murder hadn't been a spur of the moment act.

"...it's been at least forty minutes. I don't know what it is that she—"

"Excuse me," Theo Neville said to prevent one of the park rangers from continuing his statement. "My colleague, Sylvie Deering, needs assistance behind the cabin. Would one of you be able to answer her questions about the terrain?"

It wasn't long before Theo had entered the cabin, though he remained by the doorway. His dark skin contained a thin sheen of sweat at his temples, but it wasn't from being out of shape. Quite the contrary, he was very passionate about his health. He'd offered to be the one to canvass the wooded area surrounding the cabin. Brook wasn't sure if he'd truly discovered something around back or if he'd just wanted to separate the two park rangers.

As for Theo's reasoning for not entering the cabin, such a decision wasn't due to the noxious odor or the disturbing sight of the macabre corpse. He was all too familiar with the process. Less disturbance meant more evidence. Given the dust on the hardwood floor, she'd purposefully kept her own tracks separate from the others.

"Size eleven. Do you notice the break in pattern of the right sole? The unsub has a rock stuck in the tread. That probably won't help us, but you never know. There was also a smudge on the wall behind where he'd set the victim's backpack. Maybe his elbow rubbed against it." Brook began to walk toward Theo, ensuring that her hiking boots had retraced her own steps to the exit. She came to a stop about three feet from the doorway and began to point out the obvious. "No sign of damage to the lock, but I'm assuming a cabin like this one wouldn't be secure. It hasn't been used in years. Notice the disturbance here? The victim was dragged to the chair. She fought her killer."

"Anything else stand out?"

Brook motioned for Theo to exit the cabin. She joined him, but she didn't respond right away. She took a moment to breathe in the fresh mountain air. The temperature hovered in the mid-sixties, so the ninety-minute hike hadn't been too difficult. Seeing as she jogged a couple of miles every day, the long walk hadn't been difficult. She would have preferred to have used a helicopter to save time, but there hadn't been a clear area to land a chopper.

The only way in and out of this region was on foot.

"This wasn't an impromptu abduction or killing of our victim. The unsub wasn't in a rush. He took his time, and he had absolutely no fear of getting caught in the middle of his laborious efforts."

"Personal?"

"I don't know yet."

Brook was struck by the rugged and isolated beauty of the area. They were surrounded by a riot of reds, oranges, yellows, and browns as the leaves had already changed color. At least a quarter of them had already fallen from the branches overhead, covering the forest floor with what appeared to be a colorful blanket. The natural scenery was a welcome change from the hustle and bustle of the city.

"What is the protocol from this point forward?" Park Ranger Erica Ashton asked as she stood to the side and kept her hands inside the pockets of her green coat. Her auburn hair was chin length, and she wore minimal makeup. She'd been professional on the hike, but it was obvious that her curiosity had gotten the best of her. "Will you submit your findings to the FBI before handing off the investigation?"

"No," Brook replied, knowing full well that she'd caught Theo off guard with her response. She hadn't planned on extending their business trip, either. "S&E Investigations will be taking lead on this case, although we would prefer to work alongside your agency. You and your colleagues are familiar with the locals, the surrounding towns, and this terrain. Your insight would be invaluable."

Brook owned and operated S&E Investigations, Inc. with a silent partner. The private investigative firm was based in Washington, D.C. While its mission was to tackle cold cases that had long since been forgotten, giving closure to the family members left behind, S&E Investigations currently maintained a consulting contract with the Federal Bureau of Investigations.

The main reason that Brook had received a call this morning regarding a murder in the Smoky Mountains was due to her and her team wrapping up a cold case in Charlotte, N.C. The underlying justification for their presence was the domestic terrorism case that the other park ranger had mentioned mere minutes ago.

"Of course," Erica replied as she reached for the radio at her side. The black device was clipped to her belt. "I'll notify our supervisor, and he'll assign one of us to be your liaison and guide."

"I'd prefer you," Brook stated without reservation. It was her understanding that there were maybe thirty park rangers for the Smoky Mountains. That was a lot of area to cover with minimal staff. Erica Ashton had been professional, knowledgeable, and she never hesitated to give a valid opinion...unlike her colleague, who had a tendency to complain. "Would you please excuse us for a moment?"

At first, Erica seemed at a loss. It was evident that she didn't want to upset her supervisor, but there was also an underlying excitement in her eyes at being chosen over Park Ranger Hal Egger. Brook wouldn't tolerate an individual who questioned her every decision and criticized the workload. The investigation would be difficult enough without having to deal with a potential liability.

"Yes, of course," Erica replied before she made her way to the edge of the forest. She didn't look back, and her stride was purposeful now that she'd accepted her role. "Base, this is..."

Brook waited patiently for Theo to point out the obvious. She used the time to cleanse the lingering pungent odor from the lining of her nose.

"We've taken active cases before, but usually with ties to a previous investigation," Theo pointed out as he adjusted his beanie hat. The material was meant more for a jogger than a hike in the woods, but it was what he'd brought with him for the trip. He always managed to maintain his daily workouts while in the field. She'd offered to buy him one more appropriate for the cooler temperatures experienced at such a higher elevation, but he'd refused her offer. "Are you sure you want to take on one that could potentially take months—if not years—to close?"

There was another reason that Brook had been comfortable with choosing Erica as their liaison with the park rangers—the woman's interaction with Theo. He'd been injured in the line of duty during his tenure as a federal field agent. The loss of his right eye had resulted in him wearing a black eyepatch and looking at a long future of desk duty until he'd come to work at S&E Investigations. Whereas Hal Egger avoided looking directly at Theo during a conversation, Erica had no such issue.

Brook had known immediately who she'd wanted on her team upon agreeing to establish S&E Investigations. She'd initially chosen three team members who had each brought with them their own set of skills—Theo Neville, Sylvie Deering, and Bobby "Bit" Nowacki.

Theo had been raised by two loving parents who had dedicated their lives to law enforcement. His father was currently the NYPD commissioner, and Theo's mother had been an officer. She'd officially turned in her retirement papers a couple of months ago. Theo's instincts had continued to be cultivated during his training at the FBI Academy, and it was the Bureau's loss that their requirements were outdated. Theo wasn't meant to be behind a desk, and his injury only fueled him more to prove them wrong.

The Bureau's loss had turned into Brook's gain.

"The FBI lacks the resources to cover this case, unless they pull agents from other field offices," Brook said before she mulled over their options. Theo wasn't wrong that this type of investigation could take months if not years. "This isn't the unsub's first victim, though. It's too neat. Too clean. He knew what he was doing when he abducted the victim and exactly how much time he had with her. I also believe that he expected to return to the cabin in order to dispose of her body."

Her last statement had caught Theo's interest.

"You think the unsub is a local."

"Not necessarily."

Brook would need to sit down and draft a profile before she was able to make any assumptions. She'd crafted a method when creating an outline that would help her team narrow down the suspect pool. Every single aspect that she drew from the crime scene then fed into another until a profile emerged, giving her insight into their killer. She wouldn't skip steps, and she wouldn't lead her team down the wrong path by rushing her process.

"The unsub could be a local, a seasonal hiker, or maybe even someone who chooses different trails across many states as a way to remain camouflaged," Brook said as she began to study their surroundings. "The crime scene is too neat, which tells me that he wouldn't leave the victim and her belongings to be found by some random hiker. Erica mentioned that this cabin was off the grid and nowhere near the trails. Our unsub was comfortable leaving behind his victim. Too comfortable."

Theo nodded his understanding before reaching into his jacket. He pulled out a small notebook along with one of those miniature pencils. While he had access to the latest technology, his mind processed details better when they were handwritten on paper. It was a technique that he'd learned from his father.

Brook took advantage of the pause in their conversation to mentally catalogue what needed to happen within the next twenty-four hours. First and foremost, the team would need a place to stay that would allow them to setup a makeshift headquarters. The nearest town was Moonshine Valley, which they'd already visited to buy the essentials for today's hike at a local hiking shop. She'd placed the cost of everything on the corporate credit card, although they'd only bought the necessities needed for one day. They would need a lot more gear in the coming days. The town couldn't have more than a population of five hundred people, but surely there was a B&B for the tourists.

The inability to reach Bit by phone was a nuisance. There were no cell towers nearby, and they were currently relying on the park rangers to relay information. Brook wasn't looking forward to giving their talented technology expert approval to use his own corporate credit card, but they would need special equipment to communicate with one another while canvassing the mountains.

"Did Sylvie really discover something behind the cabin?" Brook asked as she caught sight of movement through the trees. She thought for a moment that the forensic techs had arrived on the scene, but it had only been a squirrel scurrying across the ground. "Or was that something you said so that I wouldn't lecture Ranger Egger on the importance of canvassing a crime scene?"

"A little of both," Theo replied with a smile as he joined her to walk around the cabin. He tucked the notebook and small pencil back into his pocket. "Sylvie and I noticed a piece of fabric stuck to a tree. It was almost as if someone's shirt got caught at one point, but it looked old. We were hoping that one of the park rangers would be able to tell us how old."

Brook was mindful of where she stepped as they rounded the corner of the small cabin, although it was doubtful that any evidence remained outdoors. The forensic techs would still take photographs and collect anything unusual, but a week had passed since Luna Breen had been reported missing by her family.

"...nothing of importance. Riggs is the man to speak to, though."

"Is that his first or last name?" Sylvie asked, raising a hand to indicate that she noticed Brook and Theo. "I take it that he's a park ranger?"

"No," Hal replied dismissively as he peered over his shoulder. He shifted so that he was facing Brook and Theo as they continued forward. "Deputy Rigby Kendric. He grew up in Moonshine Valley, and everyone just calls him Riggs. He volunteers for one of the mountain rescue teams, which is comprised of volunteers who are trained in wilderness rescue and emergency medical services. Good guy all around, but he has a chip on his shoulder."

"To my knowledge, Moonshine Valley doesn't have a sheriff's office," Sylvie stated, having done her homework when they'd arrived in town this morning. "I take it that he works out of the county sheriff's office?"

Sylvie's ability to conduct due diligence in record time was one of the reasons that Brook had requested she join the team. She also had as close to an eidetic memory as one could get, and her proficiency to compartmentalize was invaluable when dealing with sensitive cases.

Similar to Theo, Sylvie had been employed by the Bureau, but in the roll as an intelligence analyst. Unfortunately, due to circumstances out of her control, her security clearance had been suspended when an internal investigation was launched after her father's arrest and conviction of fraud. Such clearance would have eventually been reinstated, but Sylvie had taken Brook's offer to work at S&E Investigations without any regrets.

"That's correct," Hal confirmed as he hooked his thumbs inside his utility belt. "The sheriff's office is about a forty-five-minute drive from Moonshine Valley. Riggs is the point person for the town since he still lives there. As I said, he volunteers with the mountain rescue team, so he knows these trails like the back of his hand."

Hal took time to survey the area with a grimace.

"Not that this cabin is anywhere near a trail."

"You mentioned that two of the volunteers who were with a search party discovered the cabin and the body," Sylvie pointed out in her attempt to narrow down information. "Was Mr. Kendric one of those volunteers?"

"No. I believe Nate and Jules found the body," Hal responded as he pulled his hat a little lower on his forehead. The sun was low near the horizon. Brook had heard him say earlier that they had less than three hours until sunset. It had taken them about an hour and fifteen minutes to hike from town to this particular location. Given that estimate, Riggs and the two techs should be arriving soon. "Nate and Jules are both veterinarians. Like Riggs, they volunteer their time. We have a lot of hikers who do decide to veer off the trails. Most are experienced and can find their way back, but others are just idiots and—"

"Hal?" Erica called out as she rounded the corner. "Chief said that you could head back to base. Riggs has already offered to stay with the forensic techs before ensuring they make it safely back to town."

Hal narrowed his eyes and thinned his lips at the implication of Erica's words. He hadn't needed to read between the lines, and Brook met his accusatorial stare. He wasn't as obtuse as he had initially let them believe.

"Guess I'll be able to make my poker game after all," Hal said drily as he touched the brim of his hat in a mock gesture.

"Did I miss something?" Sylvie asked softly as they monitored Hal's departure. He passed by Erica without a word, walking in the same direction that they'd come from earlier. The trail was at least a thirty-minute walk from the cabin. "I definitely missed something."

"Erica will be our liaison with the park rangers," Brook explained, knowing that Theo would give Sylvie more insight to the situation later this evening. "We're taking lead on this investigation. I'll touch base with the Charlotte field office to let them know, and we'll need a place to stay that can double as our headquarters."

Sylvie automatically reached for her phone, which caused Theo to smile.

"Satellite phones are already on my list to give to Bit." Brook stepped around Sylvie to where a small piece of faded blue fabric had attached itself to a large tree. She could see why Theo had responded the way he had when she'd asked if Sylvie had truly discovered something of value behind the cabin. There was barely anything left of the material, revealing its age. She glanced up, not surprised when she found that there were very old marks on a branch that indicated a swing of some sort. "We'll need a history of this cabin, but I believe the unsub used the shelter more out of convenience than anything."

"I don't recall such a signature when we were at the Bureau." Sylvie's words gave Brook confirmation on what she'd recalled of the FBI's list of active serial killers. Sylvie hadn't gone inside the cabin upon arriving at the crime scene, but she had stood in the doorway for a moment to observe the victim. She'd seen enough to know what had taken place. "Are you saying that Luna Breen isn't the first victim?"

"I'm not saying anything right now," Brook revised, mindful not to commit to anything until she had a chance to put her thoughts down on paper. She had a process, and she'd like to stick to it. "Like I said, we'll take lead on the investigation for the moment. If we need to hand it off to the Charlotte office at a later point, I want to make sure that we've turned over every stone."

Sylvie could read between the lines, and she nodded her understanding. A strand of her blonde hair fell against the right side of her cheek. She had most of the wavy strands contained at the base of her neck with a pink hair tie, but the strenuous activity on their hike had gotten the best of them.

"Once we get settled somewhere, I'll have Bit gather information on the cabin's history, as well as a list of missing persons reports for the area." Sylvie turned her attention toward Erica. "How familiar are you with Moonshine Valley?"

"Somewhat, but I live a few towns over. You'll want to speak with Riggs," Erica said, confirming what her colleague had already professed about the deputy. "I do know that the only place for you to stay is Wyn's bar. He converted the second floor to rooms for hikers and hunters who get caught in town after an evening of celebration, if you know what I mean."

"That'll work for us," Brook replied before turning her attention to Theo. "We'll wait here until the forensic techs show up, but I'd like it if you stayed with them until they finished processing the crime scene. Erica can lead me and Sylvie back to town so that we can secure the lodging before anyone ties one on."

"I'll talk to Riggs while the scene is being processed and see what information I can gather about other cabins in the area. It might be a good idea to check them out over the next few days," Theo suggested as if he took the thoughts straight from Brook's mind. "If your theory about the unsub returning to bury the body rings true, then maybe your other speculations have roots."

The crisp air bit at Brook's cheeks, but she still held back as the others made their way toward the front of the cabin to wait for the others to arrive. She wanted a moment to herself to weigh the significance of such a case. Theo and Sylvie were both aware that this wasn't the type of investigation the firm usually accepted, and they had no obligation to do anything other than report their findings to one of the agents at the Charlotte office.

Brook couldn't get the manner of death out of her mind. She had likened the crime scene to some extreme form of interrogation. The brutality inflicted on the victim had been cruel and merciless.

Maybe Brook had it wrong, and this *was* a lone incident.

Had the violence been personal in nature?

She couldn't make sense of it, because the bloodshed left behind seemed too contained to be a mere one-off incident. Such sheer intensity was an act of unfathomable evil.

The gentle breeze began to pick up speed, causing a soft whistle to emanate from the dense forest. For the most part, it was quiet. Peaceful. Yet something lingered in the air that told of another story, and it was one that Brook needed to finish in order to see that justice was served.

Chapter Three

Brooklyn Sloane

October 2023

Thursday — 10:26pm

It was arguable that Moonshine Valley was even a town, but the townsfolk took pride in their small community. A handful of mom-and-pop shops lined the main thoroughfare through town, each one probably struggling to keep up with the modern world.

The only business that seemed to thrive in these parts was the pub.

The exterior of Wyn's Tavern was unremarkable, much like the other storefronts. A faded wooden sign with chipped lettering hung above the door with rusted chains. The entrance was sturdy, made from dark-stained wood. The brass handle was worn from years of use, and the creaky hinges announced the arrival of every patron.

Needless to say, the same clientele had gone quiet the moment that Brook and Sylvie had entered the establishment. Each and every one of them listened to Erica as she spoke to the owner on the firm's behalf about needing a place to stay while conducting their investigation. Considering that Erica wasn't a local, Brook had been impressed with the way she'd handled the situation.

In under five minutes, Wyn had handed them four sets of keys.

As Brook made her way down the staircase at the back of the bar, she took time to study the old, framed photographs hanging on the wall. Some were of hikers, others were of hunters, but she figured every single picture featured a resident of Moonshine Valley. Theo had asked her earlier if the unsub could be a local, and she hadn't been able to answer him. She still couldn't, but she also hadn't had time to work on a profile.

Brook didn't lower her gaze as the low hum of conversations at the various tables and booths once again became random whispers of curiosity. The lower level had a different odor than the greasy scent that permeated the upstairs. She breathed in deep, picking up a distinct hint of moonshine, not that such a fragrance was surprising given the name of the town.

The bar itself was long and wooden, with matching stools that lined the length of it. The dim lighting that hung above the thick countertop had been made from old-fashioned lanterns that cast a warm, amber glow over the worn surface. She glanced at the bartender, who just so happened to be the owner himself—Wyn Becket.

Apparently, Wyn was the fifth generation to carry that name. He was a burly man with black hair and a thick beard. She doubted it had been trimmed in years.

It was clear that Wyn expected her to make a couple of complaints, but Brook wouldn't give him the satisfaction. Granted, the rooms were simple, with just a bed and a dresser. It turned out that the fifth door led to a shared bathroom, which would make their stay rather interesting, but they'd been given a roof over their heads. Considering what she'd seen at today's crime scene, she wouldn't complain about a hard mattress, itchy sheets, and low water pressure.

"You must be Riggs." Brook held out her arm as she reached her destination, not surprised when the man pushed back his chair to stand and shake her hand. "Thank you for today. I know that it was your scheduled day off, but we truly appreciated you taking the time to help us."

Riggs merely nodded, obviously a man of few words.

She noticed right away that he had calloused hands and a strong grip. He was rather rugged, broad in the shoulders, and carried his service weapon on his left side. While he might have greeted her with his right hand, he was naturally left-handed. His jacket had been swung across the back of his chair, and his flannel shirt was probably more for comfort than fashion.

Brook pulled out a seat, indicating that she'd like to join him for a moment. Theo had come upstairs after the group had returned from the crime scene, but then he'd joined Bit to bring in their equipment from the tech van that had been driven from D.C. The modified 2022 Mercedes Sprinter van had been outfitted with a three-hundred-and-sixty-degree HD day/night nine camera video surveillance that came in handy on their previous case.

This one?

Not so much.

"Theo said that you were a wealth of information, and I was hoping that you might want to continue helping us out while we're here," Brook said, getting straight to the point. "I've asked Park Ranger Erica Ashton to be our liaison with her agency, and I'm sure that Theo has filled you in on our consulting agreement with the Bureau."

"I know who you are, Ms. Sloane."

Brook had gotten very good at hiding her reactions over the years, and now was no different. Riggs seemed to be testing her, and she wasn't sure of the reason. She trusted Theo when it came to character references, and he believed that Riggs would be more beneficial involved with their case than not. While she did have the final say, she would do her best to remain civil.

"Would you like to be part of the investigation, Mr. Kendric?" If the man wanted to be formal, she would be more than happy to oblige him. "I can contact your superior should your schedule be an issue."

Riggs had been enjoying his dinner, and he hadn't let her question stop him. He took another bite of his greasy cheeseburger before using his napkin to wipe his mouth. He wasn't cleanshaven, but he also didn't resemble Wyn's shaggy appearance. Riggs sported a five o-clock shadow that was a bit thicker than most. He never took his dark gaze off her as he lowered his napkin.

"No need." Riggs proceeded to pick up a steak fry. "You answer me one question, and I'll help you any way that I can."

The other patrons had somewhat gone back to their own conversations, but she could sense the weight of their curiosity. It wasn't that they were being unfriendly. She came from a small town herself, and outsiders were looked upon with reserve until something changed their minds—usually a small-town connection.

Riggs could be that specific link for her and the team.

Brook reminded herself of that detail as she forced herself to remain relaxed in her chair. She maintained direct eye contact with Riggs, even when the front door opened to reveal Theo and Bit carrying in the firm's portable 4K monitor that would serve as their murder board through software programmed by his very own hands. Their presence was a reminder that she preferred to surround herself with a tight-knit group.

Trust didn't come easy for her.

Hell, she didn't even trust herself, but she'd gradually learned over time that there were layers of such an emotion. Her team had earned a few layers, but the man sitting in front of her wasn't even on the spectrum.

"I don't make a habit of negotiating with those I choose to work with, Mr. Kendric. I'm not inclined to do so now."

"Not even for the benefit of the investigation?" Riggs asked with open curiosity as he tossed his napkin on his plate.

Once again, she didn't get the sense that he was judging her. The problem was that she wasn't sure what he thought he would gain from this exchange. She'd asked a straightforward question. If he had a problem with who she was, then there shouldn't be some kind of test.

"My colleague has a list of seven other people who know these mountains like the back of their hands, Mr. Kendric. That young man right there?" Brook nodded toward Bit, but the moment didn't technically showcase his better abilities. He was shouting the word *pivot* as he laughed at the difficulty that he and Theo were having in carrying the heavy screen. "If all seven of those men and women have a problem working with me, Bit can find me someone who can. My decision to answer or not won't hinder this investigation."

"Fair enough." Riggs reached behind him for his jacket. "Shall we? It looks like your colleagues might need a hand."

Brook made no move to leave the table. Riggs rested his jacket over one knee as he waited for her to stand, but he might be waiting awhile. She didn't like games, and she needed to ensure that he understood his role. First, though, she wanted to appease her curiosity.

"What was your question?"

"Did you know that your brother was a serial killer?"

"You wouldn't have conceded if you believed for a second that I knew my brother was capable of murder from a very young age," Brook replied evenly as she reached for the two-sided menu that was tucked between the salt and pepper shakers. She stood as she perused the limited contents on the menu. Once she'd chosen the four meals that she and the team would have before the kitchen closed its doors for the night, she placed the menu back into its spot and met Riggs' stare. "Are we done with this pissing contest?"

"Yes, ma'am," Riggs replied with a crooked smile. His jacket was too thick to sling over his shoulder, so he just held it in his hands. "I'll go see if your colleagues need my help."

Brook simply nodded and waited for Riggs to head for the stairs. Theo and Bit were no longer in sight, so she could only assume that they had been successful in getting the monitor inside the second room. Since there had only been four rooms available, Theo and Bit had chosen to share one. The makeshift office was conveniently attached to Brook's room through a connecting door, allowing her to come and go without disturbing anyone. She wasn't much of a sleeper, and she worked all hours of the night, unlike the rest of her team.

"Wyn? Could I please get three cheeseburgers, three sides of steak fries, and one club sandwich?" Brook had sent Erica home to get some rest with a directive that she join the team at seven o'clock in the morning. It would take the rest of the evening for the team to get things set up, and it would take even longer for Brook to draft a profile. It was best to start fresh with a clean slate. "I'll be back down in thirty minutes to collect them, if that's okay."

"I'll have Allie bring up your meals," Wyn said as he set a draft beer down in front of a male individual who was eyeing Brook with curiosity. "Anything to drink?"

Brook had already eyed the coffee machine that was positioned against the far wall, but the glass carafe was only half-full. Considering that the rooms didn't come equipped with anything of the sort, she figured she might as well admit to Wyn her one weakness.

"Coffee. Considering you're not a doctor and can't administer it through an IV, I guess I can settle for a cup now." Brook's comment garnered a smile from Wyn, but not so much the male subject nursing his beer. "Black."

"I think I'm going to like having you around," Wyn said with a hearty laugh. He wiped his hands on a dishtowel before reaching for a white porcelain mug. "I do have a question for you, though."

Brook was getting the sense that every single resident in Moonshine Valley had a question for her, but she bit her tongue so as not to ruin the moment between her and the bartender. He was technically their host, and his tone didn't indicate that his inquiry was about any specific topic. Given that she'd learned the hard way that each scenario required a different response, she granted Wyn his question.

"Shoot," Brook urged him as she did her best not to stare at the coffee being poured into a cup like some frenzied, dehydrated tourist lost in the mountains.

"Is that kid old enough to be in a bar?" Wyn asked skeptically as his gaze traveled toward the staircase. "We can be lenient around these parts, but I don't want to lose my liquor license, if you know what I mean."

"You'll be happy to know that Bit is in his mid-twenties." A bit of tension eased from Brook's shoulders. She'd been prepared for many questions, but Bit's age hadn't been one of them. Wyn set the coffee mug down on the counter so that she could pick it up by its handle. "Thanks, Wyn. I might just buy a carafe and have you fill it up every morning."

"I've got you covered," Wyn said as he reached underneath the counter. He pulled out a white carafe, similar to the one that her mother used when guests visited during the holidays. "I'll have Allie bring you some fresh coffee when your meals are done. Also, feel free to use the coffee pot whenever you want."

"I knew that I liked you," Brook said with a tap to the counter. She ignored the man listening in on their conversation. She made a mental note to ask Riggs if there was anything she needed to know about any of the local residents. Considering that Luna Breen was from Virginia, and she hadn't had any ties to the area, it was probable that the male subject just had idle curiosity about the case. "If I don't see you before you close, have a good night."

Wyn nodded as Brook took a tentative sip of her coffee. It wasn't as hot as she preferred it to be, but the taste of the dark roast was most welcome. She carefully ascended the wooden stairs, still sensing everyone's gaze on her. Unless they had all just crawled out from underneath rocks, it was a sure bet that they knew exactly who she was and that her brother had recently been sentenced to prison for life.

Technically, several life sentences had been handed down by a federal judge.

"...don't touch anything. Not a keyboard, not a mouse, and especially not my energy drinks."

Brook had entered her room, but Bit's voice had carried through the connected doorway. She hadn't lied to Wyn when she said that Bit was in his mid-twenties, though she could understand why the owner of the establishment had thought otherwise.

Bit wasn't like Theo and Sylvie. Brook had chosen the young man to be part of the team for completely different reasons. Bit had never been to college. He'd barely graduated high school. Everything he'd learned regarding technology had been self-taught. He also had no ties to the Bureau, if one didn't count the interest he'd garnered from several departments inside the FBI, CIA, and the NSA. If the agency had letters, then Bit's name had likely crossed their desks.

Had Bit blurred the lines of justice in his past to make ends meet?

Yes.

Multiple times, for numerous reasons, and for several parties—Brook being one of them. She wouldn't apologize to anyone for the lengths she'd gone to in order to search for her brother. It was the reason that she'd agreed to consult as a profiler with FBI for so many years before going into the private sector.

Every connection found, each contact made, with one single goal in mind had eventually come to fruition. Brook didn't believe for a moment that her brother wouldn't use every resource himself to get out of the so-called coffin that he'd found himself in, and she would monitor every single breath he took until the day he died to ensure that he didn't take another life.

People sinned daily, and she was no exception.

Brook could lie to herself and say that the end justified the means, but she would only be giving herself false hope that she wouldn't end up next to Jacob in the lowest level of hell.

"Everything okay in here?" Brook asked as she leaned a shoulder against the doorway. She took another sip of her coffee. Theo and Sylvie were getting ready to head out the main door to make another trip to the van. Bit was still explaining to Riggs why it wasn't wise to touch any of the equipment and wires. From the deputy's expression, he'd gotten the message loud and clear. "Mr. Kendric, I see that you met the rest of the team."

"Riggs. Just Riggs." His gaze was drawn to Sylvie, which wasn't all that surprising. "And yes, I met everyone. I'm just not allowed to touch the laptop."

"Laptops," Bit said, purposefully stressing the plural part of the word. Brook could only see his legs clad in denim since the rest of his body was behind the large monitor. "Basically, don't touch anything in this room. Not even the light switch."

"We'll be right back," Sylvie said with a smile. "Bit, do you have any energy drinks left that you want us to bring back?"

"Does a hard drive crash when you drop it from the top of a skyscraper?"

Sylvie and Theo left the room after a couple of good-natured moans, leaving Riggs to refocus his attention. It seemed as if he'd gotten over his reservations working with Brook rather quickly.

"It must be rather cumbersome to travel with this much equipment."

"And this is why you won't be touching anything in this room," Bit replied, finally stepping out from behind the monitor. Wyn hadn't been rude with his question regarding Bit's age. The young man's energetic vibe was that of a teenager with a zest for life. "Boss, you can go ahead and get started on your draft. I uploaded the pictures that were taken by the forensic techs earlier this evening to our software program. You'll also find the blueprint for the cabin, the property taxes, and the sale history in a separate folder. The initial background check of Luna Breen came back, as well. I'm still waiting for her financials. Oh, and I'm running an application on her social media sites while we wait for the warrant to come through for her cell phone. If anything pops, you'll be the first to know."

Brook continued to enjoy her coffee as Bit filled her in on what he'd been able to accomplish while the rest of the team had been hiking to and from the crime scene. She particularly enjoyed Rigg's surprised expression. Bit had a tendency to shock people with his ability to multitask.

"There is no way that this kid was in the FBI."

"You'd be surprised by how many young men and women just like Bit are recruited by the agencies," Brook said as Bit began to set up a second portable table. He must have borrowed one from Wyn, because it wasn't one that she'd seen before. "S&E Investigations wouldn't be where it is today if it weren't for Bit."

Bit put a hand over his heart and flashed her a smile, but she wasn't one to throw around compliments. His appearance tended to throw others off, but that was only a benefit in her opinion. He was lean with an oblong face, long nose, and blond hair that always looked in need of a wash. Genetics was to blame for the greasy appearance of the long strands that he usually kept covered by a gray knitted hat. He'd branched out to other colors, but it all depended on what yarn his older sister chose to use for her knitting projects.

"I get that your Boy Wonder has to set up his headquarters, but is there a reason that we're not working?" Riggs asked, getting right to the heart of the matter. "Neville said that you want to check out some other isolated cabins that aren't near the trails. Most of them are so old that they aren't even on the updated maps anymore. I'll need to call in some friends from the mountain rescue team. We'll be able to cover more ground that way."

From Riggs' tone, he obviously believed it was a waste of time to search the other cabins. He might very well be right, but it was beneficial to the profile to be certain that there weren't signs of similar crimes at the other locations.

"Feel free to make those calls tonight," Brook said as Riggs continued to monitor Bit as he rearranged his computer equipment. "You'll need one or two people who are willing to spend the day hiking tomorrow. I'd like there to be three groups. A guide for Sylvie, one for Theo, and you can go separate or tag along with Park Ranger Ashton.

I'm not familiar with the terrain, so I don't know if you need someone with you or not. You make that call for yourself."

"Satellite phones were delivered an hour ago," Bit interjected as he turned on his laptop. In seconds, the screen on the monitor came to life. "I bought the top of the line, Boss."

Riggs remained by the door. The room was small, which meant that they didn't have a wide area to work. Someone had pushed the bed to the far wall, placing a couple of pillows to makeshift a couch. Bit must have stolen a couple of chairs from downstairs to use at the tables. He was a creature of habit, which meant every offsite work area had to be set up in the same manner.

"And the investigation? Someone murdered that woman, and all you're going to do is waste time searching empty cabins?"

Bit had just begun to enter the code from his security token to access one of the software programs when Riggs had asked his question. He wasn't used to hearing others question Brook's process. The team had become like a well-oiled machine, so it was odd to have an outsider express his reservations.

"Do you believe someone from Moonshine Valley killed Luna Breen?" Brook had both hands wrapped around the mug, though the warmth had faded as she'd enjoyed the contents. She released her grip to hold up a finger in order to stop Riggs from answering. "Do you believe it was personal? Random? Mistaken identity? The victim's mother and sister have been notified, and it is my understanding that they are driving here from Virginia. I'll speak with them sometime tomorrow. Tell me, Riggs. Where would you start your investigation?"

Riggs' five o'clock shadow couldn't hide the tension in his jawline. She'd only pointed out that there were a million places to start the investigation.

None of them were right.

None of them were wrong.

"I'm sure you are good at your job," Brook said to preface her upcoming point. "But your talent when it comes to this investigation resides in those mountains. You know the terrain, you know the oddities, and you know the regular hikers who come and go from the trails. My specialty lies in profiling, and my process is different than other investigators. I'm open to all input, but I have final say on the steps taken in this case."

Riggs didn't reply right away, but she hadn't expected him to, especially given that Sylvie and Theo could be heard coming up the stairs. As a matter of fact, the noise level downstairs had heightened in response to someone playing songs on the jukebox. The tune was that of an old country song by a female artist that Brook's mother used to listen to during her childhood.

"This is the last of it," Theo said as he entered the open doorway with a small plastic box in his hands. Since the storage container was clear, it was easy to discern that it was full of additional USB cables. "I locked up the van."

Sylvie had two grocery bags, and Brook didn't need to look inside to know that it contained loads of candy and cans of Bit's favorite energy drink. Brook had been known to have a handful of Skittles and bars of chocolate from time to time herself.

"Over there, Big T," Bit directed as he nodded toward the corner of the room where a few other storage containers had been set on top of one another. He then took the two grocery bags from Sylvie and swiveled in his chair to place them on the bed. He'd brought in his personal seat from the van. All the other chairs were from the downstairs bar. "Little T, you're a lifesaver."

Riggs' right eyebrow had lifted upon hearing the nicknames that Bit had given Theo and Sylvie. The Ts stood for different reasons, though.

Theo's due to his muscular size, and Sylvie because of her love of tea. Brook expected there to be an adjustment period for Riggs and Park Ranger Erica Ashton, but Brook wouldn't handhold them, either.

This investigation had little leads, and they would need to come at the case from every single angle. Luna Breen's life was about to be turned upside down. The questions that Brook had posed to Riggs were significant. Had the victim's death been personal? Random? Discovering the answers to those questions was going to be key to solving her murder.

"All I'm saying is that the clock is ticking, and the victim has already been dead for a week." Riggs glanced around at Bit's setup as if to indicate he believed it was all just a waste of time. "For all we know, it's as simple as an ex-lover following Breen from Virginia to North Carolina."

"If it was a simple murder investigation, S&E Investigations wouldn't be here," Brook stated as she pushed off the doorframe. "We usually have a team meeting before starting our day, so please be here at seven o'clock sharp. In the meantime, I'm sure the team members can fill you in on our process. I have a few calls to make and a profile to draft."

She tacked on that she'd also ordered dinner for the team while she'd been downstairs, letting them know that Allie would be bringing up their meals. Brook quietly closed the connecting door. She understood Riggs' impatience, and she agreed that the clock was ticking, but he didn't seem to understand that the alarm had already gone off without any of them hearing it.

Luna Breen was dead, and her killer could already be thousands of miles away.

Chapter Four

Brooklyn Sloane

October 2023

Friday — 5:02am

The dim glow of the emergency exit sign above the back door of the pub was nestled to the side of the staircase. One of the letters flickered, tired in its continual effort to stay lit and provide a safety net for those inside. The vibrant hue cast red and black shadows on the steps as if warning the person using them to be mindful of their destination.

Brook had taken the time last night to get a layout of the bar. As she took the last step that put her on solid ground, she reached for the light switch next to the exit door. While the pub itself had security lighting tucked up underneath the decorative wood surface, she preferred to see a bit better than someone who wanted only to drown their sorrows in solitude.

She'd gotten around three and half hours of sleep. Considering that was her usual, minus around thirty minutes, she questioned her sanity upon inhaling the delicious aroma of coffee. It all made sense as she made her way behind the counter to where a note had been taped to the coffee machine.

You strike me as an early bird. ~Wyn

"I'm liking you more and more, Wyn," Brook muttered to herself as she took the glass carafe off the burner.

Brook began to pour the contents into the white carafe that Wyn had set to the side. She doubted that Wyn came in before nine or ten o'clock, but she'd return the favor. Once she'd secured the cap to the tall carafe, she set about brewing up another pot so that Wyn had something to drink when he arrived. Worst case scenario, she could enjoy another pot all to herself before having to question Luna Breen's mother and sister later in the day.

Brook's cell phone vibrated, and she pulled it out of the back pocket of her jeans. She'd only brought two pair of denim pants with her. She hadn't expected to take on an additional case and one that would require clothing that she normally reserved for her days off. Seeing the name of the person calling her, she might be able to get away without having to drive a town over to buy additional clothes.

"If it isn't my business partner," Brook greeted as she searched for the can of ground coffee. She'd expected the container to be next to the machine, but the counter space had been cleared off except for a stack of porcelain coffee mugs. "I thought you were in Somalia."

"And I thought you'd be at the office this morning," Graham replied in a rich tone that she'd surprisingly come to miss during their business trips. "Imagine my disappointment when Arden greeted me with a cup of coffee. Not that I'm complaining too much. That man makes a mean cup."

General Graham Elliott was a former Commanding General of Marine Forces Special Operations, and he also happened to be more than just her silent business partner.

She'd always had the philosophy that it was better to wake up alone.

Less worry, less stress, and less heartache.

It had taken her a very long and winding emotional road to figure out that she was more than the sister of a serial killer. Yes, there were many things she'd done in her life that she needed to atone for, and she would continue to do so until the day she drew her last breath.

Graham had taught her that she didn't need to do so alone. He'd faced his fair share of demons that had resulted in the same ugly scars that she carried on her soul. For once, she was learning to share. She just needed to be reminded of that occasionally.

He was also one hell of a lover.

"I haven't figured out Arden's secret to making coffee, either," Brook said as she struck gold after kneeling behind the bar. There were a few bags of ground coffee, and it was an unfamiliar brand. That might explain why it hadn't tasted like the dime store stuff. "I'm pretty sure that's on purpose. Arden believes if I figure it out that I'll fire him."

Arden Hinnish was the latest addition to the team. A unique one, given his age. The former private investigator was in his late sixties with a penchant for cardigan sweaters. His previous career hadn't always been on the up and up, but it was also the reason why his opinion carried weight. He came at an investigation from a completely different angle, and she could appreciate the distinctive view.

"Would you fire him if he didn't know how to make a fantastic cup of coffee?"

Brook caught herself smiling, which was something of a rarity from what she'd been told time and again by her team. She grabbed the bag and stood, not expecting the door to the bar to swing wide open. Riggs and two men came in as if they owned the place, though that was doubtful since the other individuals looked nothing like Wyn.

Had Wyn left the front door unlocked on purpose or due to the fact that he had guests staying in the upstairs room? Either way, that issue needed to be rectified this morning.

"Arden isn't in any danger of losing his job," Brook said quietly as she stopped holding her cell phone in between her cheek and shoulder. "The FBI called me for a consult on a case. Since we were already in North Carolina, I didn't think it would take up much of our time. Unfortunately, we might be here for a while. Listen, I have to go, but I'll touch base with you later this evening."

"I'm afraid that I'm catching a flight to the West Coast."

"You wouldn't want to do me a favor first, would you?" Brook asked as she turned around to finish her task. She filled the filter with ground coffee. "There was a murder in the Smokey Mountains. About an hour and a half hike from a small town called Moonshine Valley. Let's just say that my business attire isn't cutting it here."

"I'll stop by your condo on my way home. It's cool there this time of year. Do you even own sweatshirts?"

"There might be a couple of sweatshirts in the back of my closet, but my turtlenecks are in the third drawer of my dresser," Brook said as she rinsed out the glass carafe in the sink before filling it with water. "Jeans are in—"

"Fourth drawer," Graham filled in before lowering his voice. "Do you need anything out of the first drawer?"

Brook slid the glass carafe onto the burner before gently pressing the brew button. Her previous relationships consisted of sex and doors. First one, then the other. Graham had an intimate, playful side to him that he'd never revealed before they'd taken their relationship to the next level. At times, she still wasn't quite sure how to respond.

"Be safe, Brooklyn," Graham said with a soft laugh before the line disconnected.

Brook cleared her throat before lowering her phone. She then tucked it back into the pocket of her jeans before reaching for the porcelain cup that was stacked on top of the pile. Considering that she'd heard the chairs being taken off the tables and set on the floor, Riggs and his two friends had almost certainly made themselves comfortable. She distinctly recalled telling Riggs that their morning meeting was at seven o'clock, but he seemed to have his own schedule.

"You're early," Brook called out as she turned with her coffee in one hand and the carafe in the other. She reluctantly set both on the counter. "Meeting is at seven o'clock."

"Let's just say that I had a feeling you were up working on that profile of yours."

Brook was usually able to read people rather well, but Riggs wasn't making it easy. She assumed there was a hint of sarcasm to his words. He was going to have to do better than that if he wanted to offend her, which was why she wasn't so sure about her initial take on his statement.

Considering that Sylvie and Bit were still sleeping and Theo was in the shower, it wouldn't hurt to be formally introduced to the two men keenly observing Brook and Riggs' interaction. She took her time ensuring that three additional mugs were placed next to the carafe.

"Jace Mathers and Dominic Ryder, this is Brooklyn Sloane."

Brook slowly made her way out from behind the counter, wanting to catalog each of their mannerisms before she shook their hands. Jace seemed more curious of the two, and Dominic appeared to be the more reserved of the group. Jace had dark blond hair with a scruffy beard, and Dominic sported black hair while keeping himself clean-shaven.

"I take it that the two of you volunteer your time for search and rescue around these parts?" Brook asked as she pulled out a chair. "Has Riggs explained what we need from you today?"

While she'd put on jeans this morning, she'd opted to wear one of her black blazers over a long-sleeved burgundy shirt. She wasn't sure if she would be needed at one of the sites being checked on today, but she wanted to be prepared for anything. Business casual was appropriate under these circumstances to meet with Luna Breen's family members.

"Yes, ma'am," Jace replied first, though that wasn't unexpected. She got the sense that Dom wouldn't say much if he could get away with it. "We're going to split up the abandoned dwellings that we know are off the grid into three quadrants. With some rockslides over the centuries, a lot of those areas just aren't inhabitable anymore. We can still hike in and out, but I can think of four cabins off the top of my head that were just left there to rot."

"Only four?"

"There have been a couple of cabins struck by lightning and burned down." Jace glanced toward Riggs, who had walked over to the counter to collect the three mugs and carafe. He set them all on the table before filling each to the brim. "Remember Doc's hunting cabin? There was nothing left but ashes, and he never bothered to rebuild."

"That might have been due to his drinking problem," Riggs replied wryly as he leaned back in his chair. He shrugged, as if it was common knowledge. It probably was, given the size of the town. "Doc's now in his seventies, though how his liver has managed to hold out is anyone's guess."

Brook set her coffee down on the table. She leaned forward enough to reach her cell phone, feigning as if she'd received a message that needed attention. She quickly typed out the names of the two gentlemen who she'd joined at the table before sending a text to Bit with instructions to initiate background checks. They had a protocol they adhered to with anyone even loosely connected to the case. Bit would see the message when he woke up, which should be relatively soon.

"There's too much ground to cover." The statement came from Dominic. He'd wrapped his right hand around the porcelain mug, but he made no move to enjoy its contents. "You'll need us for more than a day."

"That's fine." Brook didn't see the harm in divulging some of the profile that she'd worked on last night. "There is a chance that whoever is responsible for Luna Breen's death has done this before. Her body wasn't meant to be discovered, which tells me that the killer was going back to the crime scene to clean up his mess."

"Mess? That's what you believe was left behind?"

The animosity radiating from Dominic was obvious, but Brook had dealt with individuals like him most of her career. As a profiler, she needed to be able to see things from the unsub's point of view. It's what she taught her students in the course she'd been asked to teach at a university located in D.C. Not everyone had the ability to alter their perception of reality. Those who managed to do so without effort would go on to be excellent in their chosen field.

"A mess is how the killer views the aftermath of what he's carried out," Brook explained patiently as she set her phone face down on the table. She picked up what remained of her coffee. "Why the unsub chose to carry out such torture remains to be seen, but it is key to figuring out his identity."

"You make it sound as if you sympathize with this guy," Jace said with a frown. "Riggs told us how that woman suffered, and it sounds to me as if it was some random lunatic who got off on killing someone."

"Each of you will be taking a member of my team to as many locations as possible over the next couple of days," Brook explained, not bothering to address Jace's statement. She'd already given a brief explanation about the unsub's perception of reality, and she wouldn't waste the rest of the morning by defending her process. "They'll be checking to see if there was any trace evidence left behind to indicate this has happened before."

Maybe it was due to Riggs' experience in law enforcement, but he was the one to connect the dots first. He'd pulled his chair close enough to the table that he was able to rest his elbows on the hard surface. He rubbed his five o'clock shadow as he voiced his thoughts.

"You're thinking that if there is evidence to support your theory, the killer might still be somewhere in those mountains. Maybe even a local," Riggs suggested even as doubt laced his tone. "Lack of evidence would indicate that he's long gone."

"Maybe," Brook said while purposefully remaining noncommittal. She wouldn't box herself in, nor would she hinder the case by being closeminded. "We're not sure of anything right now, which is why we need to come at this from all angles. As you know, I'll be speaking with Luna Breen's mother and sister today. We'll peel Luna's life back in layers to see if there was anyone who wanted to hurt her. Why was she hiking by herself? Why this area? Did she have an ex-lover? A profession that made her a target? These are questions that need to be answered, but we also can't take our attention off the killer. What was his motive? Why did he choose Luna Breen?"

"Is there something about this murder that we don't know about?" Dominic asked cautiously, his steady gaze never leaving her face. He'd still not taken one sip of his coffee. "Your firm consults with the feds on cold cases and serial killer investigations. You are obviously here because they don't believe this is an isolated murder."

"Federal land, federal case. And yes, it is true that S&E Investigations specializes in cold cases that involve serial murders. With that said, my firm has a special arrangement with the Bureau. The Charlotte office has a lot of irons in the fire right now, and my colleagues and I were here for another investigation. They merely asked if we'd assess the crime scene to let them know if their presence was needed, but I decided to see it through."

"Because you believe there is some serial killer stalking his victims in our mountains?" Dominic asked right when the vibrations of her phone rattled the table. She casually picked it up, not surprised that Bit had woken up upon hearing his phone. It was too soon to have the background results of those individuals sitting with her, but Bit had provided the basic information on the two men. "We're a small town, Ms. Sloane. You aren't going to make friends by accusing one of them of being a murderer."

"One, I'm not here to make friends," Brook stated matter-of-factly, keeping her voice level. She kept both her cup and cell phone in her hands. She wouldn't be sitting with these gentlemen for much longer. "Two, I'm not the kind of profiler who goes around accusing anyone of anything unless there is hardcore evidence to make an official arrest. I'm here to investigate a murder. It's as simple as that, which is more than I can say for you."

"Excuse me?" Dominic asked before his knuckles whitened due to the tightening of his grip on the coffee mug.

"Riggs, it's my turn to pose a question to you. What would possess you to choose a member of the press to guide one of my colleagues to a potential crime scene?"

Brook noticed Riggs surprise at her question, but then his gaze dropped to her phone. He inhaled slowly as he shot an apologetic look toward his friend.

"Dominic isn't here as a reporter. He's here because he knows these mountains as well as I do, and he's agreed to keep everything discussed out of the paper." Riggs shrugged, as if his friend's profession wasn't cause for concern. "Dominic has helped the sheriff's office many times on missing person cases, and never once has he printed information that wasn't meant for the public."

"That's not to say that I wouldn't like an exclusive interview with you once this is—"

"Dominic, I'd stop talking if I were you," Brook warned him as she stood from the table. "I'll make my decision before seven o'clock. In the meantime, there's another pot of fresh coffee on the burner behind the bar."

Brook turned and made it halfway to the staircase before turning back around. All three men were still focused on her, but she needed their attention elsewhere.

All three had grown up in Moonshine Valley.

Their insights were invaluable to the case, but only if they trusted her process.

"Jace, you're having marital problems. You've been twisting your wedding ring since you came into the bar, and it has nothing to do with nerves. You're staring at it like it has all the answers. Dominic, you're having money problems, which is no surprise given your profession. You're also a smoker. Stress is preventing you from quitting even though you know it's a waste of money. Given the deep yellowish stain on your thumb and index finger, you're up to at least a pack a day."

Riggs held up his hand.

"Don't profile me, Brook. I was just starting to like you."

"You respect me," Brook amended, having gotten her point across. "There's a difference. Like I said, I'll make my decision on Dominic joining the hike before our seven o'clock meeting. Enjoy the coffee."

Brook had just reached the top of the landing when Theo exited the bathroom. A towel was slung over his shoulder, but he was dressed for a day of strenuous hiking. Normally, he would have gone for a morning run.

"You don't look happy," Theo pointed out as the two of them walked towards their designated rooms. Seeing as the banister afforded a view of the downstairs, Theo caught a glimpse of their guides for the day. "Locals?"

"Yes, with one of them a reporter for a newspaper. Dominic Ryder also has a nature blog that does quite well for itself. We can use that to our advantage, but I'll wait until Bit can look more into his articles." Brook stopped in front of her door. "Do me a favor? If we do allow Dominic to make the hike today, make sure you're the one who is paired with him. I don't want to be blindsided right out of the gate."

Chapter Five

Sylvie Deering

October 2023

Friday — 7:01am

"Luna Breen."

Sylvie used the remote in her hand to ensure that the victim's picture appeared on the monitor. Underneath the photo were details that Brook would cover in this morning's briefing, but there were also tidbits of information that could be of importance at a later date if they decided the woman's murder had been committed due to personal reasons. Only time would tell, but Sylvie had learned early in her career as an intelligence analyst that there wasn't one detail that lacked significance.

"Twenty-six years old, brunette, and single," Brook said as she stood next to the monitor. Sylvie was sitting in a very uncomfortable chair next to Bit, and Theo was leaning up against the dresser that had been pushed into the corner. As for Erica, Riggs, Jace, and Dominic, the four of them had brought up chairs from downstairs and had placed them against the wall just inside the door. "Luna Breen was a physical therapist who liked to travel. She was an avid hiker, close to her younger sister, and belonged to several online groups that shared her interests. According to the missing persons report taken by Sheriff Otto Jackson, Luna's mother and sister became concerned when she didn't call them after a three-day weekend hiking a popular trail in the Smoky Mountains. One that can be easily reached near an access point from Moonshine Valley. They requested that a welfare check be performed at a B&B about six miles from here."

"Hiker's Haven," Riggs interjected after raising his left hand. He spoke to everyone, but he kept his dark gaze on Sylvie. She'd noticed his interest in her yesterday. She didn't like to mix business with pleasure, and that was the way it would stay for the foreseeable future. "Mauve Benson owns the place, and we've sealed off the room. Mauve is expecting you sometime today."

Brook nodded her appreciation, although the team had already known the name of the owner. Sylvie had spoken to Mauve yesterday over the phone to inform the woman that a forensics team would be out first thing this morning. Brook wasn't one to leave any stone unturned, and she'd assembled a team that made sure even the smallest pebble had been scrutinized during every investigation.

As Brook continued to cover the pertinent details to the case that Sylvie already knew by heart, she studied Luna Breen's picture. The photo had been taken on a hiking trail, and it was in stark contrast to the gruesome scene they had witnessed yesterday at the cabin.

The woman in the picture had been happy, carefree, and living her best life possible. Sylvie's heart always ached for the victims and their families. Luna had been robbed of a bright future, but there was no turning back time.

Luna Breen was dead, but that didn't mean her story had been brought to an end.

The vibrations of Sylvie's cell phone caught her attention, and her stomach tightened with an anxiety that she hadn't experienced since before her employment with S&E Investigations.

Sure enough, she recognized the number on the display.

It was the third time in as many days, but she purposefully declined the call. She had nothing to say to her father. He'd ruined many peoples' lives by the crimes that he'd committed over a span of many years. The charges that had been brought against him had been too many to count, but the bottom line was that he'd ruined his clients' futures by defrauding them of their savings and retirement plans. While she'd tried her best to be the forgiving daughter, there had been moments when she could sense he had no remorse for the damage that he'd done to so many families.

"We've requested a full background on Luna, as well as her family and colleagues. Bit has already modified one of his applications to comb through Luna's online presence. All social media sites, any forums that she might have visited in the last few months, dating websites, direct messages, text messages, emails, and the like will be scoured for any sign that someone wanted to hurt her." Brook paused to take a sip of coffee, giving Sylvie time to set her phone face down on the table. Bit must have sensed her agitation, because he nudged the donut box that Theo had brought in the room moments before the meeting had commenced. "Theo will be teaming up with Dominic to canvass a few sites where something similar could have occurred over the last year or so. Sylvie, you'll be with Jace. Erica and Riggs can hike together. I don't want anyone to wander off alone. Understood?"

Sylvie had nodded toward Jace after Brook had paired them together. He acknowledged her, but he didn't seem too thrilled with the thought of being her partner for the day. She'd read over the information that Bit had been able to pool together on the volunteers. While the data wasn't complete, it was enough to give the team an idea of who they would be spending time with while scouring hidden recesses of the Smoky Mountains.

It had also helped that Riggs had pulled Brook aside a few minutes before the start of the meeting to ease her concerns regarding Dominic. Having someone help them who was associated with the press wasn't typical, but Sylvie doubted that Dominic would be foolish enough to cross someone like Brooklyn Sloane. Dominic concentrated mostly on his hiking blog, only freelancing for a local paper a few times a month.

"My morning will be spent with Luna's mother and sister. In the meantime, Luna's room at Hiker's Haven will be processed by a forensics team," Brook reiterated as she stepped close to the portable monitor. Since it was a touchscreen, she had no issue navigating the tabs to pull up her profile. It wasn't complete, which was probably the only reason she'd allowed Dominic and Jace to attend the meeting. It was doubtful that they would be included in the future. As always, Sylvie was impressed with Brook's insights thus far. "Moving on to the profile of our unsub. White male, twenty-five to thirty-five years of age. I'll be able to narrow that down as more evidence is discovered throughout our investigation. He's methodical, patient, determined, and cunning. I don't believe this is the first time that he has killed someone, and I don't believe this crime was sexual in nature."

Brook used two hands as she shifted her profile to one side of the display while ensuring that crime scene photos were visible so that she could explain her reasoning behind the assigned traits. Sylvie took advantage of the pause to lean forward and read over the information that Bit had just received from one of his programs.

The numerous alerts flashing on one of his screens had the potential of proving Brook's theory right. Sylvie would hold off on giving such confirmation until the end of Brook's presentation. In the meantime, Bit leaned forward to download the data to the software the firm used for their murder board.

Sylvie and Bit had gotten extremely close over the past two years. So much so, that she hadn't immediately recognized the signs that he viewed their friendship as one that could grow into something more. The problem with that scenario was he was her best friend, and she wasn't ready to give that up. Their professional relationship couldn't be affected by either choice, and the bottom line was that she wasn't sure she would ever want their friendship to change...ever.

"According to the physical evidence, the unsub dragged the victim from the front door of the cabin to the chair. I believe the scene was set up beforehand due to there being no signs of an altercation in the middle of the room." Brook created a circular motion around the victim in the picture. "The killer never once strayed away from this path. He continually circled his victim, cutting her one slice at a time to keep her off balance. She never knew where he might strike. Then there is the fact that he set her backpack just out of reach. His intention was to keep her desperate."

"Why not younger?" Erica asked as she kept her focus on Brook. Sylvie had noticed at the crime scene yesterday that Erica always stayed to the side of the doorframe. She had been extremely uncomfortable around the bloodshed left behind. "Or older?"

"A few reasons," Brook explained as she turned to face her audience. "The unsub isn't younger than twenty-five due to the patience it would require spending hours torturing someone like Luna Breen while not straying from his objective. He's exceptionally focused, which would be rare for someone younger. As for the other end of the spectrum, the killer would need to be in remarkable physical strength to navigate the terrain while forcing another to do the same. If you see this slightly disturbed area near the wall, you'll notice that is where he set his own backpack."

"If you believe that the killer visited the cabin before he abducted his victim, then this murder was premeditated," Riggs said as he leaned forward and rested his elbows on his knees. "Wouldn't that indicate it was personal?"

"Not necessarily. The manner in which the unsub was able to create a safe place to work signifies that he's done this before. More importantly, the choice of cabin tells us that he's familiar with the area."

The room suddenly became quiet as the implication of what Brook had just stated hit home. Sylvie could sense the weight of Bit's stare. He was wondering when she was going to reveal the information collected from one of his applications that basically corroborated part of the profile.

"Just because you believe that the killer is someone who knows the area doesn't mean he's from Moonshine Valley. There are a lot of surrounding towns with hikers, hiking guides, and the like who know these trails better than us," Jace claimed as he crossed his arms. "You're making assumptions that could upset a lot of people."

Dominic was still staring at the portable monitor as if he'd been mesmerized by the photographs. Sylvie didn't want to read too much into his fascination with the crime scene. Erica was still a bit pale. As for Riggs, his dark gaze had settled on Sylvie as if he was somehow aware she was waiting for the right time to speak. She figured he was attuned with this process given his occupation, though it was doubtful that he'd ever worked such a large case before.

"I'm a profiler," Brook stated unapologetically. "Answers lie within the aftermath of all tragedies, and this crime scene is no different. Sylvie, would you like to add something?"

"Jenny Tabithson, Carissa Norman, and Helen Beckham." Sylvie didn't have to instruct Bit to pull up their pictures. "In the last ten years, these three women were reported missing by their families. Their remains have never been found, but all three were brunettes and in their mid-twenties."

There were some expletives thrown around the room, but Brook remained silent as she studied the three photographs. Bit had also added the dates that corresponded to their missing persons reports that had been filed by the local police. He then continued to work in the background to obtain more information.

"I'll contact Arden and have him reach out to the families," Sylvie said as she reached for her cell phone. Considering that she and Theo would be off the grid most of the day, the investigation would slow down the pace of researching aspects that would help them narrow down pertinent details. She swiped away the number that she'd been ignoring for the past few days to gain access to her text messages. "Once Arden has spoken to the family members, we should be able to have a clear picture on whether these women could be potential victims."

"Boss?" Bit pressed a button on his keyboard. "You can rule Jenny Tabithson out of the victim pool."

Bit had garnered Sylvie's attention as she'd been in the middle of constructing her text message. It was taking her too long to string two words together, and she was annoyed with herself that she was still allowing her father to influence her mood. She quickly read one of the headlines for Jenny Tabithson.

"Robbery?"

"Tabithson robbed a bank with two men. They were arrested, but she managed to get away with a half million dollars," Bit revealed as he began to work on another application. The code appearing on the display was like a foreign language. "I'll see what I can find on the other two missing persons."

"That actually feeds into your theory regarding the killer's age bracket," Riggs pointed out with what could only be disappointment. He was highlighting the fact that Tabithson's disappearance was over ten years ago, leaving the other two women to have disappeared within the last five years. Sylvie had amended her text to Arden, omitting Tabithson. "We all helped on those two searches, canvassing a very wide area. We never found any trace of them."

"Bit, see if you can find any link between Carissa Norman and Helen Beckham," Brook instructed as she reached for the coffee mug that she'd set down on the table earlier. "We shouldn't jump to conclusions until we have evidence to support the theory that their disappearances are related to our case."

"I'm confused," Dominic spoke up after he'd rubbed his eyes in frustration. Sylvie didn't believe that he'd be foolish enough to print or publish anything that had been discussed this morning. Then again, she never thought her father would have bilked good people out of their lives' savings. "I thought that was the point of your profile. Haven't you already jumped to conclusions that Luna Breen's murder is part of a bigger conspiracy?"

Sylvie caught the way Riggs shot his friend a glare of warning.

"The physical evidence left at the crime scene suggests that the unsub has done this before," Brook said as she turned to face them. "Until proven otherwise, we'll be working off this profile."

Sylvie was finally able to concentrate enough to send her message to Arden. If anything changed regarding the background information of the two missing persons, Bit would keep Arden in the loop. She kept her phone in hand, figuring the briefing was about to wrap up. It was going to be a long day, and she wanted to eat something hearty to last her. She appreciated the donuts, but she needed something that would stick to her ribs.

"Again, I'd like to stress to the three of you that you do not need to be here." Brook was addressing Riggs, Dominic, and Jace. Erica shifted uneasily under the weight of such a harsh tone. Brook wasn't one to cut anyone slack. "While your knowledge of the area would make the upcoming search easier on my team, we do have other resources."

"Which would cost time and money," Riggs interjected as he stood from his chair. "We're here to volunteer our time to the case. We'll see to it that your team is guided to abandoned structures that could potentially be a part of this investigation. Brook, may I speak to you in private?"

Sylvie's phone vibrated in her hand, and she all but forced herself to look at the lighted display. The tension eased from her shoulders when she glimpsed Arden's reply. He would monitor the software program they were using for any updates and proceed from there.

"Little T?"

"I know," Sylvie said, acknowledging the concern in Bit's voice. They'd already spoken about the fact that her father had been trying to reach her, and Bit had given her his thoughts on the subject. "I should just answer and get it over with, but I'm not ready, Bit. If the appeal that he filed finally gained some ground, his name is going to be plastered all over the news. I'm just not ready to deal with it."

"Want me to dig around some?" Bit offered as he took one of the chocolate donuts from the box. "I'll be discreet."

"I appreciate the offer, but I'll call my father when we're back in the city," Sylvie said with a half-smile of reassurance. Bit adjusted his knit hat higher up on his forehead. He tended to do so when he couldn't come up with the right words for any given situation. "In the meantime, maybe I shouldn't be the only one avoiding phone calls."

"I have no idea what you're talking about," Bit replied defensively before taking a very large bite of his chocolate donut.

"Uh-huh." Sylvie's chair didn't have wheels. She had to practically lift the wooden seat so that the legs wouldn't squeak on the hardwood floor. "Bit, we talked about this last week. Sometimes our timing in life is just off, and other times we are presented with opportunities that we shouldn't ignore. As your best friend, I'm telling you that you shouldn't overlook what is right in front of you."

Bit had recently met a young woman named Zoey Collins who shared his love of gaming. Sylvie hadn't needed to be told the reason that he'd ignored all the signs the young woman had thrown his way. Only Sylvie had seen the way he would smile whenever Zoey texted about some random character or level in a video game. He truly enjoyed her company, and he shouldn't be robbed of that just because of his feelings for Sylvie.

"Looks like it's going to be you and me." The interruption had been made by Riggs, who had made his way over to the table. He'd apparently spoken to Brook about whatever topic needed to be discussed in private. Sylvie focused her attention on Brook, who nodded her consent at the change in plans. "Jace can't get started until around ten o'clock today, so Erica is going to be his partner. Brook thought it would be better for the two of us to head out in the next thirty minutes."

"That will give me enough time to grab a bite to eat. I also need to pack the luminol that one of the forensic techs gave me last night," Sylvie explained as she gave Bit a fist pump. "Thanks for the satellite phone, Bit. I'll check in every hour."

"If you see a grizzly bear, take a picture."

Riggs gave Bit a rather perplexed look, but Sylvie waved a dismissive hand toward the deputy. Bit already had his headphones on and was bobbing his head to the music while finishing whatever code he'd been working on for his latest program to try and tie Luna Breen to the other two women.

"I'll explain that grizzlies don't usually stray this far east later," Sylvie said with a smile. She turned her attention to her colleague, who just so happened to be walking their way after a brief discussion with Brook. "Theo, are you eating breakfast before we go?"

Theo was very conscious about his health, but he also ate everything in moderation. He'd enjoyed a glazed donut, along with his protein shake. Given that they were about to be outdoors and hiking over rough terrain, he'd make sure to eat something that would give him energy for many hours.

"I'm going to walk over to the diner and grab some oatmeal and a bowl of fruit. I'll eat while we go over the old maps that Riggs brought with him. Brooks wants a copy of them before we head out. Want me to double the order? Triple?"

"I've already eaten, thanks," Riggs replied when the last question had been aimed at him. Sylvie had already nodded her response. "I'll spread the maps out on the table so that Sylvie can take pictures and forward them to Brook."

Theo made his way over to Erica and the others to make the same breakfast offer. Sylvie was interested about one thing, so she stopped Riggs before he could leave and collect the maps.

"I'm curious, Riggs. I thought for sure the sheriff would be joining in on this briefing," Sylvie said as she tucked her cell phone into the back pocket of her jeans. "Brook mentioned leaving Sheriff Jackson a message last night. Any particular reason that he's not here?"

While the location hadn't fallen under the jurisdiction of Sheriff Otto Jackson, surely someone in his position would want to be kept personally up to date due to the vicious nature of the crime scene. From Riggs' hesitation on answering her question, all he'd managed to do was encourage Sylvie to run a background check on the man.

"We're short-staffed, so the sheriff had to take a shift on patrol today." Riggs shrugged, as if it was a common occurrence. "I'll go grab those maps out of my backpack and meet you downstairs."

Sylvie waited for Riggs to exit the room before turning around and motioning for Bit to remove his headphones. He pulled one ear off to the side.

"Run a background check on Sheriff Otto Jackson," Sylvie instructed in a low voice. "If something pops, let Brook know immediately. Since I'll be available by satellite phone only, don't relay anything to me that shouldn't be said in front of Riggs. Okay?"

"Got it, Little T."

Sylvie turned to find Erica still on her cell phone, though the woman had quickly averted her gaze as she said something to whoever was on the other end of the line. She'd probably overheard the request, and Sylvie wasn't appreciating the odd behavior several of the parties involved were displaying this morning. She made her way over to Brook, who had been monitoring Dominic and Jace's departure with interest.

"I know that look." Sylvie shifted so that she also had sight of the door. "What are you thinking, and why am I with Riggs instead of Jace?"

"Apparently, Jace owns the bait and tackle shop here in Moonshine Valley. Whoever was going to open the store this morning had car trouble on the way into town. It'll be a couple of hours before Jace can get away." Brook twisted the worry ring on her right hand, which wasn't unusual. She had a tendency to do so when she was mulling over facts of a case. "I don't have a good read on the unsub yet, but something tells me that he'd want to be close to this case. Nothing stands out in any of their background checks, but be careful when you're up in those mountains."

"You knew that we were dealing with a serial killer yesterday, didn't you?"

"An amateur wouldn't have been able to keep a scene so contained otherwise," Brook murmured as she focused on Erica, who had just disconnected her call. "Like I said, watch your back up there."

Sylvie nodded her understanding, deciding that it might be in her best interest to take her backup piece. There were several types of holsters that the team always had on hand in the tech van, and she'd make sure to grab the boot holster. She'd be able to clip it to the inside of her hiking boot without anyone the wiser.

It was more than apparent that Brook was confident there would be some type of evidence left behind by the unsub to prove that Luna Breen hadn't been a random kill. No matter what it might look like to Dominic and Jace, Sylvie had learned one thing over the past two years—always trust Brook's profiling abilities. If she believed that they were dealing with a serial killer, then he was somewhere nearby and waiting patiently to strike again.

Chapter Six

Brooklyn Sloane

October 2023

Friday — 10:47am

"Any questions on the assignment?"

Brook set down her pen as she scanned the students gathered in the assembly hall of the college. It was important that they feel comfortable with the material that she'd given them, especially since most of it contained specific details taken from the files of a previous case. The criminal profiling class wasn't one that the students had been prepared for when they'd asked to be considered for one of the twelve coveted spots. The course certainly wasn't run-of-the-mill, and it hadn't been first come, first serve. Brook had chosen each student by hand, and she hadn't regretted her choices so far.

"I realize that I was supposed to be there in person this morning, but my firm was asked by the Bureau to consult on a case. I'm still in North Carolina."

"Is it an active serial killer?" Bryce Thielen asked from his front row seat. He was thriving in her course, and his thirst for knowledge was more acute than the others. Well, maybe apart from Melinda Reagor, but only in a more outspoken manner. "I haven't heard anything on the news."

"We're in the Smoky Mountains." Brook didn't feel the need to explain her situation, but it became apparent from her students' expressions that she should supply a bit more information. "We're in a very small town. I'm sure there will be some news coverage later today or tomorrow, but I'm doing what I can to keep a lid on the details. It would be more beneficial to the case to keep things contained for the time being."

Brook technically hadn't answered Bryce's question. Before he realized what had taken place, she gave her standard speech to them about reaching out to Arden with any questions. She hadn't thought it possible, but her students had really bonded with Arden over the past two months. Given her erratic schedule, he'd helped when he could, and the assistance so far had exceeded her expectations.

"Hey, Boss? Luna Breen's mother and sister are downstairs."

Bit must have been listening in on her lecture. She'd left the connecting door open just in case he'd needed her for something during the three hours that she'd just spent with her students. Technically, she could have continued for another ten minutes, but anything said after finishing her talking points would have been a waste of time.

"Thanks, Bit." Brook closed her laptop. "Has Sylvie and Theo been checking in regularly?"

"On the hour," Bit said as he leaned up against the doorframe. "Listen, I didn't want to say anything in front of the others this morning, but you might want to touch base with Sarah Evanston's mother again."

Bit didn't have to go into too much detail regarding the former reporter who had become infamously known as the only victim to live through one of Jacob's vicious attacks. Sarah Evanston was currently the bane of his existence. She'd lived, and his temporary sacrifice to surrender himself into the custody of the FBI had been thwarted by Brook. For the first time in their lives, she'd thought two steps ahead and managed to figure out his grand plan to escape custody.

She wasn't naïve enough to believe that her brother wouldn't try to figure another way out of prison, but for the time being, they were monitoring him to the best of their ability. Jacob thought of life like a chess board, and he was able to visualize several moves ahead of his opponent.

Bit hadn't come right out and admitted that he'd illegally been monitoring the cell phone belonging to Sarah Evanston's mother. Brook wasn't a saint, and she'd never claimed to be. Whatever judgement she faced after death, she would do so knowing that she'd sinned to save the lives of others.

"I'll take care of it."

Brook wasn't sure what she could say to Jemma Evanston without giving away the fact that they were monitoring her cell phone and online presence. Brook also couldn't alert the U.S. Marshal's Service that she was aware one of their witnesses had broken protocol. It was a delicate situation, and one that needed to be handled with care. Right now, Brook needed to concentrate on another mother.

"I'll be downstairs with Luna's family members if you need anything."

Brook had spent a good half an hour on the phone with Special Agent Landon Axel after the briefing this morning. He was her contact at the Charlotte office. She'd caught him up to speed, and then asked that he put a rush on the forensics. A lot of times a request from one of the field offices resulted in a faster outcome. If Sylvie and Theo struck out today, there was a chance that the unsub had used the same abandoned structure on previous occasions.

It didn't take long for Brook to grab the porcelain mug that she'd brought upstairs with her. She'd needed a refill for a while now, and her having her attention elsewhere might make Luna Breen's mother and sister more comfortable. Nothing was going to take away their grief, but it was Brook's job to figure out a way to extract information from them regardless of their heartbreak.

To Brook's surprise, Wyn was behind the bar. The rich aroma of coffee permeated the air, and it was clear that he'd already brewed another pot of coffee. He was in the process of sliding a mug her way. She set her empty one down on the bar, grateful for the exchange.

"Your guests are in one of the back booths. I offered them some lunch and refreshments, but they didn't want anything."

"Thanks, Wyn. For everything," Brook said, encompassing the fact that he'd programmed the coffee machine to brew at such an early hour. She hated to nitpick, but she couldn't risk the front door remaining open while such sensitive material was upstairs. "I was wondering if you wouldn't mind keeping the front door locked while we're staying here. I realize that in such a small town—"

"I locked the front door myself around three o'clock this morning," Wyn replied with a frown. He was already reaching for the phone. A lot of businesses still had landlines, and his was the old-fashioned kind that had probably been in the same place for the past twenty years. "Are you saying it wasn't locked, Ms. Sloane?"

"Brook," she corrected, not wanting to be on formal ground with their host. "Riggs and two of his friends walked in here around five o'clock this morning, so I assumed you left the bar unlocked. I'll go look for signs of—"

Wyn gave a hearty laugh before hanging up the phone. His relief was evident, and she had a sneaking suspicion as to the reason why. It didn't mean that she had to like it.

"I gave Riggs a key to this place a long time ago. He uses a room upstairs when he's had too much to drink. It's not often, but trust me when I say that man shouldn't drive when he's on a bender."

Brook was torn between asking Wyn more questions about the deputy and joining Mrs. Breen and her daughter in one of the booths. Their focus was solely on her at the moment, and she didn't want to keep them waiting.

"Wyn, I need to speak with Luna Breen's family members right now, but would you mind if I ask you a few questions about the area later on today?" Brook figured she wasn't getting one over on Wyn. He was an intelligent man, and his occupation had probably honed his abilities to read between the lines. "Maybe over lunch?"

"Sure."

Brook could sense Wyn's barriers sliding into place, and she should have known better than to give him time to think over her request. She grew up in a small town, and she understood how wary the residents were of strangers. There was nothing that she could say at this point that would ease his concern for one of their own except to display the same.

"My colleagues are up in those mountains with Riggs, Dominic Ryder, and Jace Mathers," Brook divulged, though she figured he was already privy to that information. The gossip mills in towns like this one worked overtime. "I'd just like to know that they are in good hands."

The tension visibly eased from Wyn's broad shoulders. He nodded his understanding and pursed his lips in commiseration.

"Those boys grew up in this town, Brook." Wyn had used her first name, and it was his way of telling her things between them had returned to normal. "Your colleagues are in good hands."

"Thanks, Wyn." Brook tapped the counter, but she didn't turn away quite yet. "I'd still like to treat you to lunch sometime. We do appreciate the ability to stay in town while conducting the investigation, and I'd like to show my gratitude."

"You know where to find me," Wyn said as he peered over his shoulder at a large clock hanging above the doorway to the kitchen. "My regulars will be showing up soon. Let me know if you need anything else."

Brook carried her coffee as she weaved through the tables to reach the side wall lined with booths. The first thing Brook took note of was how much Luna had resembled her mother, from the hazel eyes to the brown hair. They'd both been graced with athletic builds, good posture, and strong features that were currently etched in pain. The bags underneath Kim Breen's eyes were a testament to many sleepless nights.

"Mrs. Breen, I'm Brooklyn Sloane. I'm so sorry for your loss," Brook said softly, holding out her arm to shake the woman's hand. Kim's eyes were bloodshot and puffy from crying, and there had been a slight tremor in her fingers when she finally pulled away. "I know this is a difficult time for you and your family, but it would help with our investigation if you could answer a few questions for me."

"When can we see her?" Kim asked as she sat down next to her daughter. "When can we see Luna?"

Brook wasn't ready to answer that question, so she took a moment to introduce herself to Luna's younger sister.

"You must be Denise." Brook reached over the table, surprising the young woman. From the background checks on the Breen family members, Brook was aware that Denise was twenty-one years of age, but she looked years younger. "I know this might seem like an unusual meeting place, but we've turned the upstairs into a makeshift work area for me and my team."

"Do you know who killed my sister?"

Denise wasn't the wallflower that her hunched shoulders and clasped hands had originally signified. There was a defiance in young woman's brown eyes that would carry her through the investigation and beyond.

"I'll answer all your questions, but I'd like to fill you in a little on how the case will proceed from this point on," Brook said as she wrapped her hands around the coffee mug. She soaked in the warmth as if it would give her the strength needed to ask the difficult but necessary questions. "The FBI has officially taken over this case. My firm, S&E Investigations, has been hired as a consultant. We were originally requested to canvas the crime scene, gather the impertinent information, and then pass the case off to one of the field agents. I personally asked to remain on retainer. I'll do my best to bring Luna's killer to justice, but only if you're comfortable with my firm conducting the investigation."

"I looked you up." Denise's comment didn't come as a shock to Brook. "I know who you are."

Brook remained silent, not feeling the need to defend herself. If Denise and her mother had researched Brook's history, they also knew that she was very good at her job. She was neither humble nor narcissistic. She was a realist, and one who went above and beyond to see to it that the victims' families received closure.

"I chose to remain in the town closest to the trail that Luna took the morning of her hike. I know that the two of you are staying in the same B&B that Luna reserved a room for her weekend getaway. Forensics processed her room this morning. Any and all belongings were removed as evidence." Brook switched her focus to Kim. "Mrs. Breen, your daughter's remains were found in an abandoned cabin. An autopsy is being performed today, and I expect to have a cause of death later this afternoon."

"We saw them take away her things," Denise said as she glanced at her mother.

"Did she suffer?" Kim asked, her voice barely above a whisper. Denise reached over and grabbed her mother's hand. "Did my daughter suffer?"

"Yes." Brook wouldn't lie, but she also wouldn't give graphic details. It was bad enough that Kim's mind would forever bring forth flashes of graphic images born from the words written in the autopsy report. "And I'd like to apprehend the person responsible, which is why I need to ask you some questions. First and foremost, what brought Luna to the Smoky Mountains by herself?"

"Luna wasn't supposed to come here by herself," Kim replied as she enclosed her daughter's hand into hers. "Christina Jeffries has been Luna's best friend since middle school. She was supposed to be here, but she decided to remain back home to study for an exam. Christina is still obtaining her doctorate. The two of them had booked the weekend months ago. They always chose a random weekend in October to go hiking due to the cooler weather."

Brook was regretting not bringing down her tablet. She wasn't usually the one who interviewed family and friends. She preferred

Theo and Sylvie to handle these types of aspects of an investigation. Circumstances had forced her hand, and she needed to make up for the lack of manpower left behind.

"My sister was an avid hiker, and she loved the outdoors. As my mother said, Luna and Christina have been planning this trip for months."

"Why did Luna decide to continue with the weekend trip without Christina?"

"The B&B rate was nonrefundable," Kim replied as she finally released her daughter's hand in exchange for a napkin. She reached over and took one out of the silver dispenser. She took a moment to blow her nose and then wad the napkin into a small ball. "Luna wasn't inexperienced, Ms. Sloane. She knew what she was doing, and she was always prepared with the proper supplies."

"Did Luna mention anything unusual before she left Virginia?"

"No."

"Did Luna have a boyfriend or anyone special in her life?"

"No," Kim responded with a half-smile. "Luna was either working or hiking. She never had time for anything else."

Brook noticed the way that Denise lowered her gaze. She, too, reached for a napkin. She didn't use it the way her mother had, but instead just held it in between her hands.

"What about someone who Luna didn't get along with? Anyone who might have felt slighted by something Luna said or did recently?"

"No." Kim shook her head a bit more emphatically this time around. "Luna was kind-hearted, funny, and optimistic. She didn't have any enemies. Her patients adored her, her colleagues loved her, and..."

Kim's voice cracked, leaving Denise to fill in the rest.

"Luna didn't have any enemies."

"Did either of you speak to Luna when she arrived in North Carolina?" Brook asked, changing the direction of the conversation. "Either on the phone or through text messages?"

"Luna called me Friday and Saturday evening," Kim revealed as she used the balled-up napkin to dab the corner of her eye. "After dinner. She was supposed to call on Sunday when she was on the road, but..."

"We texted a few times, and Luna sent me some pictures that she had taken on her phone." Denise had folded her napkin to the point that it couldn't be folded anymore. She just kept turning the white square over and over in her fingers. "Nothing about this trip seemed different than the last."

"Do you have your cell phone?" Brook asked after she'd taken a sip of her coffee. She'd quietly set the mug back down on the table. "May I see the pictures?"

"Sure." Denise tossed the folded napkin onto the table. She then reached into her purse and pulled out her cell phone. After entering the passcode she'd used to protect against prying eyes, she handed over her phone. "There are about ten or twelve photos that Luna took on Friday and Saturday. None from Sunday."

"I called the police late Sunday night when Luna didn't call me. I spoke to the woman who owns the B&B, of course. Mauve Benson is her name. She said that Luna never checked out, and that was when we knew something was wrong."

Brook skimmed through the photographs. She would have to show the pictures to Riggs or Erica. Brook wasn't familiar with the area, so she couldn't tell if Luna had taken these photos from the trail or if she'd left the trail on her own. Most of the warrants had come through, and Bit was in the process of pulling all the information that Luna had uploaded to her phone. Forensics had the device itself to process, and then they would send the phone to Bit. Some pictures might have not been uploaded to the cloud.

"What are your plans right now?" Brook asked as she handed Denise her phone. "Are you staying in town for a while? Are you driving back to Virginia?"

"I want to see..."

"Mrs. Breen, your daughter's autopsy is being performed today. I'll see to it that you have the medical examiner's name and number. You can reach out to him to make arrangements," Brook said as she mulled over how to express her opinion without overstepping her bounds. No mother should remember their child the way Mrs. Breen would if she were to follow through with her request. "Sometimes, we're better off remembering our loved ones as they were in life."

"Mom, why don't you go splash some water on your face?" Denise urged as she rubbed her mother's shoulder. "I'll get the information we need for the medical examiner's office, and then we can talk about it on the drive back to the B&B."

Kim seemed hesitant, but she eventually gave into her daughter's appeal. Brook waited patiently for Denise to share whatever it was she knew about her sister that had been kept from their mother.

"Luna was having an affair with one of her colleagues. Her supervisor, in fact. She didn't think mom would understand." Denise brushed her long bangs out of the way as her eyes filled with more tears. "Kyle is a good guy. I met him once, but he wasn't into hiking as much as Luna. He stayed back in Virginia."

"What is Kyle's last name?" Brook asked, keeping her tone the same as it had been during the initial discussion. Everyone had their reasons for keeping secrets. "I'll need to speak with him."

"Kyle Ingesson. You won't say anything to my mother?"

Brook wasn't one to make promises that she couldn't keep, so she refrained from answering Denise's question. Brook pulled out a business card. She always kept one in the small, irrelevant pocket on her blazer. She'd prepared ahead today and wrote down the medical examiner's information on the back of the card.

"This is the phone number that you'll need to reach the medical examiner." Brook paused when someone entered the bar. Several someones, actually. "Denise, I understand how difficult this must be for you. For your mother. The rest of your family. Your first instinct is to remain in town, but you should know that this investigation could take weeks, months, or even years."

Brook caught sight of Kim walking back from the restroom. The four men and two women who had entered the bar were watching her with interest. Denise followed Brook's line of sight.

"I didn't want to say anything in front of Mom, but everything that I researched about you stated that you deal with serial killers. I'm assuming that's why you're here. I'm going to need to prepare my mother if—"

"Denise?" Brook reached across the table and rested her hand over the young woman's knuckles. "Your sister's remains were discovered yesterday. Give us time to investigate her murder. I give you my word that if we find evidence this wasn't some random act of violence, you and your mother will be the first ones I call."

"I'm sorry about that," Kim said as she went to reclaim her seat. Denise tried to scoot to the end, but Kim had returned more composed and determined to get answers. "A moment alone was just what I needed, and now I'd like some answers. You were inside the cabin with my daughter, Ms. Sloane. I want to know how you found her."

Someone else entered the bar, and it was clear that the place was a favorite for lunch. Brook took another sip of her coffee before leaving her mug on the table as she exited the booth.

"Why don't we take this outside? Get some fresh air while we finish our conversation?"

Denise quickly gathered her cell phone and the business card, tucking both into her purse as her mother patiently waited for her. The three of them eventually made their way outside, the cool breeze hitting them as they stepped onto the sidewalk. While the sun was shining, the warmth wasn't enough to chase away the chill of what she was about to disclose to Luna Breen's family.

Brook waited to speak until they were a block away from the bar.

"Mrs. Breen, the sheriff reached out to the park rangers after Luna didn't return to the B&B on Sunday night. They assembled search parties, and their starting point was a particular trail that Luna had mentioned to Mauve Benson during breakfast. Two of the experienced volunteers happened across an abandoned cabin quite a distance away from the trail. Once they realized what they were dealing with, they radioed back to base where someone there contacted the FBI."

"What did you find that the sheriff couldn't handle?" Denise asked as she all but pulled her mother down on a bench. Given that there weren't many storefronts on the main thoroughfare, the bench had been positioned in front of a bakery. This must have been where Theo had purchased the donuts for this morning's briefing. "What did they find that was so bad that the local police wouldn't take the case?"

"It's not that the local police wouldn't have taken the case," Brook amended as she leaned against the old-fashioned lamppost instead of joining them on the bench. She'd rather be facing them when she recited the facts of the crime scene. "It's more of a jurisdiction issue, along with what agency can best provide the resources needed for a case like this. You see, Luna's body was discovered tied to a chair. She'd been cut with a knife several times, and I believe she bled to death. Again, we won't know for sure until an autopsy is performed. I'm only telling you this so you understand the significance of this investigation."

As expected, Kim's face lost all color as she listened to Brook's toned-down description of what had been done to her daughter. Denise appeared equally horrified, her eyes wide with shock and disbelief. There were other factors that they didn't need to know right now, and Brook had glossed over the brutality of Luna's last few hours.

"I will keep you apprised every step of the way," Brook assured them as she took a step forward. She knelt before them, resting a hand on each of their knees. "There is no reason for you to stay here. I know that doing so makes you feel close to Luna, but you should return home. Plan your daughter's funeral. Say goodbye to her in a way that honors her memory. We'll handle everything else."

Denise began to whisper reassurances to her mother, though Brook wasn't sure that Kim could process anything but her own grief right now. Luna's sister was very mature for her age. There would come a time when Denise would buckle under her own grief, as well. Until then, she would be a source of strength for her mother.

Brook decided to give Kim and Denise their privacy, but she waited until the young woman nodded her consent. Brook slowly stood and began to walk back towards the bar.

She'd noticed upon exiting the pub that the same male subject who had been sitting at the counter last night had been standing outside the diner. He was dressed in jeans and a long-sleeved shirt, but he wasn't wearing an apron. She couldn't distinguish whether or not he worked at the diner.

It looked as if Wyn wasn't going to get his lunch today. Sitting down and having a conversation with the bartender was at the top of her list of things to do, but she was curious as to why the man standing in front of the diner seemed so fascinated with her and the team. She stepped off the curb, taking the time to look in both directions even though there wasn't a lot of traffic in Moonshine Valley.

When Brook refocused her gaze on the male subject, he'd already tossed his cigarette butt into the street and was halfway down the block. He never once looked back. She debated following him, but she wasn't quite ready to have a confrontation. Since she was already close to the curb, she figured she might as well take advantage of those inside the diner.

Sirens pierced the strange blanket of stillness that she'd first noticed upon driving into Moonshine Valley. Maybe it was due to the town's location and the picturesque view of the Smoky Mountains. Others might find peace in the quiet, but she found it hard to do so when a young woman had bled out not even an hour and a half away.

By the time Brook stepped onto the sidewalk, a sheriff's car had pulled alongside the curb. Whoever was inside shut off the engine, killing the siren with it.

"You must be the infamous Brooklyn Sloane."

"And you must be Sheriff Otto Jackson." Brook wasn't sure what had brought the good ol' sheriff to Moonshine Valley when Riggs had explained the small department being short on staff. She'd exchanged voicemails with the sheriff, but he hadn't seemed inclined to get too involved with the investigation. "You have perfect timing, Sheriff. I think it's time that the two of us were on a first name basis, don't you?"

Chapter Seven

Brooklyn Sloane

October 2023

Friday — 11:56am

"Not what you expected?"

Sheriff Jackson had claimed a table next to a large stone fireplace that took up most of the back right corner of what she would have called a restaurant. This wasn't a diner in the usual sense. The flickering flames cast a warm, inviting glow across the room, and the scent of burning hickory wood had greeted her over what she thought would be a greasy aroma.

The walls of Moonshine Diner were made of exposed wooden beams, and the hardwood floor had creaked slightly under her feet as she followed the sheriff's lead to a table and chairs made of sturdy, rough-hewn wood. The tablecloths were red and checkered, and each place setting had black cloth napkins.

"I'm not one who is usually surprised, but this place is a gem."

The ceiling was low and made of wooden planks, but it was the collection of antique hiking and climbing gear that hung from the walls that were the center of attention. She considered herself intelligent, but there were items included from nails and hooks that she wouldn't have been able to name if her life depended on it.

"You must not read those traveling magazines then." The sheriff removed his sunglasses and set them off to the side. He'd never put on his hat after exiting his vehicle, but he did have it in hand. He used it to cover his sunglasses before flipping over a black ceramic mug. "Moonshine Diner has been featured in a few of them over the years. People come from all over to eat here. Unfortunately, they'll all be coming to Moonshine Valley for another reason."

Brook reached out and turned over her mug, as well.

"I'm surprised you weren't up at the crime scene yesterday, Sheriff Jackson." Brook reached for the black cloth napkin and removed the silverware from the thick fabric. She spread the napkin out on her lap before meeting his stare. "I understand that this case falls under federal jurisdiction, but surely you're not one of those lawmen whose lack of interest gets in the way of justice. Unless, of course, your position is just a paycheck to you."

"Call me Otto." He lifted one side of his mouth as he leaned back to allow the waitress to pour his coffee. "And if this were about money, I'd be working here as a cook instead of spending all my time keeping meth heads out of my county."

Otto Jackson was at least four inches over six feet with dark skin and brown eyes that were more caramel in color than chocolate. Brook got the sense that there was still more to his absence yesterday than he was letting on, but they would get to that a little bit later.

"You're not the typical fed."

"You run into a lot of them out here?" Brook asked after she'd thanked her waitress. "And just for clarification, my firm consults with the Bureau."

"You and I are going to get along just fine," Otto said with a laugh. He reached for the container that held the sugar packets, holding it out to her first. She clearly surprised him when she declined his offer. He set the black container back down before taking two packets out for himself. "I appreciate the updates on the case. Keep them coming, and let me know if there is anything I can do to help."

"I've got to be honest with you, Otto. I didn't expect the offer after speaking with Riggs earlier this morning."

"Riggs didn't like to hear what I had to say about him spending more time in those mountains than he has in uniform lately," Otto amended as he stirred in his sugar. "I'm short-staffed, and Riggs is my go-to guy. He knows this area inside and out. I've already got two other deputies pulling twelve hours shifts, and now I'm going to be doing the same over the next couple of days until Riggs is done playing Grizzly Adams. No offense. I'm sure he's been a great asset to you over the past two days, but I've got an entire county comprised of numerous towns that I'm responsible for, and I don't like being left holding the bag."

Again, Brook sensed that there was something more to the situation than she was being told, but she would concentrate on the case right now. She took a tentative sip of her coffee, realizing immediately that she would be getting her coffee here instead of brewing it at the bar for the remainder of her stay.

"Trust me, you can become addicted to the stuff," Otto replied wryly as he sat back in his chair. He'd chosen a table so that they could both keep an eye on the entrance. There were other signs, such as his hair and the way his shoes shined that pointed toward a history in the military. "Wait until you try their Shepherd's Pie."

"You didn't require Luna Breen to be missing for a full twenty-four hours before sending Riggs up in those mountains, did you?"

"You and I both know that twenty-four-hour line is bullshit." Otto shrugged, as if to say that anyone would have handled Mrs. Breen's phone call the way he had last weekend. "I got the call around twenty-two hundred hours. I drove over to the B&B, spoke with Mauve, and then radioed Riggs. He was scheduled for second shift, so he was already on the clock. Mauve mentioned that Luna only took a day-pack, so I knew that she didn't have the supplies or equipment to spend the night up there. I'm a big believer that one can never be too cautious."

"And when did Riggs report back to you?"

"Right before dawn." Otto took a sip of his coffee. "Riggs had taken a satellite phone with him. Kept in touch every couple of hours, but there was nothing to be found. I sealed off Breen's room at the B&B, officially filed the missing persons report, and then contacted the park rangers first thing Monday morning."

"Did you join the search parties?"

"Do you swim in the ocean?"

It took a moment for Otto's question to register.

"I couldn't tell you the last time that I was at the ocean, Otto."

"You're reserved, cunning, and you know the lay of the land before you ever take one step to advance into a situation," Otto said as he lifted his coffee cup. He paused long enough to take another drink. "I'm guessing that if you did swim in the ocean, it would be to prove a point rather than for the sheer enjoyment of it. Too many unknowns. I'm the same when it comes to those mountains. I'm not a man who likes to waste time. I've got a job to do, and that job is to protect and serve my community. The best way for me to do that is to use my skills and resources where they are most needed. In this case, that means staying here and keeping an eye on things while the parker rangers cover their territory. Once in a while, that means loaning out my deputies. There will usually be a better outcome if everyone stays in their designated lanes."

"I would have initially guessed Army, but now I've revised my opinion. Career Navy?"

"Twenty years, one day, and nine hours served," Otto replied as he set his mug back down on the table. He didn't look a day over thirty, let alone forty. "It's not that I couldn't survive up there, Brook. I could, I have, and I will again...if ever needed. As it stands, the park rangers called the FBI, and the FBI chose to utilize a consultant. I'm not one to interfere with someone else's job unless it's absolutely necessary."

Otto was a completely different man than the one Riggs' had described, and Brook found the sheriff to be dedicated, competent, and had a presence about him that commanded respect. She wouldn't have minded his insights during this morning's briefing.

"Do the names Carissa Norman and Helen Beckham mean anything to you?"

"Beckham. Young woman who went missing about two or three years ago." Otto rubbed his index finger and thumb together as he recalled the details of the report. "Case is still open. She was never found."

"And Norman?"

"Sounds familiar, but I'd have to refresh my memory."

"Norman went missing five years ago, before you started serving the community as sheriff," Brook replied as she caught movement from behind the long wooden counter. Their waitress was bringing a tray of food out from the kitchen. Since they hadn't placed their lunch orders, Brook was guessing that the bowls held Shepherd's Pie. "You used the siren in your cruiser to let the server know you would be arriving soon."

"Guilty as charged," Otto said with a laugh. "Irene and I came to an agreement in the first few months of my term to help save me time. I've gotten called away from here too often waiting for my lunch. This way, I at least have a few minutes to swallow some food."

"Whatever we have as the special is what Otto is served," Irene said with a smile. Brook realized that Irene wasn't just on the wait staff. She was the owner and operator of Moonshine Diner. "I'll be back to top off your coffees."

"Where's Ned?" Otto asked as he squared his chair with the table. "Don't tell me that he went hiking, either. I know for a fact that he has an afternoon appointment scheduled with his parole officer."

"Ned's running a few minutes late, that's all." Irene cleared her throat. "I'll bring the two of you some waters, as well."

Otto narrowed his eyes as he monitored Irene's departure from the table. Brook wondered if Ned was the man who'd been smoking out front, but she didn't want to stray too far off topic.

"What can you tell me about Helen Beckham?"

"Other than she stayed at Hiker's Haven, not much. She was with a couple of friends who had too much to drink one night. She decided to hike on her own the following morning, and she was never seen again. We suspected the boyfriend had something to do with her disappearance, but there was no evidence to support that theory. Search parties were deployed, weeks were spent canvassing the trails and surrounding area, and eventually life moved on...as it always does. The flyer with her face plastered on the front is still hanging on the bulletin board at the station."

The two of them spent the next half an hour eating their lunches and discussing possible connections between the missing women. Brook had taken a moment to call Bit. She gave him details regarding her meeting with Kim and Denise Breen, explained that she was having lunch with the sheriff, and then gave her word that she would bring Bit back a pizza. Apparently, Moonshine Diner made an excellent one.

"Carissa Norman, Helen Beckham, and Luna Breen were all brunettes. All in their mid-twenties." Otto wiped his mouth with his napkin before setting it next to his plate. "And now you have one of my deputies searching other abandoned structures that aren't near the trails. I don't like where you're going with this, Brook."

"Who is Ned, and why is he on parole?"

Brook had made sure that Irene wasn't within earshot. The woman had obviously lied to cover for the man after Otto had asked about Ned's whereabouts. Irene cared for him. Employee? Son? Nephew? Brook had been there and done that herself. Unfortunately, Irene had no idea what those so-called loved ones were capable of outside of the bubble that had been self-imposed.

"Ned Proehl. Irene's nephew. Assault and battery."

Brook leaned back in her chair, still holding onto her napkin. There was an edge to Otto's voice that told her there was more to the story.

"It was due to a domestic disturbance about a year ago. Ned served three months, but he claims his actions were in self-defense." Otto clicked his tongue on the roof of his mouth. "Before you ask, the incident took place outside of my jurisdiction. My deputies and I had nothing to do with his arrest."

Brook remained silent, because Otto knew damn well that wasn't the question she had on her mind. Considering that Otto ate at the Moonshine Diner at least three times a week, he would have insight as to whether or not Ned was the type of man to hurt a woman.

"From my standpoint, Ned has followed the parameters set forth by his parole officer. He's kept his nose clean, has a job here at the diner helping out in the kitchen, and seems to be on the right path." Otto rested an elbow on the table. "I keep a close eye on him because of Irene. She does a lot for this community."

"What about Nate and Jules Knowles, Dominic Ryder, and Jace Mathers?"

"I'm not sure what you're asking me," Otto said as he once again rubbed his index finger and thumb together. The tic seemed to occur when there was something placed in front of him that he couldn't figure out. "Nate and Jules Knowles are volunteers on the mountain rescue teams from time to time when needed. Local veterinarians who cover multiple counties. Good people."

"I'm just trying to get a feel for those volunteering their time, that's all."

"Dominic is mostly a blogger, although he does freelance for a local paper now and again. If you're worried about him having access to the case, he has helped us out numerous times without issue. If I recall correctly, I overheard someone say that he got lost in the mountains when he was a young boy. A search party found him a day later. A bit dehydrated, but otherwise fine. As for Jace, he owns the bait and tackle shop a block down the street. I feel for him, though. Lost his brother in a climbing accident back in 2003, and then he lost his father some years back. I heard through the grapevine that he and his wife are on the outs."

Hearing Otto describe some of the reasons that the volunteers offered their free time to help others struck a chord, and Brook found herself being pulled in that direction.

"What about Nate and Jules? Why do they volunteer their time?"

"Nate Knowles?" Irene had overheard the conversation, but Brook hadn't minded since she and Otto had moved on from the woman's nephew. "Nate's one of the good ones. Loves animals. Met his wife in college. As for why he helps out with the search parties, it's because he wants to pay back what some of the volunteers did for him back in the day. You see, Nate was a late bloomer. He wasn't athletic back then, and he didn't fit in well with the other boys his age who liked to spend their time outdoors. One day, his dog chased a deer into the woods. That chocolate lab was his best friend. Anyway, the town couldn't stand to see that boy so unhappy, so a bunch of people joined together and went searching for the pup. Took two days, but that dog was finally found with an injured leg. Nate never forgot the help that he received, and he never forgot his roots. He and Jules set up their practice after graduation and have given back to the community in many ways."

"There you have it," Otto said with a smile and a wink. Brook had noticed an underlying chemistry between the two of them. Irene was at least ten years older, but that hadn't seemed to dampen their attraction to one another. Considering that Graham was more than twenty years her senior, she understood more than most that age meant nothing in the grand scheme of things. "No more coffee for me, Irene. I need to head back out and cover Riggs' shift."

Brook reached for her phone, which happened to be in a case that allowed her to keep a corporate credit card in a sleeve. She preferred to carry a purse, but there were many times it was more convenient just to carry her cell phone.

"Put that away," Otto instructed as he reached for his hat and sunglasses. "Lunch is on me. I'm glad that we got to know one another, Brook. I'd like to be kept apprised of any new information regarding the case. Should you need any additional help, I'm a phone call away."

Brook took a moment to thank Irene for such a delicious lunch, picked up Bit's pizza, and also snagged a large to-go cup of coffee. While there was nothing wrong with Wyn's coffee behind the bar, the diner's rich grounds won the contest hands down.

"Otto?" Brook had waited until they were outside to ask her question. He'd been about to step off the curb when she'd called out his name. "Most everyone seems to have a reason as to why they volunteer their time when emergencies arise in the surrounding area, but you never mentioned what Riggs' motivation was to join in these mountain rescue teams."

"Moonshine Valley is Riggs' hometown," Otto replied as he slipped on his sunglasses. He didn't bother to put on his hat since he was about to get behind the steering wheel of his cruiser. "He grew up in these mountains."

"Then why not be a park ranger?"

Otto had been turning his hat over in his hands as they talked, but he stilled his movements upon hearing her question. She made sure that her grip on the pizza box and coffee didn't change, but she sensed the ripple of tension in the air. She'd hit on something, and she braced herself for a possible shift in the case.

It wasn't unheard of for a killer to involve himself in an investigation.

"I trust Riggs, Brook."

"That isn't what I asked, Otto."

The sheriff's audible sigh reflected his reluctance to share personal information, but he also knew that she would find out what she needed with a background check and a few phone calls. Bit had submitted for information on all parties involved with the case, but the results given so far were just surface details. The next few days would have continuous information funneling in from numerous agencies.

"Why would Riggs opt to work as a deputy for the county sheriff's office instead of the park rangers?"

"Because Riggs wouldn't have been able to pass a federal background check." Otto turned, stepped off the curb, and walked around his cruiser. He unlocked the car door and opened it so that he could toss his hat onto the passenger seat. Only then did he meet her gaze over the hood. "As a county sheriff's office, we have different requirements, and I was permitted to make an exception. I did, and I've had no regrets. People can change, Brook. Bear that in mind when you look at Riggs' file."

Chapter Eight

Theo Neville

October 2023

Friday — 1:12pm

The thick underbrush had become quite dense, forming what could only be described as a wall of green. Tangled vines had wrapped themselves around the wide tree trunks, and there was what one might label a natural tapestry overhead that filtered sunlight into illuminating beams. A musty odor of fallen leaves had replaced the pleasant scent of pine, and the various birds' melodies seemed quite stifled by the concentrated vegetation.

"I've got to tell you, Dominic." Theo fortunately hadn't been bothered by mosquitos during the hike yesterday, and he'd chalked it up to the cooler weather in October. Unfortunately, he'd decided that those annoying insects had all been hiding in the dense foliage all along. "We seem relatively far from the trail. Just how confident are you that there is a cabin out this way?"

"Eight percent chance we're on the right path."

There was no path, but Theo figured he didn't need to point that out. He'd spent the majority of his childhood in Queens before moving to one of the suburbs after his father received his first promotion within the NYPD. Most of Theo's family members were more accustomed to city life than the suburbs. Not even some of his friends in the FBI academy who grew up on a back country road would be able to survive in these mountains.

"You're not instilling a lot of confidence in me, Dominic."

Theo considered himself in shape, but he'd experienced a cramp or two in his calves since they'd started out this morning. He usually ran several miles a day, worked out regularly with the free weights in the office back in D.C., and he ate everything in moderation. While he didn't mind the strenuous activity of hiking in the general sense, he could have done without having to be on the constant look out for black bears and coyotes. He was also mindful of where he stepped, because he didn't need Dominic to return to town with some wild story that Theo wouldn't be able to live down for years to come.

Theo had asked several times about the odds of them stepping on a snake, and Dominic had explained each and every time that snakes were more afraid of humans than the other way around. The likelihood of them seeing a snake was low. It had taken every ounce of willpower for Theo not to call Dominic out for being a liar.

The terrain had become more rugged with large boulders and fallen trees blocking their way, but Theo suddenly found himself in somewhat of a clearing. The ground was still uneven and rocky, and there were even gnarled roots and dead tree trunks, but at least the sun was able to reach them given the lack of tall trees in the immediate region.

"There," Dominic said as he came to a stop about a few yards away from what turned out to be more of a shed than a cabin. "Not much, but I remember it being there from when I was young. Believe it or not, a trail from the main path did exist at one point."

The exterior of the dwelling was weathered and worn from being exposed to the elements. From where they were standing, Theo guessed that there was only one window. He could see the jagged glass against a board that someone had used to cover the opening.

"This wasn't on those maps that Riggs showed us earlier."

Theo pulled out his cell phone, but not to make any calls. There was no service for miles, which was why he'd been using the satellite phone to check in with Bit. Theo had been using his cell phone to take pictures of the places that they'd been able to access.

They had yet to find any structures that had been disturbed or shown signs of any type of crime scene. Sylvie had made sure that he'd had the luminol and flashlight needed to uncover blood. From the hourly check-ins with Bit, it appeared that she and Riggs hadn't had any luck in that department, either.

"Am I reading this right?" Once Theo had finished taking a couple of pictures, he accessed his photographs. He then pulled up an image of the old map that Riggs had shown them earlier. After studying it for a moment, he zoomed into the area where he believed they were currently standing, but he could have been way off base. "Are we about here?"

"That's right." Dominic adjusted the ballcap that he'd pulled out of his backpack hours ago. He then leaned in close and pointed at a specific point on the display. "See this line? That's the main trail. This here...is basically the one we took to reach this place. Not sure who built it, though. No records on the place, either."

Theo often wondered where people went when they wanted to disappear. Take Jacob Walsh as an example. He'd somehow been able to hide in plain sight without anyone the wiser. No one could tell Theo that the man hadn't found some secluded place to live for extended periods of time. What better place than the mountains off the main trails and far from civilization?

As they advanced toward the door, Theo thought over the time frame that Brook had given in this morning's briefing. If Carissa Norman turned out to be a victim of the unsub, then her murder had occurred close to five years ago. There would be nothing left of her but skeletal bones. What Brook hadn't covered in the meeting was how the unsub disposed of the bodies. She'd mentioned yesterday that she believed the killer would have eventually returned to the crime scene, but why wait so long?

"This door is barely hanging on by the hinges," Theo said as he studied the entrance. The dry rot was evident, and he was afraid one push would disintegrate the wood into a thousand pieces. He hadn't needed to turn the handle, either. "There's nothing in here."

A sense of emptiness and abandonment permeated the shed. Theo had half-expected to find something, anything that would give them a break in the case. Not that any results had been yielded from the previous abandoned structures. While he'd never witnessed Brook swing wide on a profile, there was a good chance that Luna Breen's death had been personal.

The air inside the small shack was stale, and the mustiness had only amplified as he'd stepped inside. Theo removed his backpack and reached into the side pocket for the small spray bottle. Dominic remained outside while Theo worked, as he had with the other sites.

"Anything?" Domonic called out after a few minutes.

"No." Theo had already finished and stored the spray bottle and flashlight into his pack. He slung one of the straps over his shoulder before doing the same with the other. He then made sure both thick strips of fabric were snug before stepping back outside into the fresh air. "Nothing. Where to next?"

Dominic pointed toward the north, but Theo's interest was to the east.

"Dominic?" Theo stopped short as he stared off into the distance. Had they still been in the dense part of the woods, he never would have noticed the faint smoke billowing into the air. "What is that?"

By the time that Dominic had turned around, the hazy smolder had faded into nothing. Theo figured they were a quarter of a mile away from whoever had obviously burned something, and he couldn't just leave well enough alone.

"I want to head in that direction."

"Are you sure?" Dominic asked as he adjusted the bill of his ballcap once more. "This detour took a good hour off our day as it is, but to veer off on a course that will take us an additional hour or two might mean we don't clear some of these cabins you wanted to check out."

"I'll come back up here tomorrow if necessary."

Theo would take full responsibility for them not being able to clear as many sites as possible, but he didn't want to risk missing something because such a deviation from the schedule might be a waste of time. Granted, there were only so many hours of daylight left, but he wouldn't risk missing something pertinent just because he might have to drag his ass up this mountain tomorrow.

"You'd have to come up here with Jace, Riggs, or Erica," Dominic said as he fell into step beside Theo. He kept an eye on the sky for any sign of more smoke while they walked, mindful that they were about to enter another area of thick vegetation. "I'm supposed to interview Chad Thompson tomorrow for my blog."

"Chad Thompson?"

Dominic shot Theo a sideways look of disbelief before carefully stepping over a fallen log. They were once again walking over rough terrain, and Theo began to pay more attention to where he was stepping than Dominic's facial expressions.

"A legendary climber, though he retired a few years ago."

"You climb?"

"Nah," Dominic said as he continued forward. His voice was a bit muffled, but Theo could still hear him clear enough. "I'm not an adrenaline junky."

"You volunteer for search parties when a hiker goes missing," Theo pointed out as he followed behind. Every now and then he would scan the area around them, as was his habit in any setting. "I've had adrenaline pumping through my veins all day at the thought of crossing paths with a black bear."

"Didn't you say your injury was from a case involving a serial killer?"

Theo shrugged, not that Dominic caught the movement considering he was focused on the path in front of them. Both fell silent as they navigated over some rocky landscape. Once they were back on solid soil, Theo explained the main difference between a human and a wild animal.

"I can read the body language of an individual. Granted, I was a little too late in reacting to the man who we'd closed in on, but that error was mine and mine alone. A black bear? Coyote? Snake? They're unpredictable."

"Hiking comes second nature to me, I guess. I grew up in Moonshine Valley, as did Riggs and Jace. We weren't in the same class or anything. Riggs is three years older than me, and I'm two years older than Jace." Dominic came to a stop so that he could take a drink from his water bottle. It wasn't a canteen, but instead one of those travel bottles that could easily be hooked to his backpack. "We all know the trails well enough, but I got lost when I was young. Spent a night roaming these mountains, wondering if I would ever see my parents again."

Theo could see where this conversation was heading, and he now understood Dominic a bit better than before. Getting lost in the mall as a child could leave a lasting impression, but to be lost in the Smoky Mountains without water, food, or other supplies could be a death sentence.

"I give back when I can, but hiking isn't about the adrenaline rush. It's connecting with nature, although there's no denying that she can be brutal at times." Dominic grimaced, as if he'd heard his own words. "Sorry. What happened to Luna Breen was awful. Like I said, I want to help. How far away do you think that smoke was located? I caught the tail end of it, so it's difficult to calculate the distance."

"Maybe a quarter of a mile."

They continued to walk with Dominic asking questions about the investigation. Theo wanted to believe the man regarding his claims of wanting to help, but it was challenging to separate the man from his job. Regardless that Dominic mostly concentrated on a hiking blog, it would be best for everyone on the team to remember that Dominic freelanced for a local paper. Anything said could be taken out of context, and Theo refused to be responsible for details being leaked to the public. Brook had been mindful of that very fact during this morning's briefing.

At least twenty minutes had passed before Theo and Dominic stopped in front of a slight incline. Dominic studied the terrain before pointing at something in the distance.

"We can access higher ground from those rocks, or we can take the long way around." Dominic took off his cap and ran a hand down his face. There had been some perspiration on his forehead, but Theo doubted the man was too hot. There was a slight chill in the air. Their exertion from the hike kept their body temperatures raised to the point of comfort. "The longer way around would probably only add five to ten minutes."

Theo figured that he would be hiking these mountains tomorrow given the detour, so a little more time added for safety wouldn't matter in the long run.

"Better safe than sorry," Theo replied as he fell behind Dominic. The blogger set his cap back on his head. "When we reach the top of this peak, we'll take a small break so that I can touch base with Bit."

"Wasn't your boss supposed to meet with Luna Breen's family members today?"

Seeing as Dominic already knew the answer to his own question, Theo didn't bother to respond. He'd prefer not to talk about the case in specifics. He also recognized when someone was trying to dig for information. Dominic should probably spend more of his free time blogging than freelance writing for the newspaper. He wasn't experienced enough to pull one over on someone who had dealt with the press numerous times over the years.

"I'm curious," Dominic said with an intense interest, causing tension to settle into Theo's shoulders. Dominic was going to try for the direct route. He was a nice enough guy, but he'd been slowly doing his best to work Brook into the conversation all morning. Not only wasn't Theo going to discuss the case in specifics, he sure as hell wasn't going to talk about Brook. "Does your boss ever talk about her brother?"

"Dominic, you seem like a good guy," Theo stated as they went into the final stretch of the angled terrain. They'd avoided the rocks, but there was no avoiding the steep landscape. "I really don't want to find out otherwise. Do you understand me?"

By this time, they'd finally reached the peak.

They both came to a stop, and Dominic seemed to hesitate with his answer. Theo's gaze never wavered, because he wasn't about to be worked over by a blogger who saw a way to increase his viewership.

Brooklyn Sloane wasn't fodder to be used in such a manner.

She'd worked hard to get where she was today. There had been many missteps, but she'd finally reached a point where she wasn't going through the motions. She was no longer living just for the sake of apprehending her brother.

It had taken close to two years, but she no longer viewed the team as mere colleagues. They'd become a family of sorts, and she was learning that it was okay to form relationships. Having Jacob behind bars was just the icing on the cake, and Theo wasn't about to let anyone steal Brook's dessert.

"I didn't mean any harm," Dominic said as he lifted both hands in mock surrender. "I was just curious."

As far as Theo was concerned, the conversation was over.

There was a large boulder off to the right, so Theo made his way in that direction while shrugging out of his backpack. He set it down on the large rock so that it was easier for him to retrieve the satellite phone. It didn't take him long to connect with Bit.

"Hey, Big T. Boss just brought back the best pizza that I have ever tasted in my life. I was going to save you a slice, but I definitely don't have that kind of willpower. How's that protein bar of yours?"

"You're lucky that I'm over two hours away, Bit," Theo replied wryly as he scanned the area. They were in a region that didn't have as many trees, and there didn't seem to be any sign of life other than a few birds flapping their wings in the trees above. Most of them had fallen silent the moment he and Dominic had come into view. "Nothing to report. Anything from Sylvie?"

"Little T didn't find any sign of a crime scene, but she did say that there was some disturbance in one of the abandoned structures. Probably from wildlife, but she took some pictures just in case. Boss had lunch with Sheriff Jackson."

Theo had gotten to know Bit's tones rather well, and there was something more to know regarding Brook's lunch with the sheriff.

"I'm sure that I'll hear all about it over that pizza you owe me, but not right now." Theo noticed the slight shake of Dominic's head. He'd slid his tongue over his teeth in exasperation, as if Theo had taken their previous conversation out of context. Well, Dominic would just have to get over the intended slight. "I'll touch base in an hour."

Theo signed off before Bit could say anything else, fully expecting Dominic to launch into a speech about how he could be trusted with information. That might be the case, but Theo didn't see any reason to test that pledge. Oddly enough, Dominic's attention had been diverted to the reason Theo had wanted to canvass this particular area in the first place.

"Smoke," Theo murmured as he stared at the wisp weaving itself through the air. The thin, elongated line twisted with the gentle breeze and was eventually carried off as if it had never existed. "What do you think?"

"Someone is trying to start a fire. They're probably using too much kindling," Dominic said as he glanced around their immediate surroundings. "You know, that might be one of the trails that Erika and Jace are working off of today."

"You think they're in trouble?"

"Nah," Dominic immediately replied. He started to walk in that direction, and Theo followed suit. "Both are competent hikers. I wager that it's probably some hikers trying to set up camp."

"Isn't it a little early?"

"Some hikers like to camp for the weekend, but some don't want to be too far from town. Moonshine Valley is about two hours from here, but Black Oak is about an hour hike from the west." Dominic sidestepped uneven ground for more solid footing. Theo did the same while keeping an eye on the area where the smoke seemed to have originated from. "Hikers set up camp, and then they explore."

Theo and Dominic might have walked for another eight minutes when the campsite finally came into view. Sure enough, there were three tents set up and one person tending to a small flame that wasn't even large enough to call a campfire.

"Need help?" Dominic asked loudly so as not to startle the woman.

"I think I've got it now," she said with a laugh. "I spilled some water when I went to put the pot on the tripod, and then I had to start over."

The flames began to dance and grow, casting another faint line of smoke into the air. There was a pot off to the side, but she made no attempt to hook the handle over the tripod.

"See? All good now." The woman flashed a smile before tilting her head in curiosity. "I'm Selena, by the way. I volunteered to stay behind and get started on a late lunch. The others should be back soon."

Selena appeared to be in her mid-twenties. She had brown hair that she wore in a messy bun, and she couldn't have been two or three inches over five feet. She'd been smart to say that she didn't expect to be alone for too long.

"I'm Dominic, and this is Theo. We've been—"

"We're just passing through," Theo interrupted to reassure her that she wouldn't have to make small talk for long. Dominic had obviously been going to share the reason they were hiking, but Theo didn't want to frighten the woman. "Enjoy your weekend."

Theo made sure that Dominic had no choice but to follow him. It wasn't long before they'd hit the trail that Dominic had mentioned earlier. Theo didn't want to overlap the territory that Erika and Jace were covering, so he finally came to a stop.

"You don't think that we should have warned Selena? Your boss talked a lot about that profile of hers, and Selena seems to check all the boxes, doesn't she?"

"Selena isn't hiking alone, and there's no need to start a wave of panic that would surely circulate throughout Moonshine Valley, Big Oak, and the other surrounding towns that feed into these trails." Theo wouldn't divulge to Dominic how strong the urge had been to instruct Selena to pack up her things and head home. He'd learned long ago that guilt wasn't a useful emotion. Such sentiment caused knee-jerk reactions that weren't necessarily the right decisions later on down the line. "I get it, Dominic. I do. I'd like to clear out every hiker on this mountain, but that's unrealistic. Until we have proof that Luna Breen was one in a long line of victims, we keep searching for answers and allow life around here to carry on as usual."

Dominic didn't seem to agree, but he motioned that they should veer off the trail so that they could resume their search.

The detour had been a waste of time.

Maybe.

"Stay here," Theo requested as he began to retrace his steps. "I want to ask Selena a question. I'll be right back."

Considering that they hadn't gotten too far away from the campsite, it hadn't taken more than a minute for Theo to find Selena still sitting next to the fire. She'd managed to get the pot on the tripod, though the contents weren't hot enough to give off any aroma yet.

"Selena? I don't mean to bother you again, but have you seen any other hikers today?" Theo realized that his question was rather broad, and that she probably had seen many hikers. He and Dominic had crossed paths with a lot of people on the main trail until they'd deviated into more natural territory. "We're just trying to meet up with a friend, but we can't recall what trail that he was hiking today. He would have been alone."

Selena's smile had faded upon hearing Theo's first question, but she relaxed somewhat after he'd explained the reason behind his inquiry. Still, she'd crossed her arms as she rested them against her knees in a defensive gesture.

"I did see someone in a dark blue jacket up ahead of us on the trail, but he must have been walking fast. When we came up over the hill, he was nowhere to be found." Selena gave a slight shrug, as if to say she wished she could have helped more. "I couldn't even tell you what the guy looked like, though. I do know that he had on a dark beanie."

"Our friend wears one," Theo said with a smile. He didn't want to leave Selena feeling uneasy. "Then again, I'm sure a lot of other hikers wear beanies, too. Gives us hope, though. Thanks. Enjoy your weekend."

Theo had gotten maybe two feet away when Selena called out to him.

"Oh, wait! Does your friend use a walking stick? I'm pretty sure the guy was using a walking stick, if that helps."

Theo thought back to the crime scene. Brook had mentioned that there had been a smudge on the wall that stood out. She'd thought that maybe the unsub had rubbed against the wall when setting the victims backpack on the floor. Given the amount of dust and cobwebs, such a disturbance would have been evident.

What if the killer had rested a trekking pole against the wall?

"As a matter of fact, he does," Theo replied as he scanned the area. "Which way did you say he went?"

"Like I said, I lost sight of him on the trail," Selena said regretfully as she cast a glance toward the contents in the pot. "Good luck, though."

Theo bid Selena goodbye and began to make his way back toward Dominic. His so-called partner for the day hadn't been patient enough, and he'd retraced his steps until they met on middle ground.

"What was that about?" Dominic asked, completely in the dark as to why Theo had returned to speak with Selena. "What did I miss?"

"I want to walk the trail for a while," Theo said as he scanned the area for the easiest way to reach the main path. Selena and her friends had set up camp near the trail, but far enough away so that they wouldn't be bothered by day hikers. "Selena mentioned seeing a male individual with a dark jacket."

"Do you know how many hikers are out here? I don't think that I need to tell you that—"

"You don't," Theo reassured him as they both began to walk in that direction. "Just humor me, okay? You said yourself that you felt bad about not telling Selena about Luna Breen. If Selena did hike from Big Oak, there's a chance she has no idea that a murder was even committed nearby. While Luna Breen's death has hit the local channels, it hasn't done so with the national news outlets. As I said, the last thing we want to do is cause a panic within the community."

"We'll be heading back toward Moonshine Valley if we follow this trail."

"I need to hike up here tomorrow anyway. We'll walk the trail, and then call it an early day."

"Suit yourself."

There seemed to be a bit of disappointment in Dominic's tone over the fact that they weren't going to get a chance to check out the remaining dwellings that they'd circled on the map. There had to be many more that weren't even listed, but Theo didn't think this day was a waste at all.

"Hey, Dominic. Tell me again the various reasons why hikers use walking sticks."

CHAPTER NINE

Brooklyn Sloane

October 2023

Friday — 3:26pm

The crisp autumn air whistled through the colorful foliage of the trees behind a two-story log cabin that had been converted into a charming inn. The bed and breakfast, aptly named Hiker's Haven, stood proudly amidst the splendor of the fall season. Its weathered wooden exterior blended harmoniously with the vibrant reds and oranges of the leaves that had managed not to fall from the branches above. Even the front porch, which was adorned with matching rustic rocking chairs, offered a serene spot to enjoy the breathtaking view of the Smoky Mountains.

Brook had pulled the rental SUV into a spot next to a Jeep Wrangler. She closed the door before taking notice of an elderly gentleman looking out one of the windows on the lower level. He didn't seem to mind that she'd caught him staring at her. It wasn't until she began to walk up the wooden steps of the porch that he let the curtain fall back into place.

She'd wanted to see Luna Breen's room herself, though the forensics team had already taken the victim's belongings. They wouldn't release the room for Mauve Benson to rent out for another few days. It was standard procedure, just in case the team found something that would initiate their return.

Brook readjusted the strap of her purse as she reached for the silver knob and turned it to the right. Stepping inside, the quaint lobby exuded an inviting charm with its exposed wooden beams and cozy seating area. A grand fireplace made of river rock took up most of the far wall, with bookshelves on either side on the mantel. The blazing fire crackled and popped, casting a warm glow that mirrored the gentle hues of the garland made of autumn leaves that had been draped over the mantel.

A middle-aged woman was sitting in a rocking chair while knitting, but she'd immediately set her project to the side upon hearing someone come through the front entrance. The check-in counter was to the left of the door, and there was a very large bulletin board to the right covered with maps of the immediate area. Trails were listed with specific overlooks, along with popular campsites for those hikers who preferred company.

"May I help you?" the woman asked with a welcoming smile as she stepped behind the counter. The older gentleman who Brook had spotted at the window must have vacated the area, because he was nowhere to be seen. "I'm Mauve, owner of Hiker's Haven."

"My name is Brook Sloane, and I'm a consultant working with the FBI on the Breen case," Brook explained as she took out her identification. Mauve glanced down at the credentials, but she had clearly taken Brook's word at face value. She wasn't so sure how she felt about that, but it wasn't like there was anything left behind to tamper with in the room. "I was hoping to ask you a few questions."

"My heart breaks every time that I see that girl's mother and sister. They arrived this morning, you know. I had Kirk take them some of my chili for lunch, though I doubt they'll eat anything. They didn't even eat breakfast," Mauve said as she retraced her steps and came back around the counter.

Mauve pulled the sides of her cardigan sweater together as she motioned toward the fireplace. Plush chairs and couches that were adorned with soft blankets offered a large cozy area for the guests. Brook understood why the hikers, especially those who only went out for the day, stayed at Hiker's Haven.

"When Luna didn't return that evening, her mother had called several times," Mauve explained as she sat on the couch. "It wasn't a surprise when Sheriff Jackson stopped in. He asked me if there was a chance that Luna decided to camp out, but I saw her leave Sunday morning. She only had her day pack."

"How was Luna's demeanor?" Brook asked as she claimed one of the overstuffed chairs. "Did she seem preoccupied? Upset?"

The beige pillow gave Brook's back some support so that she wasn't swallowed by the cushions. A part of her was tempted to call Bit and have him pack up the portable monitor and all the materials that they'd only just started to collect before it became too cumbersome to move. Then she thought of the bar and its patrons, specifically Ned Proehl. There was a reason that she'd chosen to stay in Moonshine Valley, and that reason hadn't changed.

"Goodness, no. That girl was all smiles, all the time."

"And Luna checked in by herself?"

"Yes, although Luna had originally booked a room with two beds. Her friend was supposed to have joined her for the weekend, but I guess something came up and the other girl had to cancel." Mauve shook her head in despair. "I couldn't believe it when I heard that she'd been found murdered yesterday. I told those people who were here earlier this morning that I didn't let anyone besides the sheriff and his deputy inside Luna's room last weekend."

Those people were members of the forensics team.

"Which deputy would that have been?" Brook asked, keeping all judgement out of her voice. "From my understanding, there are several deputies working under Sheriff Jackson."

"My dear Riggs," Mauve said with another smile before gently resting her hand on her chest. "He's worked so hard to make something of himself, and I'd like to think that I pitched in and helped in some way."

The moment that Brook had returned to her room above the bar after having lunch with the sheriff, she'd immediately crossed the threshold of the connecting doorway. Bit had practically lunged for the pizza, but he'd been extremely productive while she'd been gone.

Bit not only had background checks available on all the volunteers who'd given their time and effort to the mountain rescue team earlier in the week, but he'd also collected more information on Riggs, Jace, Dominic, Erica, and even Hal Eggers. While Erica didn't fit the profile, and neither did Hal Eggers given his age, one could never discount an oddity here and there.

Brook had discovered that Riggs hadn't had the best childhood, and he'd basically grown up without parents. His older brother had hidden the fact that their father had up and left when Riggs was still in diapers and their mother had been a drug addict. She had frequented the neighboring towns where the people dealing drugs could be found, and she'd be gone for days, sometimes weeks at a time. By the time that Riggs was a senior in high school, his mother had been found dead in a seedy hotel thirty miles from Moonshine Valley with a needle in her arm.

While his parents' transgressions would not have prevented Riggs from applying for a federal agency, his juvenile record had the courtesy of sealing that coffin shut. Brook had to place a discreet call and phone in a favor to discover that Riggs had been arrested three days prior to his eighteenth birthday...for pulling a knife on another kid.

The other seventeen-year-old boy had needed stitches in his hand by the time a teacher had intervened and stopped someone from being seriously hurt.

It would have been easy for the sheriff—Roger Kitt, at the time—to press the prosecuting attorney to try Riggs as an adult. Hell, she'd been surprised that the prosecuting attorney himself hadn't taken it upon himself to do so. It hadn't made any sense to her until she'd dug a little deeper and discovered that the prosecuting attorney's wife had been the guidance counselor for the high school where the incident had taken place.

There was obviously more to the story than what had been reported by the hospital, which was who had followed protocol and called the sheriff in the first place. It was very interesting to Brook that the staff members of the school hadn't been the ones to place that call.

"Riggs came by the B&B on Sunday night?" Brook asked as she caught movement by the stairs. She kept her gaze on Mauve, needing the woman to be very specific about that day. The sheriff had mentioned that he was the one to stop by Hiker's Haven. According to Otto, Riggs had been working second shift and then was the one to hike up in the mountains. "Or Monday?"

"I believe Monday or Tuesday." Mauve waved her hand in the air as if the detail was minor. "Both he and the sheriff searched through Luna's room, hoping that she might have left town without checking out. Unfortunately, her clothes and toiletries were still in her room."

"Did anyone stop by the B&B to speak with Luna?" Brook inquired, casually skimming her gaze throughout the room. The movement she'd caught near the stairs hadn't been the older gentleman. Instead, a younger man had come to a stop on the last step. He was staring down at his phone, only she wasn't so sure that his attention was on the screen. "Did Luna make any friends while she was here? Maybe she connected with some of the other hikers?"

"Luna arrived on Friday, and she ate here that evening. She mingled with some of the other hikers, but I wouldn't say she hit it off with anyone." Mauve gestured toward a very long dining room table. "We always have a dinner buffet for our guests, as well as breakfast. Since no one is usually around for lunch, we don't serve food then."

"What about Saturday evening?" Brook asked as the male subject finally moved off the last step, but he only made it as far as the bulletin board. She doubted that there had been anything interesting on his phone, just as she suspected that he wasn't really standing in front of the bulletin board in search of a trail to hike. "Did Luna eat breakfast and dinner here on Saturday?"

"Yes, and she even joined us for breakfast on Sunday morning," Mauve revealed, her attention diverted slightly as well after she realized that someone was standing in front of the large bulletin board. She frowned a bit, but she made no move to check on her guest. "Luna and another hiker were talking about the trails, which was why I was able to let the sheriff know which one she'd chosen to hike that morning."

"You wouldn't happen to remember the name of the hiker, would you?"

For the first time since Brook had started to question Mauve, the older woman hesitated to respond. She pursed her lips and laced her fingers together in uncertainty over giving names to an investigator.

"Mauve, Luna Breen was abducted, dragged through the mountains, and killed in an extremely brutal manner." Brook's words hit her target. "I'd like to be able to let her mother and sister know that the person responsible will never be able to hurt another soul. I can't do that without ruling out those who Luna interacted with in the days leading up to her death."

"A lot of my guests are regulars who have been coming here for years," Mauve explained after she'd given Brook's compassionate speech some thought. "They're good people."

"I'm sure they are, which is why it's important to rule them out. The sheriff already sent over your guest list for the weekend that Luna stayed here, but I'd like your insight." Brook paused, giving Mauve some time to think over the request. "Did anyone seem to show Luna any special interest? The other way around, maybe?"

"Luna was talking to Ryan Atley about the trails, but he's been a regular for years. He wouldn't hurt a fly. His family are regulars, too."

"And did Ryan return to the inn on Sunday evening?"

"Yes. He and his fiancé, Becky, left here to return to Charlotte around eight o'clock that night." Mauve once again turned her focus to the male subject in front of the bulletin board. "Lance, is there something that I can help you with? I believe Kirk is helping another guest right now."

"No, thank you," Lance called out, not really looking their way. "I'm just killing time, waiting for my fiancé."

Brook didn't recall seeing the name Kirk in any section of the missing persons report sent over by Otto. Seeing as Mauve was rather protective of her guests, Brook figured such defense mechanisms would only be tenfold for employees. There was a way around such a strong reaction, though.

"Speaking of Kirk, would you mind if I speak with him while I'm here?" Brook asked, continuing without pause so that Mauve wouldn't be upset by the request. "It sounds as if he often socializes with the guests, and I'm hoping that he might have some insight on Luna's conduct while she was here."

"Of course," Mauve said as she stood from the couch. "Will you be speaking with Mrs. Breen, too? She and her daughter came back around lunchtime, and they've been in their room ever since."

"I spoke with Mrs. Breen and her daughter earlier today," Brook said right as she noticed Lance peering up to the second level. The wooden railing of the staircase wrapped around so that the entrances to the rooms were visible from the front door. The spindles were made of thick natural wood and matched the rest of the exposed beams throughout the inn. Had someone been listening in from above? "It's been an emotional two days for them, and I think it's best to give them some privacy right now."

"Of course, of course." Mauve made her way around the counter. She was in the midst of reaching for the phone when her lips spread into a smile. "Kirk. I was just going to call you. I thought you were around back with those folks from Utah. Do you have a moment to speak with Agent Sloane?"

Brook didn't bother to correct Mauve about the assigned title. Most people assumed that she and her team were federal agents, and it was pointless to get into a lengthy explanation of how a consulting relationship worked between the Bureau and her firm. What wasn't futile was this visit. Otherwise, Brook never would have known about Kirk.

Why hadn't his name been listed in the missing persons report?

"Kirk, I won't keep you long," Brook said as the man finally made his way down the wide staircase. It was only after they shook hands that she pressed for a bit more information. "I apologize for being so informal. I wasn't given your surname."

"Sampson." Kirk appeared to be in his early thirties. He was tan, lean, athletic, and there were calluses on his hands. The flannel shirt he wore was only half-buttoned, but Mauve didn't seem to mind his casual appearance. "I'm not sure what I can tell you that would help your investigation. Luna arrived on a Friday. She seemed like a nice enough girl, but she was an experienced hiker. We didn't talk much."

"Why was that?"

"Mauve keeps me around to help the beginners," Kirk said before flashing a smile Mauve's way. "She cares about her guests, and these mountains can be dangerous. They should be treated with respect."

"Was there anything unusual that you noticed about Luna?" Brook paused when the front door opened and revealed a young woman. She lifted her sunglasses and zeroed in on Lance, though she seemed to hesitate before greeting him with an embrace. "Did Luna seem upset to you at any time? Did you witness anyone bother her?"

"No," Kirk replied with a shake of his head. He crossed his arms without giving the couple near the front a second glance. "Mauve's business slows down in the month of October. The weather changes can be pretty dramatic up here, especially late in the month. Fifty-degree temps can plummet in hours. We've even been known to have a snowstorm or two this time of year. Rare, but it's happened before. What I'm getting at is there were only a handful of guests last weekend. Everyone ate their meals, talked about the trails, and then went their separate ways."

"I appreciate your time." Brook saw no reason to keep Kirk any longer. Both he and Mauve agreed that Luna hadn't been distressed in any way, and there were only so many ways to ask the same question over and over again. "I won't keep you."

Kirk merely nodded without saying a word as he walked away. He didn't retrace his steps back up the staircase, but instead strolled over to have a discussion with Lance and his fiancé. Brook found it odd that there wasn't a ring on her left hand.

"Mauve, I'd like to see Luna's room now that forensics has finished processing the scene. I'd also like to know the names of the guests who were staying in the rooms on either side of her on the off chance they might have heard something," Brook requested right as the sound of her ringtone indicated that she was receiving an incoming call. "If you'll excuse me a moment."

Mauve nodded as she turned to reach for the appropriate key. Brook stepped away from the counter as she pulled her cell phone out from the side pocket of her purse. She wasn't surprised by the name on the lighted display.

"What have you got for me, Bit?"

"Confirmation that your profile was spot on," Bit said, his tone a mixture of triumph and remorse. "Sylvie and Riggs discovered a cabin where a lot of blood was spilled in the middle of the floor. At least, according to the luminol spray. Someone went to a lot of trouble to clean up. No body, though."

"Alert forensics," Brook said as Helen Beckham and Carissa Norman's faces came to mind. Would the DNA of the second crime scene match one of the two women? "See if the team can't get up there tonight. The faster we process that cabin, the quicker we have results. I'll be back in a half hour."

Brook disconnected the line, but she might have just been given a valid reason to officially link Hiker's Haven to Luna Breen's disappearance. Mauve had come around the counter with a key in her hand, but Brook first had another request that might be crucial to solving what was turning out to be a series of murders.

"Mauve, I know that Helen Beckham stayed here before she was reported missing three years ago." Brook wouldn't sugarcoat anything from this point forward. While Mauve was the type of individual who needed reassurances and a bit of handholding, the case took precedent, especially since they could be hours away from connecting the two women. "I need a list of guests who were here during Helen's stay."

Mauve lost some color in her face and her fingers tightened around the key in her hand. She didn't need to be explained the reason for such a request.

"Mauve?" Kirk must have been keeping an eye on Brook and Mauve, because he didn't hesitate to come to the woman's side. It wasn't as if Mauve was in her seventies or eighties. She was a middle-aged woman. Given her reactions this afternoon and the way Kirk's protective instincts had kicked in, Brook could only assume the woman was sick. Heart issue? Cancer? "Why don't you sit down for a while? Go back to knitting. I'll see to it that Agent Sloane has access to the guest room."

"I'm fine," Mauve reassured him, going so far as to pat his shoulder. She wasn't too convincing, and Kirk didn't seem inclined to leave her. "I just hadn't thought of Helen in a very long time. I remember her well, because it was the first time that she and her friends had hiked the Smoky Mountains. She wasn't murdered, though. She's still missing, so there's still hope."

"And Carissa Norman?" Brook asked, going out on a limb. There had been nothing in the woman's missing persons report that had linked her to Hiker's Haven. Still, the former sheriff had been the one assigned to the case, which meant that she'd gone missing from this very county. "Carissa went missing five years ago. Do you recall the name?"

From the way that Mauve's grip had tightened on Kirk's arm, the investigation had just taken another surprising turn. It was evident that had Luna Breen not been killed, no one ever would have made the connection to the other two missing women.

"Kirk, I think you should call a lawyer," Mauve whispered as she tried to push him in the direction of the counter. "Don't say another word."

"A lawyer?" Brook repeated, needing confirmation that she'd heard Mauve correctly. "Why would you need a lawyer, Mr. Sampson?"

"Kirk, don't—"

"I did nothing wrong, Mauve. It's okay," Kirk said reassuringly as he wrapped an arm around Mauve before addressing Brook. "The night before Carissa Norman went missing, she spent the night with me. I was the last one to see her alive."

Chapter Ten

Sylvie Deering

October 2023

Friday — 5:29pm

"We should have stayed overnight," Sylvie said with a bit of frustration as she reached for the zipper on her jacket. The sun was setting, and the temperature had dropped a couple of degrees in the last hour. They'd reached one of the main trails about ten minutes ago and were walking at a slower clip than when they'd hiked it this morning. "Forensics had no one who could process the scene tonight. It's a sitting duck."

"If you do believe that one of the other two women were killed in that cabin, it's not like the evidence is going anywhere." Riggs was ahead of her since they were on part of the trail that didn't allow for two people to walk side by side. "The abandoned structure has been there for decades. Another twelve hours isn't going to hurt anything."

"You saw the amount of blood that was spilled in that cabin once I'd sprayed it with luminol. The blood had been contained in the middle, just like it was with Luna Breen."

"Why clean it up?" Riggs asked, skepticism lacing his tone. "Luna Breen had been dead for days. I don't understand why your boss thinks the killer would have returned for the body and the cleanup. Was he going to bury her? It's a little late for remorse, don't you think?"

"Society tends to think of serial killers as individuals who can't control themselves," Sylvie said as she kept her gaze lowered to the ground. The angle in which the sun was still shining over the horizon was casting shadows all around them. "Let's stop for a minute. I want to get out my flashlight."

Riggs didn't argue. He stopped, turned, and began to take off his own backpack. She did the same, and it didn't take them long to retrieve their flashlights. She took the opportunity to drink some water. She continued their conversation as she hooked the bottle back to a clip on the side of her pack.

"Brook is good at what she does," Sylvie explained as she rotated both shoulders to loosen up her muscles. "The best, really. She had the best closure rate during her tenure with the Bureau. Still holds that record, too. You can't argue with the points that she made in her profile this morning. The unsub all but dragged Luna Breen to that cabin, but the lack of disturbance in the rest of the room displays his need for order. She was most likely a random and convenient choice, but something about her caught his attention. Looks? Age? All signs point to that, and Brook knows the answers to our questions can be found with the first victim."

"What do you mean? Wouldn't they all be important?"

"To a degree, but the first victim is where the unsub usually makes all the mistakes." Sylvie grimaced when she thought back to the cabin that they'd just left. "The blood that the luminol emphasized on the floor is very similar to yesterday's crime scene. If we are dealing with a serial murderer—and it's certainly looking that way—then I'm going to assume that we just came from the place that Helen Beckham was killed. You saw how concentrated the stain was on the floor, and how the killer tried to erase and destroy all evidence."

"Do you know how many people go missing in these mountains? Hundreds, and that's not an exaggeration," Riggs said solemnly as he picked up his backpack. "The blood that we found could be from an animal. The door was hanging wide open, Deering. For all we know, a coyote was looking for a place to heal."

"And did this coyote also bring with it cleaning supplies?" Sylvie held up a hand when Riggs would have tried to reason with her that years had passed since then. The blood could have absorbed into the wood, or maybe the large hole in the ceiling had allowed rain to wash it away. Yes, there were a lot of rational explanations as to what could have happened inside that cabin. But considering the facts of what they were dealing with today, the blood left behind almost certainly belonged to Carissa or Helen. "It's pointless to debate this when we'll have our answers soon. All I'm saying is that our presence in town could alter the behavior of the unsub. I've been involved with many investigations in small towns like this one, and word travels fast."

"Tell me about it," Riggs muttered as he waited for her to secure her backpack. Once they were prepared for the rest of their hike back to town, he pressed the button on his flashlight. She did the same, more confident in her ability to walk the trail now that dusk had mostly fallen. "Everyone in town knows everyone else's business. That's why I know the killer doesn't reside in Moonshine Valley."

"I don't mean to steer this discussion into another debate, but you work in law enforcement. You know more than anyone that people have secrets. We don't really know what people are like behind closed doors," Sylvie theorized, reflecting over the brutality of the crimes that she'd witnessed over the last two years. During her own time with the Bureau, she'd mostly been behind a computer screen. "We only see what they want us to see."

Riggs was quiet for a time. He'd hinted several times throughout the day that he'd like to get to know her better. He wasn't her type, but she also couldn't deny that he brought an underlying sensual tension to the table. She also wasn't the type of woman who indulged in one-night stands, either.

"And what is it that you don't want anyone to see, Deering? The fact that you and that kid blurred professional lines?" Riggs was still focused on what was in front of him, but that hadn't stopped him from waving his hand to ward off her ire. He'd been right to do so, because her flash of anger would have left behind blisters. "I overheard the two of you earlier this morning. Something about your timing being off. I'm not one to judge, because I've crossed those lines myself. The woman in question left the area to join the state police, so I don't see her much anymore. You, on the other hand, have to work side by side with—"

"You call Bit a kid one more time, and you'll be the one speaking with a high-pitched voice."

"Duly noted," Riggs said with a laugh, but Sylvie wasn't in a forgiving mood.

"Believe it or not, Bit is in his mid-twenties. He's kind, compassionate, intelligent, and beyond loyal. He'd give his life for any one of us, and I'd do the same in return." Sylvie shrugged, though Riggs couldn't see it. "Bit is my best friend, though our relationship is none of your business. Getting back to your question, there will always be things about me that I keep hidden from the world. You don't strike me as naïve, Riggs."

"Look, I've done some things in my past that I'm not proud of," Riggs admitted as he walked around a large fallen branch. Sylvie followed suit, though the crunching of some dead leaves underneath her boot echoed behind her. Just to be sure, she paused long enough to skim the beam of her flashlight over the area. She hadn't realized just how dark it had become until she'd focused on something other than the beam of light. "But when it comes down to it, someone knows everything. Family members, friends, colleagues...you name it, someone always knows."

"An example?" Sylvie asked as she refocused on the path ahead of them.

"Tori Mills. A girl who I dated in high school. She was there when I spray-painted our history teacher's car. Only Stan Beachman was the one who got expelled, because the spray can was found in his locker." Riggs came to a stop. She could still see him clearly as he turned around to face her. "My point is that while Tori might not have ratted me out, she still has knowledge of something that I'd rather not be made public. I made some really bad choices when I was younger, but the town and its residents know me for who I am now."

"We'll have to agree to disagree." Sylvie switched the base of her flashlight into her left hand. "Let me ask you this, though. What is the one thing in common when you hear family members, friends, and neighbors being interviewed on the news when asked about an arrest of a murderer, pedophile, or rapist? I'll answer for you to save time—*but he seemed so nice.*"

Sylvie noticed immediately when Rigg's gaze slid away from hers. He never let on that he wasn't listening to her side of the conversation.

If others were observing them from afar, they would never have known that the deputy was surveilling the immediate area.

"I thought I heard something myself," Sylvie murmured before continuing their conversation. Their words might have carried before, and she didn't want for whoever might be monitoring them to think they were aware of such observation. "We all have things in our past that we'd rather not have come to light. If spray-painting the history teacher's car was the worst thing you did in your past, I applaud you."

Sylvie glanced down at her boots.

"I'm glad we stopped," she said as she leaned down, placing her flashlight on the ground in such a way that she would be able to seize it easily if she needed to palm her weapon. It would be easier to reach for her backup piece without any suspicion than it would be to unzip her jacket. "My shoelace is untied. Give me a minute."

"You can take your time, Deering." There was humor lacing his tone. He'd also swung his flashlight up the slight incline. Two beady eyes were trained on them. "Looks like you have an admirer."

Sylvie wasn't as relieved as Riggs seemed to be about the racoon staring back at them from maybe eleven yards away. The rustling that she'd heard before had seemed to be from something...or someone...heavier. Granted, sound carried and bounced off the surrounding trees in such a way that any disturbance seemed amplified.

"Do you know what the chances are that Luna Breen's killer followed us through the Smoky Mountains the entire day without us being any the wiser?"

"Not as low as you seem to think given that most of the townsfolk knew what we were doing today," Sylvie countered as she picked up her flashlight and stood, causing their little voyeur to scurry off into the darkness. Riggs would have argued with her had she not continued to explain her reasoning. "We're on the main trail. We followed said trail for quite a while this morning before veering off into the unknown. We passed several hikers, bird watchers, and campers. It's not that farfetched to think that someone could have followed us without us noticing them."

Riggs didn't respond right away, but she could tell that he was considering her point of view. For once, they seemed to be on the same page.

"Let's keep moving." Riggs had driven through town to where a small parking lot had fed into several trails for the hikers to choose from. "We've lost quite a lot of daylight. It will be completely dark by the time we reach my truck. By the way, I regret to say that the spray-painting incident wasn't the worst thing that I did when I was young."

Sylvie chose not to take the bait.

At least, not until they reached the parking lot.

They had walked in silence the rest of the way, and Sylvie couldn't shake that something other than a racoon had been behind them. She still wasn't certain that they were making the right choice in leaving the cabin sit for another twelve hours or so. Now that they were back in cell phone range, she would text Bit to press forensics into taking a hike up that way first thing in the morning.

"What's your schedule tomorrow?"

"Whatever you want it to be."

Sylvie caught the additional meaning behind Riggs' words.

By this time, he had pulled down the tailgate of his F150. When he went to take her backpack, his warm fingers wrapped around hers. It was then that she broached the subject that seemed to have weight behind it as they brought their day to an end.

"What *was* the worst thing you did when you were younger, Riggs?"

Chapter Eleven

Brooklyn Sloane

October 2023

Saturday — 8:58am

"Impressive."

"You must be Sheriff Jackson. I'm Sylvie. It's nice to..."

Brook rubbed her eyes while ignoring the sensation of sand being trapped underneath her lashes. While she could thrive on little sleep, last night had been one for the record books. The noise level from the bar on Friday night had been a lot louder than she would have thought possible for a town this size. What should have been a two o'clock close happened much closer to four o'clock. Add on that she'd wanted to meet with the members of the forensic team at six o'clock before they hiked to a potential second crime scene, and there wasn't enough coffee in this town to keep her energy at a working level.

"Brook is through there," Sylvie directed the sheriff, who would no doubt make an appearance inside the connecting doorway any moment. Seeing as the rooms were small, she'd wanted some additional space to work. Hence the reason that there were numerous files open on the bed while her laptop and tablet were on the wooden desk. "Mark my words, Sheriff. You'll be her favorite person today."

The comment had Brook opening her eyes and turning in her chair. Sure enough, Sylvie had been right.

"Please tell me that coffee is from the Moonshine Diner."

"This coffee is from the Moonshine Diner." Otto had walked into her room not only with a cupholder carrying two cups of coffee, but also a large box. He handed her the cardboard holder before scanning the room. Since the bedspread was covered in open files, he ended up setting the box down near the nightstand. "Overnight delivery from D.C. It was left by the front door of the bar."

Brook's lips curled at knowing that Graham had come through for her. He'd texted her yesterday before his flight out of the city to let her know that warm, comfortable clothes were on the way. She would change out of the jeans that she'd worn for three days in a row the moment the sheriff gave her some privacy.

"Thanks, Otto."

"You certainly know how to bring people out of the woodwork," Otto said wryly as he stood in front of her bed with his arms crossed. He took time to peruse the open folders that she'd collected at the police station yesterday. All of them were the full files of the missing persons reports that were in connection to Luna Breen's case. "Kirk Sampson has retained Lee Rohan as his attorney. They are scheduled to come into the station at fourteen hundred hours."

"You can handle the questioning," Brook said after she'd taken a healthy drink of her coffee. The contents were the perfect temperature. "Let me know if anything of interest is discovered during the interview."

"You don't want to be there?" Otto asked in surprise as he turned back to her. His sunglasses were hanging from the pocket of his uniform, and he was once again without his hat. "You surprise me, Sloane. I would have figured that you'd want to run with that meeting."

"Kirk Sampson might have had a one-night stand with Carissa Norman, but he wasn't in town the week that Helen Beckham went missing," Brook said as she leaned back in her chair. "And in regard to that alibi, I mean that Mauve mentioned that Kirk was with her for a doctor's appointment at John Hopkins. Bit confirmed the alibi. I can only go on the assumption that Sampson kept quiet after Carissa Norman went missing because he didn't want to be a suspect in her disappearance."

Otto was right about one thing—a lot had taken place in the span of twenty-four hours. It was as if their presence had rattled everyone in town, and the townsfolk were talking amongst themselves more than usual. While they could have been looking at a long-drawn out investigation, she believed their mere presence had caused enough pressure to break the silence.

"By the way, you could have told me that Mauve was dying from pancreatic cancer." Brook reached out and pushed the cupholder a few inches toward the edge. Otto shook his head at the offer, and she couldn't say that she was sad at such a denial. She needed all the help she could get to keep her thoughts in order today. "From my understanding, she's going to leave Hiker's Haven to Kirk."

"That's the rumor," Otto said as he closed the distance to the open doorway. He wasn't leaving the room. He'd changed locations so that he could lean a shoulder against the wall. "Mauve thinks of Kirk as the son she never had. By the way, do you want to tell me why you're targeting Riggs?"

"I'm not targeting anyone."

"You requested his personnel file from one of my deputies."

"I did," Brook agreed without reservation. She wouldn't apologize for doing her job. What she could do was treat the sheriff with the respect she'd want in return if they were speaking about one of her team members. "Forensics used the satellite phone to call in about thirty minutes ago. While we won't have the results from the lab for days, if not weeks, the pattern of blood left behind suggests that the scene was similar to that of what we discovered with Luna Breen."

"And you believe there is a chance that Riggs murdered those women." Otto was rubbing his index finger and thumb together as he considered the context of her words. "I understand why you need to look at those with shady pasts, but that accounts for a lot of people in this town."

"I'm aware," Brook said knowingly as she gestured toward the bed. The file on the end summed up Riggs' performance as a deputy for the county sheriff's office. "Riggs isn't being singled out. He shared with Sylvie last night his version of events that almost landed him a lengthy stint in prison. The knife belonged to a young man who attempted to assault Tori Mills. She didn't want to cause any trouble since the young man in question was the mayor's nephew, so she denied Riggs' claims of what took place."

"You believe him then," Otto said as he relaxed somewhat, but she couldn't ease his concern just yet.

"I think that Riggs has some anger management issues that has come to the forefront every now and then. By the way, Riggs and Theo accompanied the forensics team up to the second cabin."

Brook would have cleared off the bed to give Otto a place to sit down, but he would only turn her down once she shared with him her updated profile.

"You want to keep Riggs close," Otto stated with some reserve, obviously not pleased with her motives. "Does he know that you suspect him of murdering two or three women?"

"You're making assumptions without looking at the broader picture. I understand that you investigate your cases based on the facts in front of you, but my method is slightly different."

"Slightly?"

"I base my profile on the evidence left behind, such as the fact that had Luna Breen been the only victim, one could fathom the killer enjoyed torturing her. With a second victim, one needs to step back and view it from a different angle. What if I were to ask you for an opinion on a crime scene where a male individual was tied to a chair in close quarters and systematically tortured for hours? Water just out of reach. No one to hear him scream."

Otto straightened a bit, his own experiences while in the military coming to the forefront. She'd captured his attention.

"I would say to you that it was some type of an interrogation."

"We didn't immediately view it as such given the odd surroundings and the fact that the victim was a woman. A civilian woman."

"Are you saying the unsub is or was a service member?"

"No. Quite the opposite." Brook reached out and turned her laptop on the desk so that Otto could see the screen. "You and I both know that true interrogation techniques weren't used on Luna Breen. This torture was inflicted by a civilian who wanted answers that Luna and at least two other women couldn't answer. We have no idea whose blood was left in that second cabin, and we won't know for a while. In the meantime, we work with the evidence."

"It's still all assumption," Otto pointed out after he'd leaned in to read what was on the screen. His attempt at redirecting her own words back at her fell flat. "There's a good chance that he was turned down by the military. It's all conjecture. And as far as I'm aware, Riggs never even attempted to enter the service."

Brook didn't get a chance to argue that point. She even had proof to the contrary. Riggs had spoken to a recruiter about enlisting in the Army. His high school guidance counselor had even made a note in Riggs' file that a meeting had been set up before his arrest. Unfortunately, the rest of their conversation would have to wait until they confirmed the call that had come over Otto's radio. Not for him specifically, but the dispatcher thought he should be aware of a particular issue since it could involve one of his deputies.

Smoke had been spotted somewhere in the Smoky Mountains.

"Sylvie, would you please reach Theo over the radio?" Brook called out before she stood from the chair. Both she and Otto walked into the other room. "Make sure that everything is okay up where they are, please."

"Is that satellite footage?" Otto asked as he walked closer to the portable monitor. He pointed toward a specific location. "Riggs told me last night that the cabin in question is here, so the smoke can't be originating more than a half a mile from their location. Wait. Is this live footage?"

"Yes," Bit replied after he'd flashed a smile at Otto. "Don't worry, Sheriff. It's on the up and up."

"Brook, do you want Theo and Riggs to check it out?" Sylvie asked, holding the phone away from her mouth. "They can see the smoke from where they are, but the forensics team isn't finished processing the scene."

"You realize that the chances of that fire having anything to do with your case is almost nonexistent," Otto said skeptically, and Brook agreed. It wasn't worth the waste in manpower when the rangers would be sent to check it out and make sure the fire wasn't about to spread. Rain wasn't due in the area for a few more days, either. "It's probably from a campfire that someone didn't snuff out properly."

"Otto's right. I'd rather Theo and Riggs stay where they are," Brook said as she monitored the small wisp of smoke begin to darken and thicken as it rose into the air. "The park rangers have a process for handling these types of situations, and if it was a structure versus a campsite, there's nothing we'd be able to change about the situation now."

"Speaking of rangers, wasn't Erika supposed to be your point person?" Otto asked without taking his gaze off the screen.

"Dominic had an interview for his blog that got cancelled this morning. Since he had knowledge of where he and Theo left off yesterday, he accompanied Erika to finish searching the various shelters that were marked on an older map of the area," Brook explained as she walked up behind Bit. One of his monitors seemed to be pulling pictures from some database. "Are those the photographs from Luna Breen's phone?"

"Yeah." Bit wiped his hand on a napkin. He'd been eating one of the stale donuts still in the box from yesterday. "I created a program to see if anyone else was caught in the lens. Little T is in touch with the cell phone providers that Carissa Norman and Helen Beckham used in hopes of them granting us access to their accounts. We've already requested warrants, but it could take a day or two. Since their belongings were never found, we'll be limited to what was uploaded at the time."

"Limited?" Otto asked as he joined Brook to watch the program scan a picture before moving onto the next. "Impressive. What software are you using?"

"Mine," Bit replied with another smile.

Otto switched his focus to Brook, who nodded her confirmation.

"We keep him around for a reason," Brook said as she patted Bit on the shoulder. She then moved away to where Sylvie was sitting on the bed, leaning back against a bunch of pillows. She'd just set the satellite phone down next to her on the comforter. "Are Erika and Dominic checking in on the hour?"

"Yes. I spoke to them right after the sheriff arrived," Sylvie said as she stretched out both legs. She steadied her laptop with one hand. "I spoke with Luna Breen's friend who was supposed to join her last weekend. Nothing stood out, but she's going to need a lot of counseling after this. Let's just say that she's harboring a lot of survivor's guilt."

Otto was in the midst of asking Bit numerous questions about the applications that were open and operating in the background. Since the two of them seemed to be in their own world of tech jargon, Brook quietly broached a more sensitive subject with Sylvie.

"I received an interesting call around an hour ago," Brook said gently as she took a seat on the edge of the mattress near the foot of the bed. She was about to bring up a topic that Sylvie avoided, but with good reason. "Your father needs to speak with you, Sylvie. He assured me that it has nothing to do with an appeal or him requesting anything else from you but a few minutes of your time."

Sylvie was fair-skinned with golden blonde hair that she mostly always kept contained in a bun at the base of her neck. Her blue eyes darkened, and she pulled her legs up underneath her.

"I'm sorry that my dad bothered you with this, Brook."

"It's no bother," Brook reassured her before extending the offer of personal leave. Doing so would clue Sylvie in on the seriousness of her father's situation. "If you want to fly back to D.C. today, we can arrange accommodations for you to do so."

"He's dying."

Brook didn't confirm nor deny the statement.

She'd given her word to Nigel Deering that she would keep his diagnosis under wraps until he'd had a chance to speak with his daughter. It was obvious that he'd wanted to try and make some amends before he was no longer able to do so. Sylvie might not see it as such, but those close to a situation tended to have a skewed view of things.

"You need to speak with your father in person, Sylvie. I've already spoken to the warden, and he's willing to waive visiting hours." Brook could hear Otto and Bit's conversation ending, so she stood from the bed. "Look, I'm the last one who should be giving family advice, but you don't want to look back on this with regret."

"You don't believe in regrets."

Sylvie wasn't wrong, because Brook had come to the realization with the help of therapy that there shouldn't be regret. At least in her situation. Every choice, every decision, and every consequence had molded her soul. There were stains of sin, but there were also marks of redemption.

"No, I don't believe in regrets," Brook murmured before imparting one more piece of advice, not that she was an expert in family affairs. "I do believe in closure, though. Whatever you decide to do, Sylvie, make sure you find closure."

Brook motioned to Otto that she would be in her room. Bit was now talking about some computer role-playing game that he'd created and how he'd gotten a few online friends of his to join. He was explaining prompts and such things as she walked over to where Otto had set down the box that had been delivered to her this morning. She used a pen that she'd tossed onto the bed and reamed it down the middle before pulling the two edges apart.

"Let me get this straight, Sloane." Otto had finally rejoined her, but she quickly closed the two sides of the box. Graham had sent something else besides clothes, and she'd wait to open the gift in private. "Your firm is a consultant to the FBI on a possible string of murders, and you allow one of your employees to play online games?"

"First off, I don't view Bit, Sylvie, or Theo as my employees," Brook corrected the sheriff as she tossed the pen on the bed. "I view them as my colleagues. They add the same value as I do to the cases that we take on, and they deserve the same respect. Second, we all take moments to ourselves to clear our thoughts. Sylvie drinks as much tea throughout the day as I do coffee, and she spends a lot of time in the kitchen brewing different blends. Theo works out at the office whenever he can, and Arden likes to look up recipes when he's sitting at his desk. We all have our different ways when mulling over information on cases. Bit? He can multitask better than any of us. The roles we've chosen to take on as our careers aren't the type with timecards. Neither is yours, for that matter."

"Maybe I am a hard ass," Otto muttered more to himself than her before his radio came to life once more. This time, for a potential missing person. He met her stare with interest. As far as they were aware, the unsub took his time between abducting and killing his victims. Years, in fact. His dispatcher gave the details on a private channel. "I'm across the street. Heading there now."

"Did I hear that name right?" Brook asked for clarification. Otto was already shaking his head, but she wouldn't be sitting on the sidelines for this one. She fastened the button of her blazer before sidestepping him to alert the team. "Ned Proehl never showed up for work yesterday or today. Until proven otherwise, we treat his disappearance as potentially being connected to Luna Breen's murder."

Chapter Twelve

Bobby "Bit" Nowacki

October 2023

Saturday — 7:14pm

Even though it was still relatively early in the evening, the bar buzzed with energy and anticipation of a fun night ahead. The only thing louder than the country music spilling from the jukebox was the laughter of the patrons and the clicking of glasses. Warm hues from the dim lighting flickered shadows on the wood paneling, but what really stood out above all else was the aroma of delicious pub food. Nothing was better than a greasy cheeseburger with bacon and a side of steak fries.

"You're a walking heart attack, Bit."

"Nah," Bit replied to Sylvie as they strolled up to the bar. "My genetics won't allow it. My family tends to go from..."

Bit winced before allowing his words to trail off. He hadn't meant to remind Sylvie that her father could be dying, and he'd gone the extra mile to reassure her that such a supposition could be wrong. Brook hadn't technically said anything of the sort.

"Bit, you and I both know that Brook wouldn't have urged me to fly back to D.C. and all but abandon this investigation otherwise." Sylvie took a seat on the last empty stool, although neither one of them intended on staying and eating at the bar. He couldn't leave the programs that he currently had running, and Sylvie wanted to comb through more files before turning in for the night. She had an early flight to catch. "I'm okay with it."

Bit highly doubted that Sylvie was okay with her father dying in prison.

Considering that the bar was packed with locals and hikers from out of town, Bit barely managed to squeeze in next to Sylvie. At least she had claimed the last stool on the end near the corner. This way, his right shoulder was against the wall.

"Big T just walked in with Erika." Bit monitored their progress, and someone at one of the tables had reached out to grab the park ranger. She stopped and chatted a bit, leaving Theo to continue toward the stairs. "I don't think I've ever seen him so tired. You'd think hiking an hour or two would be a breeze. See? This is why I would never give up my greasy way of life."

Bit was glad that he could still garner a laugh from her, which just so happened to cause several heads to turn. Her blonde hair was still contained in a bun, but a few of the strands had come loose to frame her face. He wouldn't deny falling in love with her upon first sight, but he was reconsidering the strong attachment he felt toward her.

It was obvious that Sylvie didn't think of him in that manner, and he couldn't really blame her. He certainly wasn't book cover material.

It was the reason that he went the extra mile to make her laugh. Still, he couldn't deny that she had a point about their friendship.

Sylvie Deering was his best friend.

And once she'd gotten him to see that, he wasn't so sure he wanted their status to change. Hence his hesitation on accepting Zoey's coffee invitation. He'd also never met the woman. She was merely an online friend who had wanted to participate in his new role-playing game that he'd created a couple of months ago. Her humor matched his, though. And he couldn't deny having a strong desire to meet her in person.

"Trust me, Bit. Lifting weights and jogging is nothing like hiking in these mountains. Different muscle groups. Honestly, it's also a different mindset. I didn't want to say anything this morning, but it took me ten minutes to lean down and tie my shoes."

"Think a cheeseburger will make Big T feel better? He enjoys one from time to time, you know."

"I think that Theo won't even be awake by the time we make it up those stairs. Besides, we got him a bowl of chili," Sylvie said before bumping shoulders with him. Bit realized why when she lowered her voice. The twang of the singer blaring from the jukebox made it hard to hear what she had to say, but he put it together when her blue gaze traveled across the bar. "Does that man look familiar to you?"

Bit took a moment to distinguish which male subject that Sylvie had been referring to, because there were quite a few men sitting on stools or standing nearby attempting to get Wyn's attention. The bartender had turned his back on them all as he'd entered the kitchen, hopefully for their dinner. Bit was famished, and he'd been monitoring Ned Proehl's credit card all day long, hoping that the man was foolish enough to use it.

Unfortunately, the longer that Proehl went without being spotted by anyone, there was a good chance that he might have taken off into the mountains. Was Proehl their unsub? He was in the age range, and he had been arrested before for domestic assault.

The only thing that Bit could tell Sylvie was that the man staring at the muted television above the bar wasn't Ned Proehl. Granted, the stranger did look familiar, but Bit couldn't place him. Sylvie was the one with a steel trap that was as close to an eidetic memory as possible.

"Sorry," Bit replied with a shrug. "I see what you're saying, but I don't think he is part of our case. Hey, could he be the clerk at the gas station? Didn't that guy have a mole on his face, too?"

"No, that was a birthmark."

"Is there a chance you saw him hiking?" The two of them had gotten into the habit of bouncing questions and answers off one another. "There are some serious campers still up in those mountains freezing their asses off. Maybe he was one of them."

Bit couldn't see the appeal of spending the night out in the wilderness where any type of wild animal could sneak up on him. Not to mention mosquitos. Theo had come back with several bites yesterday, and he'd still been itching them this morning. There had even been a freeze last week when the temperatures had dropped, and Bit had always believed such cold got rid of those pesky bloodsuckers. Theo mentioned something about them hiding in the vegetation, but it was still a good reminder of why Bit should be grateful to be the one behind the scenes.

"No," Sylvie said, drawing out her answer. Wyn finally came out from the kitchen with their food in hand. "Bingo."

"Bingo? When did you have time to play bingo?"

"Not that kind of bingo."

Bit gave Wyn a half-hearted smile, because Sylvie still wasn't making too much sense. He handed over his corporate credit card to the burly bartender.

"I made sure to put extra barbeque sauce in there for you," Wyn said after he took the credit card. He continued to carry on the conversation as he cashed out their order. "You ever consider moving to a small town? Your business alone could keep this place functioning on a daily basis."

"I'm more of a city guy," Bit replied as he pulled the two white bags closer to him. "Have you ever considered D.C.? You could make a killing there with these cheeseburgers."

"Hey, Wyn?" Sylvie had waited for Wyn to hand back Bit's credit card, receipt, and a pen. "Is that your brother?"

"Son. His name is Gabe." Wyn cleared his throat before leaning down and resting his forearms on the bar. "I know that I don't look it, but I was wild back in my day. I wasn't always around for Gabe when I should have been, and as a result, he lived a hard life. Proud of him, though. He's turned things around, got a steady job as a raft guide, and built himself a place not too far from here."

"Gabe Raskins?"

Bit had signed his name before stuffing the small receipt into the back pocket of his jeans. Gabe's surname brought him up short, though. Bit managed to push the pen back toward Wyn without drawing the man's attention. Bit was always in awe of Brook, Theo, and Sylvie. The process in which they usually pieced together investigations was astounding, although Wyn seemed to sense that something was wrong. His bushy eyebrows practically touched in suspicion.

"Yes," Wyn responded cautiously as he pulled back from the counter and straightened his shoulders. "Why?"

"I saw his name on the list of volunteers who joined the search party for Luna Breen," Sylvie explained with a smile. "Thank him for us. Not a lot of people would give up their time like that, and those volunteers don't get enough credit."

Bit was reminded of why he wouldn't be as good in the field as he was behind his computer screens. Sylvie's excuse had done the job it was intended, and Wyn smiled proudly at the compliment that she'd given his son.

Only the bartender had no idea that his son would now be put at the top of the list to have a background check completed as soon as possible. Lying was part of the job that he would never get used to, and there would be no erasing the guilt that he experienced over deceiving someone as kind-hearted as Wyn.

"Just holler if you need anything else," Wyn said as he finally turned his attention to the men who'd been waiting rather impatiently to place their drink orders. "What are you having tonight, gentlemen?"

"Bit, you read the updated profile. Brook believes that the unsub is returning to the scene a week or two later to bury the body and clean up any evidence left behind."

"Which would mean there is a good chance that the killer inserts himself into the search parties with the sole intention of leading them away from whatever cabin or dwelling that he used as his interrogation room," Bit finished, still not comfortable with the conversation they'd just had with Wyn. The man who fed them delicious cheeseburgers, and who made sure there was additional barbeque sauce. "I get it, Little T. I do, but there were a lot of volunteers. What makes Wyn's son stand out?"

"The local news is on the television, Bit. They had a picture of Luna Breen in the top righthand corner while they interviewed the sister. Who, by the way, is still staying at Hiker's Haven. Do you see anyone else in this bar watching the news?"

"No," Bit replied reluctantly as he grabbed the bags of food. "Doesn't mean I feel good about misleading Wyn like that."

Sylvie hopped off her seat, giving Bit more room to maneuver around the stool. It was no wonder that no one ever claimed it. His hat had snagged on a portion of the wooden wall that hadn't been sanded down. He'd felt the tug, so he'd quickly grabbed onto the knitted material before any damage could be done to his sister's creation. She'd knitted him many hats, but the gray one was his favorite.

"I know you don't want to hear this, Bit, but we're not here to make friends."

The two of them made their way up the stairs, with Sylvie leading the way. Bit hoped that Theo was still awake to enjoy his bowl of chili. It should help to warm him up after such a long day in the mountains. Thankfully, the fire that had been reported had been nothing of significance. As for Brook, she was still with the sheriff hoping to locate Ned Proehl. Thinking about the changes to the profile, Bit couldn't help but glance back at the bar.

Gabe Raskins was no longer watching the muted television. Instead, he was monitoring their retreat without an ounce of embarrassment. His stare came across as almost mocking, and every ounce of guilt that had plagued Bit moments earlier vanished into thin air.

Chapter Thirteen

Brooklyn Sloane

October 2023

Monday — 6:16am

"Sloane."

"Meet me at Hiker's Haven in twenty minutes."

Brook was prevented from asking what had transpired at the B&B when the sheriff disconnected the line. She'd been in the process of gathering her notes together for the upcoming meeting that was supposed to have included the sheriff. It appeared that she wouldn't be briefing her team on the adjusted profile until later today.

"Good morning to you, too," she murmured before setting her phone back down on the desk. She wasn't surprised when Bit poked his head around the connecting doorway. "That wasn't Sylvie, Bit. I have to meet the sheriff out at Hiker's Haven. I'm not sure if it's about Proehl or not. Can you let Theo and Erika know that the morning meeting has been moved to ten o'clock? That should give me enough time to meet the sheriff and drive back to town."

"In that case, I'm going to walk down the street and grab a box of donuts."

"Would you please grab me some coffee cake while you're there?" Brook asked as she began to shut down her laptop. "And maybe take the carafe over to the diner for a refill?"

"Sure thing, Boss. I won't say anything to Gumshoe, either."

"You don't need to say anything to Arden, because he still makes the best caramel macchiato on the East Coast." Brook wasn't exaggerating, and the mere mention of their other team member had her reaching for the phone. She made sure it was on speaker before straightening the manilla folders that she'd acquired since arriving in town last Thursday. "Good morning, Arden."

Only Bit referred to Arden by the nickname given to a lot of private investigators back in the day. Bit basically had a nickname for everyone.

"Top of the morning to you, Brook," Arden greeted, his voice gruff from years of smoking. She'd gotten used to him arriving at the office before her. It wasn't that she expected anyone to put in the same number of hours that she worked on a daily, weekly, or even annual basis. However, having the lights turned on and a special caramel macchiato waiting for her when she arrived had definitely spoiled her. "What can I do for you?"

With Ned Proehl still missing, there was quite a list of volunteers who needed to be interviewed over the next few days, and Sylvie had flown back to D.C. Being short a team member required that Otto be a little more involved in the case, because Erika had no idea how to conduct an interview. The team's liaison to the park ranger service was outstanding in her own job responsibilities, but she'd never worked a murder investigation before.

"Arden, how do you feel about taking a drive over to the college?"

"Do I get to join in on a game of beer pong?" Arden laughed at his own reply.

"Let me guess," Brook said as she closed the lid on her laptop. "You were the only semi-sober one at your frat parties."

"And you weren't," Arden asked with a knowing cadence in his tone. "I don't think I've known you to take second place, Brook."

Memories from college came flooding back, making it hard for Brook to breathe.

Cara Jordan had been the worst partner to have for beer pong, but Brook hadn't been able to bring herself to choose anyone other than her roommate. They'd been inseparable starting their freshman year, and they'd requested to share a dorm room from that point on...until Jacob had intervened and ended Cara's life.

"...time do you need me to be there?"

"Eight o'clock," Brook answered after clearing her throat. She did her best to push aside the past that always seemed to hit her out of nowhere. "They're working on an assignment. They can use the three hours of class today to conduct some research, but I'd like you to be there if they have any questions."

"It would be my pleasure."

"Thanks, Arden."

Brook reached out and disconnected the call. Her firearm, holster, and credentials were off to the side, so she picked them up and secured them to the cream belt that she'd chosen this morning. The black turtleneck was a nice change from the business blazers that she'd worn for their previous case, and she was able to wear a more comfortable jacket. Theo had mentioned before taking a shower this morning that the high of the day was only fifty-eight degrees. Relatively normal for the end of October.

"I ran into Bit walking down the hallway," Theo said right as Brook finished tying the laces on her right hiking boot. The cream and brown material came above her ankle. Since she wasn't sure exactly why the sheriff wanted her to drive out to Hiker's Haven, it was best to be prepared. "He said the morning briefing is postponed?"

"Otto called and requested that I meet him at the B&B." Brook walked back to the desk where she'd left her cell phone. After double-checking that her driver's license, corporate credit, and personal credit card were in their designated spots inside the phone case, she slid the contents into her right pocket. "Erika should be here soon with a list of volunteers who searched for Carissa Norman. Since we have the names of those in the search parties for Helen Beckham and Luna Breen, compare them so that we have one comprehensive list of who was involved with all three. You don't have to wait for me to start questioning them, but I don't want Erika on her own. Keep her with you or let her remain back here with Bit. I'm sure he has something for her to do."

"Have you heard from Sylvie?"

"No." Brook was aware that Theo and Bit knew of her phone conversation with Nigel Deering, but she'd given her word that she wouldn't reveal what had been said between them. Should Sylvie want to share with them her personal feelings in regard to her father's devastating diagnosis and what could only amount to unresolved feelings over such news, then that was her personal choice to do so. "The sheriff said that he'd loan us a couple of deputies, but I'd rather he be personally involved than someone we don't know."

"And Riggs?"

"Riggs is back on patrol as a deputy until such time that we need someone else besides Erika to help us out in that area. Jace is back minding his bait and tackle shop, and Dominic has that interview rescheduled with that famous climber. Those two were only helping us search the mountains for places the unsub could have taken more victims." Brook didn't need to give her reasons as to why the two men were no longer involved in the investigation. Theo understood completely, but he would have to speak with each of them regarding their previous experience with the mountain rescue teams. "I've witnessed you several times during interviews such as these. There's no one better."

"Yeah, well, the interviews aren't typically with the ones who've helped us out the way Jace and Dominic did last week," Theo said grudgingly as he unscrewed the cap of his protein shake. "I want to look over their background investigations once more before speaking with them. I wanted to see if we missed anything, especially since you amended the profile to include that the unsub would most likely insert himself into the search groups. Why not the investigation? Hey, that reminds me. You left out the unsub's relationship status."

"I need more to go on," Brook replied reluctantly as she walked over to her suitcase. She'd tucked her gloves into one of the corners, along with a scarf. She pulled the scarf out first before draping it around her neck. "There's a reason that the unsub needs to leave after spending a day in the mountains with his victim. Job, marriage, kids? The profile is definitely a work in progress."

Unfortunately, the team still hadn't heard back from forensics regarding the evidence at either crime scene. There was always the possibility that the killer had left behind his DNA. If he was in the system, the investigation could be wrapped up in hours. As it stood, they could be waiting for such a call for a while.

"Your birthday isn't until December," Theo commented as he gestured toward the small gift box that she'd set on her nightstand. "Did I miss some holiday?"

"You know that you didn't miss any holiday," Brook said good-naturedly as she grabbed the keys to the SUV that they'd rented over a month ago. She'd have to allocate the expense properly between cases when the time came. "Graham sent me a keycard."

"You mean, a hotel keycard?"

"Considering the pink flower printed on both sides of the access card, I'd say it was more symbolic." Brook stood in the middle of the room as she stared at the square giftbox with torn emotions. "Graham wants us to take a four-day weekend somewhere on a private tropical island."

Theo leaned back against the wall. He'd become her sounding board, and vice versa. She was still quite awkward when it came to these talks, but it wasn't like she could call her therapist at six o'clock in the morning, two o'clock at night, or whenever her thoughts began to spiral out of control.

"I'm still getting used to..." Brook was at a loss for words, so she made a circle with her right hand. "All of this."

"Having a life?"

Brook shot Theo a glare, but he simply laughed it off.

"I'm serious." Brook glanced down at the ring that Graham had given her last Christmas, and she twisted the outer band in contemplation. The worry ring had signified his knowledge of her most intimate fears. "I'm not sure I know how to do anything other than work. I'm not sure I can be someone who can take time out for herself. Is it possible to change?"

"Is it possible for *you* to change?" Theo clarified, because they both had come face to face with murderers who would never be able stop until they'd taken their last breath. It was all in their wiring, just as it was with Jacob. She'd often asked herself the nature versus nurture question, and she'd yet to find the answer. "Yes, you can change the way you view life. You didn't start out as a sister who would become dedicated to the righting the wrongs committed by her older brother."

"But that *is* who I am," Brook murmured as she released the ring to get a better grip on her gloves and keys. She met Theo's stare. "Jacob might be behind bars, but you and I both know that he doesn't intend to stay there. Bit mentioned that Sarah Evanston broke the protocol of her witness protection deal. She called her mother, which means that it's only a matter of time before she opts out of the program. It's what Jacob wanted all along, and he's about to get his wish if I can't somehow convince Sarah's mother to stop her daughter from making such a destructive decision."

"And you've put yourself in a position to monitor your brother on a daily basis," Theo pointed out as he tightened the cap on his protein drink. "You've also got a team under your employment, friends who care for you so much that they worry you *will* work yourself to death, and the start of a relationship with a man who just so happens to come with some baggage himself. All in all, I'd say it's okay to take a few days away from all the responsibility. Let's face it. We all know that you've never taken a vacation in your life. Don't tell me that you don't want to know what it feels like to lay on a beach while soaking up the warm rays from the sun and being served those tropical drinks with those tiny fancy umbrellas. Hell, I might have actually talked myself into a singles cruise."

Brook let out a small laugh, because she knew for a fact that Theo would never be caught dead on a singles cruise. He had made some very good points, but she still needed time to think Graham's proposal over. They were in the middle of an investigation, and there was no telling how long that it would drag out. If nothing came to light in a few weeks, they would return to D.C., but the case would remain open with team members making occasional trips to and from North Carolina for the foreseeable future.

"I should get going," Brook said as she tucked her gloves in the pocket opposite of the one that she'd stored her phone. "Otto didn't say why he wanted me to meet him over at the B&B. I'm going to be late as it is."

Theo nodded, but he stopped just inside the connecting doorway.

"I'm going to speak with Riggs, Jace, and Dominic this morning," Theo said before she could turn exit her room. He usually didn't feel the need to give her specific details on his fieldwork. His following statement gave light to the reason. "You mentioned that we're looking for someone on the list of people who joined the search parties, but that includes every park ranger that's assigned to this area. I just thought you'd want a heads up that you'll be receiving a phone call or two later today after I speak with some park rangers—including Hal Eggers."

"We both know that we're not here to make friends, Theo." Brook wasn't a stranger to those types of phone calls. In fact, the team wouldn't be doing their jobs if such communication was nonexistent. "We're here to stop a killer."

Chapter Fourteen

Brooklyn Sloane

October 2023

Monday — 6:51am

The red and blue lights that danced across the porch of the hikers' retreat in a mesmerizing pattern disrupted what should have been a peaceful morning. The vibrant hues flickered over the dark wood, causing the pumpkins and the cornstalks to appear as if they were in motion.

The moment Brook stepped out of the SUV, she caught the subtle hint of anticipation that lingered in the air. Not even the birds were singing their morning melodies. She figured that had a lot to do with two reporters standing off to the side with their news camera crews. She tamped down her irritation over the fact that Otto had withheld vital information from her.

It didn't take long for Brook to ascend the porch stairs and walk across the wooden planks. She pulled open the screen door and was greeted by the delicious aroma of coffee. The fact that a deputy was standing at the foot of the staircase told her that she probably wouldn't be enjoying a cup.

"Brooklyn Sloane."

She had pulled out her credentials, but the deputy didn't seem to be too caught up in formality. He titled his head toward the stairs. She'd already taken notice of the fact that Mauve and Kirk were in the dining room with five other individuals, none of whom were Kim or Denise Breen. They'd contacted Brook on Saturday night to inform her that they were catching an early flight out yesterday morning, so she highly doubted that whatever had taken place at Hiker's Haven had anything to do with the Breen family.

Mauve wasn't hiding her displeasure of seeing Brook again, and Kirk was simply avoiding her stare. Brook had mentioned to Theo earlier that they weren't in town to make friends, but she understood his concern about questioning Riggs, Dominic, and Jace. The three of them had given their time voluntarily, and their upcoming interviews would undoubtedly notify them on their position within the investigation.

Muffled voices could be heard coming from the only room that had its door open. She listened closely as she slowly took one step at a time. While Otto had kept her in the dark, she'd caught enough of the subdued conversation to know that another woman had gone missing. She'd wait to alert the team until she had more details, but they were already stretched thin.

Brook also didn't want to jump to conclusions. If she were to base the timeline off Helen Beckham, Carissa Norman, and Luna Breen, years had passed between their abductions and subsequent murders.

While a lot of the evidence would take weeks and months to process by forensics, lab results should be given soon on any possible DNA matches from the site discovered by Riggs and Sylvie.

"...gone. It was like she simply vanished into thin air."

The deputy who had been standing near the bedroom door had noticed Brook's presence. She made sure to lift her credentials, which had garnered a slight nod of recognition from the female officer. She'd clearly been waiting for Brook, which meant that Otto had informed his deputies that she would soon be on site.

"We all know about the murder that happened last week," Lance said, his voice cracking with emotion. Brook had recognized his tone from her last visit to the B&B. "Darlene almost canceled our trip because of it, but I was the one who insisted we come. Like I said before, we were a couple hours into our hike. I thought that we should refill our water bottles. Darlene's sock was bothering her, so while she sat down to take off her boot, I walked over to a stream. When I returned, she was gone. She never would have just wandered off on her own, so that means..."

"Who is *we*?" Brook asked softly as she entered the room. The simplistic yet rustic décor complemented the rest of the B&B. The rich wood blended with the earth tones of the furnishings, creating a cozy atmosphere that contrasted starkly with the grim discussion taking place. "Who all knew about the murder?"

After Lance's voice had trailed off as if he didn't understand her question, he'd shifted his focus from the sheriff to the floor. Before too long, he lifted his defiant gaze to meet hers.

Brook was the one who now had Lance's full attention.

Otto remained silent, but his puzzled expression was just as prevalent as the one Lance was exhibiting in his confusion.

"Everyone who is staying here," Lance explained as his gaze flickered to the doorway. It was apparent that he wasn't sure how he should take her inquiry. "Everyone in town, and probably everyone in the state. In case you didn't notice, it's all over the news. What kind of question is that? Darlene is missing. It's obvious that psychopath took her, and you need to organize a search party. You shouldn't be wasting time asking asinine questions."

"I recognize the seriousness of the situation, Mr..."

"Griffin." Lance directed an irritated glance toward the sheriff. "Lance Griffin. I was downstairs last Friday when you were speaking with Mauve. You saw Darlene. You know that she is a brunette. The second that I realized she was gone, I should have returned to town instead of searching for her. I wasted precious time, and now it might be too late."

Brook lifted the corner of her lip in commiseration, giving Lance the appearance that she was agreeing with him. In reality, she'd already made the judgement that Darlene's disappearance had nothing to do with the unsub.

"Mr. Griffin, I know this is a very stressful time. You must understand that we need to ask you some very difficult questions."

While Brook had spent most of her career conversing with field agents regarding their interactions with victims, witnesses, and even those responsible for the crimes, she'd always found the saying odd—*we need to ask you a difficult question*. The inquiries weren't challenging to ask. The difficulty resided in believing the responses.

"You told Sheriff Jackson that Darlene almost canceled on you because she'd heard about the murders," Brook reiterated as she gestured toward a suitcase. "You live where, Mr. Griffin?"

"Kentucky."

"I take it that there was coverage of the murder on television?" For the first time since Brook had walked into the room, she witnessed Lance hesitate with his answer. "Maybe Darlene read an article? If she wanted to cancel, then that would mean she knew about Luna Breen's murder before your trip."

"I'm sure that was it," Lance replied as he curled his fingers into fists. "I should have listened to her. We never should have come here."

"What time did you and Darlene leave the B&B yesterday morning?"

"Sunrise."

"And you returned to town this morning?"

"Yes. I spent all night searching for her." Lance's voice had cracked, but she noticed that his eyes had remained free of any tears. "I called out to her so many times, hoping to hear something...anything that might lead me to her."

"The sheriff is going to do everything in his power to ensure that Darlene is brought home safe. Right now, I'm going to ask that you wait downstairs so that a forensics team can be brought in to process the room." Brook wasn't surprised when Lance appeared encouraged by her statement, but he then immediately became wary until she reassured him that it was all part of their protocol. He stood and wiped the palms of his hands on his jeans. "Mr. Griffin, would you please give a detailed description of what Darlene was wearing? Those details are important and will be given to those joining the mountain rescue team."

Brook and Otto remained silent as Lance began to walk toward the deputy. Now that he'd cleared the room, she had a better view of his backpack. What she discovered helped to solidify her belief that Darlene hadn't been abducted by the unsub.

"Griffin will lawyer up within the next few hours," Brook informed Otto quietly, ensuring that her voice didn't travel outside the room. "You'll want to bag his clothes, jacket, gloves, and anything that was on his person when he left the B&B yesterday morning. I'd also instruct the search party to canvas a much larger area. Chances are you'll discover Darlene's body at least a mile or two away from where Griffin claims she went missing, especially given that he had all day to dispose of her body."

"This is a federal case, Brook. Either you take it under the possibility that Darlene Hummel is connected to your investigation, or I hand it over to the feds."

"I don't believe that Darlene Hummel was abducted by the same individual who killed Luna Breen." Brook thought it over before coming to a quick decision, and one that she would prefer Otto go along with for the time being. "Let's keep this under our investigation for now, but we'll work separately. I'll notify the Charlotte office, as well as make sure the park rangers work with you on this. We'll say that it's a joint investigation to keep things contained."

"Did you notice the scratches on the back of Griffin's right hand?" Otto asked as he focused on the doorway. "Griffin explained the wounds away by saying he tripped and caught the back of his hand on some twigs."

"I had the ability to observe Ms. Hummel enter the B&B last Friday," Brook explained as she deliberately scanned the room for other inconsistencies. "She was reserved when she greeted Griffin. While it is possible that Hummel saw coverage of Breen's murder on the news or read about what happened in an article posted online, there was never any coverage about a serial killer. The only way Griffin could have known about the other possible victims was by overhearing my conversation with Mauve and Kirk. It was during that conversation that I inquired about Carissa Norman and Helen Beckham."

Otto's facial expression lit with recognition.

"There's also the small detail that Griffin returned with only one water bottle, which just so happens to still be connected to his backpack. Do you have any gloves on you?" Brook figured there was a slight chance Darlene's water bottle could be inside Griffin's backpack, but there was only one way to find out. Otto pulled out a pair of nitrile gloves from his pocket and handed them to her. "I was going to ask Griffin about the water bottle, but I do believe that he will request a lawyer upon hearing such a question."

Brook worked the nitrile gloves over her hands before kneeling in front of the backpack. A relatively heavy one. She unzipped the bag and carefully began to search through its contents.

Day hiking was very different than those hikers who spent the night out in the wilderness. She expected to find a hat, sunscreen, insect repellant, bear spray, lip balm, first aid kit, and maybe even a whistle. She also wasn't surprised to discover a roll of toilet paper, a lighter, a small pocketknife, and a spare blanket. It was the tightly rolled-up sleeping bag that Griffin could easily say was only taken in case of an emergency, but such unnecessary weight told of a different story. There were even remnants of some dead leaves stuck to the cord that was wrapped around the nylon fabric.

"It appears that Griffin took a break from searching for Ms. Hummel," Brook murmured before announcing confirmation of her previous deduction. "No water bottle belonging to Hummel. Griffin spent the night up in those mountains. He'll say that he was searching for his fiancé, but he used that time to find a spot and hide her body. You could play it two ways, Otto. You could ask Griffin about Hummel's water bottle, or you could continue along with his story until he trips himself."

"Not very bright, is he?"

"Bright enough that he used an opportunity to his advantage," Brook said as a thought occurred to her. More like an inspiration on how to narrow their suspect pool. "Otto, keep in touch. Oh, and do you mind if I borrow Riggs again?"

"I thought you didn't trust Riggs?"

"I don't, but that doesn't mean I can't take advantage of his knowledge," Brook replied without hesitation. She then brought herself up short before she could exit the room. Had someone spoken about her team in such a manner, she would have taken offense. She could at least give Otto the respect that he'd given her. "Do you trust him, Otto?"

"Yes."

There had been absolutely no hesitation in the sheriff's response.

Brook turned around so that she could face him. She studied the lines around his eyes and mouth, and his facial expression matched the confidence in his belief. She slowly nodded her recognition to his response.

"I'll keep you posted, Otto."

Brook had pulled out her phone before she'd even made it to the top of the staircase. She didn't want Theo speaking to anyone just yet. Instead, she wanted to explain her objective in utilizing Riggs' hiking experience and connection to the surrounding towns to lay some groundwork.

The profile suggested the unsub was a local, but the term was loose in its meaning within the context of the investigation. Riggs would be able to filter false information through to the communities that another cabin had been discovered, and that something had been left behind that could possibly produce DNA of the killer.

If the team deployed their strategy carefully and correctly, there was a possibility that they could lure the unsub out of hiding by spreading a rumor that a forensics team couldn't be deployed for a certain number of days.

Would the unsub attempt to remove said evidence?

Before Brook could access her speed dial list, her phone chimed with an incoming call. She recognized the number. It was the federal forensics lab that had collected the evidence discovered in the abandoned cabin. She answered immediately and listened to the results as she descended the staircase. By the time she reached the main level, she'd received her answer.

"Thank you for the information," Brook replied as she passed by the deputy and Lance Griffin. He was monitoring her exit, but she didn't pay him any attention. He was Otto's problem, and she wasn't about to get mixed up with another investigation. "What about the Breen crime scene?"

The brisk air was quite the change from the warmth inside the B&B. She reached into the pocket of her jacket to pull out the key fob that would unlock the driver's side door of the rental SUV. While forensics had found nothing useful inside the cabin where Luna Breen had been brutally murdered, the forensic results were all that was needed to confirm the profile. She once again thanked the forensics tech as she settled in behind the steering wheel before disconnecting the call.

Brook pressed Theo's name on her screen, and he answered on the first ring.

"Helen Beckham was killed in the cabin that Riggs and Sylvie found last week," Brook stated as she pressed the ignition button. The SUV purred to life. "We are officially hunting a serial killer preying on female hikers in the Smoky Mountains."

Chapter Fifteen

Brooklyn Sloane

October 2023

Monday — 11:14am

"Wayne Uriel, Shawn Cannon, and Allen Brixton. Oh, and we also have to include Gabe Raskins. He was also part of all three mountain rescue teams who searched for Carissa Norman, Helen Beckham, and Luna Breen."

"Hold on, Little T." Bit managed to lower the background noise of the prison's waiting room. Sylvie had called Brook via phone video as she waited to visit her father. Sylvie might have returned to Washington D.C., but she hadn't stopped working to put together a list of volunteers who had offered their time and effort to search for all three women. While there was no evidence to support Carissa Norman's involvement with the case, they couldn't discount her similarities to the other two victims. "That's better. Go ahead."

Brook leaned forward to grab her coffee. The carafes that the Moonshine Diner had provided had prompted her to make a cash offer in order to take them with her when she returned home. She wasn't sure what made them so different from the typical carafes like the one Wyn had provided from the bar, but these things could sell for hundreds of dollars and still be underpriced. She settled back in her chair as she monitored Bit type in the three names to one of his miraculous programs.

"Bit, keep your focus on Carissa Norman," Brook instructed in a low voice so as not to disrupt Sylvie's update. Her blonde hair was contained in its usual bun, but her cheeks lacked their natural rosy color. She also had blemishes underneath her eyes that told of her recent sleepless nights. "Remember, mistakes are usually made with the first victim."

Brook had no idea if Carissa Norman was the first female hiker who the unsub had targeted, but that was the name they needed to focus on right now. It might be wise to speak with Kirk Sampson again, but nothing had come to light in the interview that Otto had initiated with the man last week.

"Those are the only four male subjects who fit the profile, besides Riggs, Jace, and Dominic," Sylvie said as she glanced away from her phone. She paused for a moment before continuing. "Oh, wait. There were two other men, but I discounted them due to blatant alibis. One has been out of the country for the past month, and the other one moved to the West Coast earlier this year. Neither were in the area at the time of Luna Breen's disappearance and subsequent murder. Of course, those names are in addition to the list Erika provided us of the park rangers who fit the profile. Anyway, I've already initiated background checks on the three volunteers. You shouldn't have long to wait for the initial results."

"Fantastic work, Sylvie," Brook said before glancing down at her phone. She'd set the device to vibrate so as not to interrupt their meeting. Agent Russell Houser's name appeared on the lighted display, but she wasn't too concerned that something had taken place with her brother. Bit would have been alerted immediately, and he'd been rather relaxed this morning, which was a feat considering that he'd already consumed two energy drinks. "We'll take it from here. I don't want you worrying about anything other than the meeting with your father and his oncologist."

Sylvie had touched base with the team earlier this morning after her father had broken the news to her. Her voice had been relatively flat as she'd shared the details with everyone, and it hadn't been long afterward that she'd announced that she'd spent most of the night diving into the lists of volunteers provided by Erika.

Brook highly doubted that Sylvie had even left the prison this morning, which meant that she either hadn't eaten or she'd hit up one of the vending machines. Either way, it was time for Sylvie to take care of herself.

"Give us a call if you need anything," Brook said in a tone that would hopefully prevent Sylvie from putting up an argument. Brook then offered up a caveat so as to avoid any reluctance on Sylvie's part. "Feel free to check up on Arden. He gets lonely when the rest of us are out in the field."

"You could be there for another month or two," Sylvie argued with a shake of her head. Bit's eyes widened when Sylvie had completely ignored the subtle order. "I'll be back in a couple of days."

"No, Sylvie, you won't." Brook wasn't just looking out for Sylvie, but the team. "There is a very likely chance this investigation could continue into next year. If that's the case, we'll all be back periodically. In the meantime, you're to remain in the city unless something changes."

"Brook, don't treat me as if I—"

"I'm treating you no different than I would any other member of this team, Sylvie." Brook stood with her coffee, but she had no intention of leaving the room. "And as your friend, I'm telling you that work doesn't fix everything. Okay?"

Brook sensed the weight of Theo's stare from across the room. He had somehow managed to carry a small table up the staircase and fit it through the doorframe. The additional piece of furniture cramped the room even more, but it had provided an additional workspace. He was no longer studying the screen of his laptop, but instead scrutinizing her after such a comment.

It had taken a lot for her to make that last statement.

Ever so slowly, she was finally allowing herself to have a life outside of Jacob. It sure as hell wasn't easy, but it was long overdue.

"Okay," Sylvie replied in such a way that it was the first time a hint of fear could be heard about the reality of losing her father. There was no denying that he'd hurt a lot of people by his terrible choices. Unfortunately, no one was able to choose their family. "Will you at least keep me posted?"

"Considering that you wouldn't allow Bit to get one second of sleep otherwise, the answer is yes," Brook said as she picked up her phone. "We'll let you know of any new developments. Take care, Sylvie."

Bit smiled and waved at the camera on the 4k monitor. The special feature had allowed Sylvie to see the entire room, so she no doubt had caught Theo's wave, as well. He'd returned his attention to the information on his screen. They had all decided it was best to hold off with the interviews now that Darlene Hummel's abduction had muddied the waters.

"Hiker's Haven is still the only connection between all three women," Bit said as he reached for one of the donuts that he'd brought back from the bakery this morning. "I ran their list of employees through our system, but none of them fit the profile."

Brook had already accessed her voicemail to hear what Agent Houser had to say this morning. She lowered the bottom of her phone to speak with Bit.

"What about guests? Mauve gave us access to her guest list. Was there anyone who had a room booked on the same weekends as our victims?" Brook asked before sidestepping her chair. "I need to place a call. I'll be right back."

Brook took her coffee with her and enjoyed a sip while returning Agent Houser's call. The tension in his voice when he'd answered had her squaring her shoulders for the upcoming announcement.

"I received a call from the U.S. Marshals Service this morning," Russell said without a greeting. "Sarah Evanston has officially backed out of the program."

Brook remained silent as she thought through her options. There really were none given the scope of the situation. Sarah Evanston had barely had any skin attached to her face when they'd found her lying in a pool of her own blood. The only reason that she'd lived after such a brutal attack was because Jacob hadn't had time to slit her throat. Considering the numerous surgeries and the pain that Sarah must have endured since then, she had probably wished she had died several times over.

Jacob was going to finally get his wish.

Sarah Evanston was going to come out of hiding, though it wasn't like she could return to her previous life as a reporter. Those days were long over.

"I want to speak with her."

"Brook, you and I both know that's not going to happen. Next to Jacob Walsh, you are the last person who she wants to speak to under the circumstances."

"I don't care. Make it happen."

Brook disconnected the call. She had no idea what she would say to Sarah Evanston, but Brook needed to convince her to stay hidden. Word would eventually reach Jacob that the only woman to survive his attacks had dared to flaunt it by living her life while he sat to rot behind bars.

"Everything okay?" Theo asked with concern as she walked back into the room. He'd leaned back against the spindles of the chair that he'd also brought up from downstairs. "Erika texted a few seconds ago. She's pulling up to the bar now. Her supervisor wasn't happy that we requested she not join the search party for Darlene Hummel."

"Considering this is a federal investigation, I'm sure he'll get over it," Brook murmured as she studied the portable monitor. Bit had pulled up the information that Sylvie had added to the files. The names of the male subjects that she'd highlighted definitely fit the profile, and each one of them would need to be interviewed at some point. "You should know that Sarah Evanston has decided to leave the witness protection program."

Theo muttered some expletives while Bit readjusted his knit hat.

"I requested a sit down with her, though I'm not so sure that Agent Houser will be able to accommodate my request. Either way, I thought you should know in case I need to take an afternoon off," Brook warned them as she reclaimed her seat. "Getting back to the business at hand, I think that—"

A knock came at the door. Theo called out for whoever it was to enter, and no one was surprised to find that Erika had arrived with several bags in hand. She juggled one until Theo was able to relieve her load.

"I think I've died and gone to heaven," Bit muttered when he realized that Erika had brought them Chinese food. "Where did you get this from, Erika?"

"There's a Chinese restaurant about three miles from here," she said with a smile. "I figured you'd be sick and tired of bar food, and even the diner only has so many meals on the menu."

Erika's smile began to gradually fade when she caught sight of the monitor. Theo and Bit hadn't noticed since they were busy removing the white containers from the bags, but Brook attempted to gauge which of the three names on the board bothered her so much. Brook didn't have to wait long before the answer was revealed, exposing another problem.

"Why is Allen Brixton's name on the board?" Erika asked cautiously as she pulled at the collar of her uniform. "You can't possibly think that he murdered Luna Breen."

"About that," Brook said after taking a sip of her coffee. "Luna Breen wasn't the only victim. Helen Beckham was murdered in that abandoned cabin that Sylvie and Riggs discovered last week. We're still waiting for the other trace evidence from both crime scenes."

"That means that there is a good chance another cabin or structure is somewhere in the mountains that contains Carissa Norman's blood." Erika raised a hand to her mouth as if she could lessen her nausea. "Where are the other two bodies? What is the killer doing with their remains?"

"Burying them. What's left of them," Brook amended as she attempted to fill in the profile. "I believe that the unsub left their bodies in the cabins with resentment that they couldn't give the answer or answers to what he was asking of them. A week or two later, remorse settled in. Whether that's because the unsub went back to his regular life and the memories of what he'd done was too much or merely to hide the result of such an impulsive action isn't clear."

"But I thought you said this was premeditated?"

"In a manner of speaking, yes." Brook reached for the remote. She then pressed a few buttons so that a crime scene picture of Luna Breen appeared in the top righthand corner of the screen. "Whatever it is the unsub wants to know from these women becomes an obsession over the years. He constantly thinks about torturing someone who he believes can supply him with some type of response. So much so, that he was able to pick which locations that he would apply the torture. Considering all the victims were brunette and in their twenties, I can only assume that the sight of them triggered his urge. The compulsion to follow through with his thoughts overcame his sense of right and wrong. Only when he returned back home did repentance become heavy enough to cause his need to bury them."

"Could the unsub have properly buried his other victims?" Theo asked as he picked up a set of chopsticks. Erika seemed repulsed that Theo and Bit could eat lunch after what had just been discussed, but that was only because she typically wasn't used to handling these types of investigations. "Do you think we could attempt to find a burial ground with actual headstones?"

"In theory, yes," Brook answered as she reached for her tablet. She quickly inserted some additional notes into the profile so that the team had access to them. "Although I doubt that he would have left a marker large enough for anyone to know what they truly stood for. That last piece of the puzzle brings us as close to a full profile as possible. The unsub could be single, married, divorced, children, no children. He'll be someone who the town knows well, which is why you need to accept that even Allen Brixton could be a person of interest."

"Allen can't even kill a spider," Erika said in defense of the man. The disbelief in her voice came through with a nervous laugh. "He'd be devastated to know that his name was even mentioned with this case."

"I take it that you're involved with him?"

"No." Erika finally released her collar. "Allen Brixton is my future brother-in-law."

Chapter Sixteen

Theo Neville

October 2023

Monday — 3:23pm

Billowing clouds had gathered and were slowly rolling in from the west, their shadows drifting across the main thoroughfare of Moonshine Valley. The temperature had already dropped a few degrees, and there was nothing subtle about the chill that had settled into the air. With it came the familiar scent of petrichor.

"It's going to rain," Theo said after he and Erika had exited the bar. Their intended destination was an outdoor outfitter shop two blocks down. Allen Brixton happened to own the storefront, which just so happened to sell hiking equipment. "Or maybe a mixture of rain and snow. Once we finish speaking with Brixton, we'll drive to Wayne Uriel's residence."

The shift in weather wasn't lost on Theo. It was almost as if Mother Nature was letting them know they were running out of time. Brook had mentioned to Sylvie that it could take them months or longer to apprehend the unsub. With winter approaching, searching for a burial ground or even another abandoned structure where the killer had taken another victim would be impossible.

"We shouldn't be wasting our time like this," Erika muttered as she pulled the zipper a little higher on her jacket so that the collar protected her neck. "Like I said, Allen can't even kill a spider."

The wind had picked up a bit as the cold front began to move into the area. Dead leaves swirled on the sidewalk up ahead as if to lead them to their destination. While there were a couple of vehicles in sight, a news van stood out the most. It wouldn't be too long before more reporters showed up to cover the latest news about another woman's disappearance.

Brook would have no choice but to make a statement. She'd been hoping that the sheriff would be able to contain the situation, but it was clear that someone had tipped off a local reporter. Theo could only imagine the chaotic scene at the bed and breakfast, but he needed to focus on the task at hand.

Allen Brixton hadn't been mentioned in Erika's background information. She'd informed them that Allen had just proposed to her sister. The connection would have eventually come to light with Bit's software program. The way his application could search through online sites was incredible, but the manner in which he could then utilize said information to garner additional correlations between suspects and victims was simply astonishing.

"What do the victims all have in common beyond physical features and age?" Theo asked as they crossed the street. "I'll answer for you. Hiker's Haven."

"Right," Erika said in agreement as she shoved her hands into her pockets. "Mauve's bed and breakfast. Plus, we know that Kirk Sampson was personally involved with Carissa Norman. Shouldn't our focus be on Hiker's Haven and Kirk?"

"We need to look beyond that, because we also know that Sampson couldn't have murdered all three victims."

"What if there is more than one killer?"

"The profile doesn't suggest that there is more than one unsub, which means we need to find another connection. Whether that connection lies with the victims or Hiker's Haven remains to be seen, but we don't stop looking just because we don't like where the investigation is headed."

"You're talking about Brook's situation."

Truthfully, Theo hadn't been talking about Brook's relationship with her brother, but even he could admit that her childhood was the perfect example. He would never betray her by discussing her personal demons with someone else just to make a point.

"I'm talking about every case in general. As I said before, we're looking into any and all connections. Hiker's Haven is just one of many. What if all the victims shopped at these stores? What if they all ate at the diner? Or drank at the pub? Just because there was no financial transaction confirmed on their bank statements doesn't mean that they didn't visit other places and use cash."

"But I know Allen, and he isn't capable of murder," Erika insisted as she slowed down her pace. Theo finally came to a stop, because it was becoming clear that she couldn't bring herself to cross some invisible line that she'd drawn in the sand. "Please trust me when I say that he couldn't have done this. Why aren't we focusing on Ned Proehl? He's still missing, and he fits the profile."

Theo studied Erika as he thought through the different ways to explain the benefit of having her with him when he questioned Allen Brixton. Not just Brixton, either. The list of individuals who Theo needed to speak with over the next couple of days was long, and having someone next to him who knew the townsfolk was imperative. Erika would be able to sense when a local wasn't being truthful, and she also had facts about them that could be useful in such interviews.

A park ranger wasn't used to handling an investigation of this magnitude. The dynamics of such brutal crimes were outside of her realm of expertise. Unless Theo was able to change her perception of the case, she would only be a detriment to him.

"Erika, forget Allen Brixton right now." Theo slid his hands into the pockets of his jacket. "Besides physical features and age, the victims also enjoyed hiking. It was the reason that they were in town. Bit was able to link two of the victims to Moonshine Outfitters—Carissa Norman and Helen Beckham. According to their credit card receipts, they both made purchases at the shop. We need to know if Luna Breen entered the store at any point during her weekend stay at Hiker's Haven. Did she buy something using cash? Did she just browse through the aisles? Did she ask a store clerk any questions? It would help to know if Allen Brixton or maybe one of his employees noticed her that weekend. If they don't recognize her from the picture on my phone, do they have a security camera? Are they willing to give us the footage or do we need to obtain a warrant? And just because there is a chance that all three victims were customers of Moonshine Outfitters doesn't mean that anyone connected with the shop is guilty of murdering them. Look around you. For some of these serial killers, all it takes is a glance to stir them into action. There's a post office across the street. For all we know, someone inside has been monitoring the shop for potential victims."

Theo had needed to prove his point, and he might have just succeeded. The way that Erika was looking across the street at the other shops told him that he'd made some progress.

"We have a lot of ground to cover today, Erika. It would help to have someone with me, but I can interview these suspects solo if you want to ask Brook for another assignment."

"No," Erika replied instantly with a shake of her head. Technically, she fit the physical attributes of the victims. The only difference was that her strands contained a reddish hue, but there could have been several other reasons that the unsub hadn't set his sights on the park ranger, such as they personally knew one another. "I get it now, Theo."

"Okay, then."

Without another word, Theo continued to close the distance to the front entrance of Moonshine Outfitters. He opened the door and stood back, allowing Erika to enter the shop first. The moment he crossed the threshold behind her, a heavy scent of leather hit him. There was also an underlying fragrance of coconut, which emanated from the display of sunscreens near the entrance. The smell of leather clearly came from a section of hiking boots near the back. Tents, sleeping bags, trekking poles, and other miscellaneous hiking equipment were all on display to catch the attention of a customer.

Theo and the team had stopped into the shop on their first day in town to buy the essential items needed to hike to the crime scene. He didn't recall meeting or even seeing Allen Brixton. The picture that Bit had pulled up on the screen had displayed a thirty-one-year-old man who'd lost his hair at a young age. Either that, or he'd purposefully shaven his head for other reasons.

"Allen?" Erika called out when it was obvious that no one was manning the checkout counter. There was one person sitting in a chair near the hiking boot section. He was an older man, maybe in his sixties. "You around?"

"In back," the man responded gruffly as he leaned down to untie his shoes. "How you doing, Erika? Any word on that missing woman?"

"No, Stanley. Hal and the others are out looking for her now," Erika replied before making a proper introduction. "Stanley Schneider, this is Theo Neville. He's investigating the murder of Luna Breen."

"I don't envy you, son." Stanley removed one shoe before reaching for the laces on the other while keeping his focus on Theo. "Now with this other gal gone missing, I guess the rumors are true. There's a serial killer hunting hikers in those mountains."

Theo managed not to react to the man's statement.

"Are you any closer to finding the son of a bitch?"

"We're working on it, sir."

"Well, I'll be joining the search party. I'll be breaking in a new pair of boots, too. My old ones are shot." Stanley set his other shoe to the side. "The first group left the meeting spot around ten o'clock this morning. I guess they haven't found her yet, which is why Riggs requested another group."

"We appreciate your help, Stanley," Erika said as she unzipped her jacket. Theo had done the same upon entering the shop. The difference in temperature was quite stark. "You aren't going up tonight, are you? Sunset is less than three hours away."

"We're meeting at dawn."

"You're in luck, Stanley. I have one pair of those boots in a size eleven, and—" Allen stopped talking mid-sentence after he'd spotted Erika. He smiled as he closed the distance between them. "I heard the chime above the door, but I didn't expect to see you today. Need something special? Stanley was just telling me that there's another missing woman, and she was staying at Hiker's Haven."

"Hi, Allen." Erika leaned in to kiss the man on the cheek. She quickly made another round of introductions before gesturing toward Allen's customer. "You finish up with Stanley. Theo and I just have a few questions about your security camera."

"Sure thing." Allen didn't appear to be nervous or upset over the statement. If anything, he came across as wanting to do what he could to help his future sister-in-law. "You want to wait in the back office?"

"No," Theo answered for Erika. His intention was to keep Brixton relaxed enough to talk. "We appreciate the offer, but this won't take long."

Theo took a step back before he began to browse some of the display items. Erika quietly followed him around while they patiently waited for Stanley to try on the pair of boots that Allen had brought out from the backroom.

"Does Allen do a lot of hiking?" Theo asked as he came to a stop in front of the trekking poles.

"Maybe once a month? Unless it's to help out the mountain rescue team. Allen has one employee—Huck Rishi. You can usually find him at the pub every night. We can speak with him after our other interviews."

"I'd rather speak with Huck this afternoon," Theo said, having every intention of asking Huck about Allen's proclivities. As the sister of the man's fiancé, it was highly doubtful that Erika knew every single detail about the man. "We'll stop by Huck's residence after speaking with Allen. We'll swing back around to speak with Wayne Uriel."

Theo didn't give Erika much time to mull over his decision. Instead, he asked the question that had been weighing on his mind after speaking with Dominic about walking sticks. They'd discussed the pros and cons of such a hiking aid, but Theo hadn't had the chance to ask if any locals were known to usually use one.

"Do you know if Allen uses a trekking pole when he finds the time to hike?"

"Not usually," Erika answered with a frown. "My sister does, though."

"What about anyone else who was listed on the monitor this morning?"

"Honestly, I think I've seen every single one of those men use a walking stick at one point or another, but it's not a regular thing."

Stanley had decided to purchase the boots, and it wasn't long before Allen was standing behind the cash register. Once payment was made and Stanley had his purchase in hand, the man gave into his own curiosity.

"Why do you need Allen's security footage?" Stanley asked as he adjusted the bill of his ballcap. "Do you think that son of a bitch was in here? I think you should check the other guests who stay at Hiker's Haven. All the victim's stayed there. Makes sense that is where the killer set his sights on them."

"We're exploring every avenue, Mr. Schneider." Theo shook the man's hand. "We're working around the clock."

"Good, good. Will I see you tomorrow morning?"

"Maybe," Theo replied as he kept his options open. "We are working in collaboration with the sheriff on the disappearance of Darlene Hummel. We don't want to assume that her missing persons case is connected to Luna Breen just yet."

"Oh, really?" Stanley asked, his displeasure evident. "I don't see why not. Brunette. Right age. What am I missing?"

"You aren't missing anything, Stanley," Erika reassured the man before patting his arm. It was obvious that Stanley wasn't buying it. "All agencies involved are keeping in close contact with one another."

"Erika is right, Mr. Schneider. An investigation this large has several components to it, and we don't want anything to fall through the cracks."

"Well, then," Stanley said with a satisfied nod. "I'll leave you to it."

"Thanks, Stanley," Allen called out good-naturedly. Theo noted that the business owner had chosen not to remain behind the counter. Such a reaction meant that he didn't feel the need to be defensive. "You want access to the shop's security feed? It's not one of those fancy cameras that is monitored by an outside company. I set it up myself, but I keep the footage on my hard drive. I can't afford those expensive monthly fees."

"You wouldn't mind giving us access?" Theo asked, confirming that Allen wasn't going to make them jump through hoops to obtain a warrant. "My colleague can be here in a few minutes."

"If searching through the shop's security footage can prevent another woman from going missing or being killed, then go for it." Allen ran a hand over his bald head until his palm rested on the back of his neck. "I take it's true, then? There is a serial killer targeting brunettes on the hiking trails?"

"We're investigating all leads." Theo pulled out his phone and accessed his pictures. He then turned it around to show the display to Allen. "Do you recognize this woman?"

"The face looks familiar, but I can't place her." Allen frowned before tilting his head slightly to the side. "Wait a second. This woman is on a missing persons flyer that's hanging up at the police station."

"You go to the police station often?" Theo asked, ensuring that he'd injected some humor into his question. He noticed that Erika had tensed upon hearing the inquiry, but Allen just laughed it off.

"I do when I need a police report for my insurance company." Allen gestured to the entrance of his shop. "Some asshole sideswiped my car.

I called the sheriff's office, and one his deputies came out to take the report."

"I'm sorry to hear that. The woman in this picture is Carissa Norman. She went missing around five years ago, and her financials show that she made a purchase here." Theo monitored the man's reaction, but he didn't seem at all nervous. "You don't remember waiting on her?"

"That's like asking if you remember someone you interviewed five years ago," Allen countered with a slight shrug. "Maybe? Moonshine Valley doesn't get as many tourists as some of the surrounding towns, but we still get enough that there are just too many names and faces to keep track of."

"What about this photo?" Theo said as he swiped to the left before holding up his phone once more. "Do you recognize her? Helen Beckham went missing three years ago."

This time, recognition dawned on Allen's face.

"I know this woman." Allen shook his finger at the phone. "I remember her, because she bumped into the sunscreen display and knocked half of them off the shelves. I think she ended up buying something just because she felt bad."

"Did anything else strike you as odd?" Theo asked as he turned the phone so that he could access another picture. "Do you recall if she was with anyone?"

"She was definitely with a friend, because the woman couldn't stop laughing," Allen said with a smile that gradually faded. "Her name is Helen? And she's missing?"

"I'm afraid so," Erika said as Theo once more held up his phone. "This is Luna Breen. Her body was discovered last week in an abandoned cabin around an hour and a half from town. Do you remember seeing her in the shop a few weeks ago? It would have been either a Friday night or Saturday morning."

Theo figured it wouldn't take long before Allen realized that they weren't here just because the missing women had opted to buy something in his store. He finally crossed his arms as his gaze flickered to the display on Theo's phone.

"Three weeks ago? I was with your sister, remember? That was the weekend we went to Las Vegas with Tom and Valerie." Allen didn't seem to notice Erika's subtle exhalation of relief. He was too busy focusing his attention on Theo. "Do you think that I had something to do with the abductions of these women? Were they all murdered? Did you find their bodies? Why would you think that I—"

"Allen, it's not like that," Erika said as she attempted to reassure her future brother-in-law that he'd gotten the wrong idea. "We happened to notice that they stopped in here to purchase hiking equipment, and it's standard procedure to follow up on these things."

Theo debated on whether or not to interrupt Erika's speech, but he decided against it. He used the time to send a message to Bit regarding the approval of accessing the shop's security system. Within seconds, Bit responded that he was on his way.

"...would tell you if there was anything to worry about. There isn't, Allen."

"If it helps to reassure you, we're taking the next few days to speak with other shop owners," Theo said as he tucked his phone back into one of his pockets. "My colleague should be here any minute to take a look at your security footage."

"It's only three years old," Allen replied reluctantly as he switched his attention back to Theo. "There isn't much crime in Moonshine Valley. I only bought the security camera because someone broke into the bakery once. Turned out to be the owner's underage son who wanted cash to buy some booze down at the corner store. Of course, we didn't know that at the time. Spent two hundred dollars on that camera, and there were no refunds."

"You never know, Mr. Brixton. That two hundred dollars might just help solve a federal investigation." Theo detected a reduction of tension in the man's shoulders. "Is there anything else that you can remember about Helen Beckham? You mentioned that she purchased sunscreen, but you believed at the time that she only did so out of guilt for bumping into the display case. Did she and her friend come inside the shop for anything specific?"

"Not that I remem—" Allen snapped his fingers. "Wait a second. She was looking for a trekking pole, but she decided against it. Honestly, I think she was too embarrassed to stay around to choose one."

"A walking stick?" Theo asked, needing confirmation. Granted, Bit would be able to pull up the footage, because Helen's disappearance was in the time frame that Allen had set up his security camera. "Are you sure?"

"Trekking pole, hiking pole, walking stick. They go by a lot of names, but yes. It's all coming back to me now." Allen glanced over at the display of various trekking poles. "The woman said she saw some guy on the trail with one, and she thought it would be nice to have one if she were to hike the harder trails later that day. I think he even suggested she come here, but I don't know if I'm remembering our conversation right. It was shortly after she bumped into the sunscreen display."

"Theo, that would mean..."

"Helen Beckham spoke to her abductor two days before she went missing."

Chapter Seventeen

Brooklyn Sloane

October 2023

Monday — 5:59pm

"You were right. Griffin lawyered up the second after I asked about Hummel's water bottle." Otto released an exhausted sigh that practically resonated through the cell phone. "The search party didn't find anything today. Riggs is taking a group out tomorrow."

"About that," Brook said as she weaved her way through a few tables to reach the exit of the bar. She'd waved to Wyn, but he was in deep conversation with his son. She almost stopped and made her way over to the man, but Bit had mentioned seeing Riggs walking into the bait and tackle shop a few minutes ago. "I'd like it if Riggs could join Theo on searching the area around the location where Helen Beckham's blood was found on the floor of that cabin."

Brook opened the door and couldn't brace herself in time. She'd known that it was raining, which only made the efforts to locate Darlene Hummel's body all the more difficult. While some might think the woman was still alive, Brook didn't have such expectations. What she hadn't anticipated was how severe the drop in temperature could be from earlier today.

"Damn," Brook muttered as she reached back and pulled the hood of her jacket until she was covered enough to release her hold on the door. "It feels like winter out here."

"It's the end of October in the Smoky Mountains. If you don't like the weather, wait a day."

"I hear you," Brook muttered as she began to walk down the sidewalk. She grimaced when she noticed the media vans lined up in front of the diner. "Listen, there's a good chance that the woman who was with Helen Beckham can give us a description of the unsub. Apparently, Beckham stopped into Moonshine Outfitters searching for a trekking pole. The two of them mentioned running into someone while they were hiking on Friday."

"And you believe that particular individual is the killer?"

"Maybe." Brook figured she shouldn't be too offended by the weather. The rain was preventing members of the press from making her life difficult at the moment. She wasn't looking forward to when they were informed that the rooms above the bar were being rented out to the consultants of the FBI. It was only a matter of time, and there was a really good chance that they were already aware of such arrangements. "Could be a coincidence, but there was a mark on the wall at a very specific height."

"I don't need to remind you that many hikers use trekking poles, right?"

"Reach out to Darlene Hummel's friends," Brook suggested, purposefully ignoring Otto's question. "Chances are she told one of them that she was ending things with Griffin this weekend."

"Hummel's parents should be arriving sometime this evening."

"Friends, not family."

"I will, though probably not until tomorrow. I have limited staff, and you're about to borrow my best deputy once again."

"I'm going to keep Erika in town for a while. With Sylvie back in D.C., we need the additional assistance."

"Oh, one more thing," Otto said before his title was being called out by someone in the background. "I should have mentioned it before, but if you're really focused on the trekking pole, you might want to speak with a man by the name of Wayne Uriel. He's a woodworker who lives at the base of the mountain about a mile from town, smack dab in between two of the townships."

Brook's step faltered upon hearing the name.

"Wayne Uriel?"

"Yeah. Good guy. Helped out with the search for Hummel today. I've got to go. We'll talk soon."

"Shit," Brook muttered before she reached the entrance to the bait and tackle shop. She'd known that Uriel was a woodworker, but she hadn't put two and two together. Most trekking poles were made out of carbon fiber. "Double shit."

Riggs' patrol car was still parked out front. Bit had noticed the vehicle on his walk back to the bar from the hiking shop. She yanked on the handle to open the door and was met with a distinct odor. It was difficult to describe, but it was the same pungent smell that used to fill her parents' garage in the days leading up to her father's fishing trips.

Brook pushed back her hood.

"...can't, Riggs. I don't have anyone to mind the shop tomorrow morning." Jace materialized from the back room carrying a tackle box. "Did you ask Dominic?"

Riggs wasn't far behind Jace, but he'd spotted Brook immediately.

"Your colleague already spoke to me," Riggs replied without seemingly any resentment. "Don't worry. I know it's protocol. I take it Jace is next up on the list?"

Jace slowly set the tackle box next to the cash register, his right eyebrow higher than the left as he waited to hear Brook's response. The ringing of a telephone broke the silence.

"Moonshine Bait & Tackle." Jace listened to the caller on the other end of the line while keeping a curious gaze on Brook to witness her exchange with his friend. "Yes, Mitch. I just received your new tackle box, and I've set it aside those lures that you..."

"What do you know about Wayne Uriel?" Brook asked quietly as she closed enough distance to speak with Riggs privately. It had helped that he'd stepped aside far enough from the counter so as not to interrupt Jace's phone call. "I just received information that he carves walking sticks."

"Wayne is private. Doesn't like to get involved in the town's business."

"Really? He's one of the main volunteers on the mountain rescue team," Brook pointed out as she wiped a few drops of rain from the back of her hand. "I'd say such a role puts Wayne Uriel right smack dab in the middle of the town's business."

Riggs shook his head in disagreement. He rested his thumbs just inside his utility belt while widening his stance. Brook decided against bringing up Riggs' conversation with Theo and Erika today. Considering Riggs' profession, he understood more than most the standard procedure of any investigation. Such questioning hadn't been personal, and she wouldn't apologize on behalf of the team for them doing their jobs.

"Wayne has a woodworking shop in a shed behind his house. He sells his products online, and he likes to keep to himself. Takes after his old man. Loves the outdoors, and he spends as much time in those mountains as he does in his workshop." Riggs observed Jace finish up his phone call. "You might say that Wayne is a prepper. You know, the doomsday type."

Jace had set a small white bag next to the large tackle box, and it was obvious that he wanted to give his two cents about Wayne Uriel. The only reason that Jace and Dominic had been included in that first briefing was to give them a sense of what to look for when they had guided Theo and Sylvie over some of the rough terrain. There was no need for them to hear explicit details regarding other local residents.

"I'd like for you to join Theo tomorrow on another hike," Brook requested, stopping short of giving an explanation as to why. "Otto is going to let the park rangers know that you won't be available in the morning."

"I take it that you don't think Hummel is alive?"

"No, I don't." Brook once again didn't want to get into specifics. From Jace's phone call, it sounded as if someone named Mitch was due to enter the shop to pick up his order. "Sylvie had to return to D.C., which means that we'll need your assistance. Do you happen to have a change of clothes? I'm going to brief the team in a few minutes."

"Do I have time to return the patrol car to the station?"

"Yes," Brook responded, knowing that the station was a good forty-five minutes from town. That would give her an hour and a half to mull over the pros and cons of her plan. She made no move to join Riggs as he began to walk toward the front of the shop. He stopped midstride before casting a curious glance back. "I need to speak with Jace for a moment. You go on ahead and return your patrol car."

Riggs' features hardened at the implication that his friend was considered a suspect, but he didn't argue. She monitored his progress as he exited through the front door. He didn't care that he'd fallen on that same list, but his concern for his friends was evident. Such loyalty was lacking in most people these days, and his understanding of her role as lead investigator was all the more impressive.

"You think Wayne Uriel could have killed that girl?" Jace asked warily as his gaze switched from the front entrance to Brook. "Wayne can be a bit extreme about end-of-the-world scenarios, but a killer?"

"We appreciated your help last week," Brook said as she stepped up to the counter. "I'm sure you've heard the rumors around town, but we don't believe that Luna Breen was the first woman to have been murdered in a such a brutal manner. The press has already caught wind that we could be dealing with a serial killer, and I'll be giving a statement first thing in the morning. For now, we're asking most of the shop owners if any of these women stopped into their shops."

"I saw Luna Breen's picture before Riggs led one of the search parties, and I know that she didn't stop in here that weekend," Jace said as Brook pulled out her cell phone. "I didn't work the Sunday that she went missing, but I checked with my brother-in-law at the request of the sheriff. He wanted to see if she stopped into town before hiking that morning."

"Why weren't you working that Sunday?" Brook asked, not bothering to reword the question to make him more comfortable. He wasn't obtuse, and she wouldn't treat him as such. "And would you please provide me with your brother-in-law's name?"

"My wife and I recently separated, and I was in the process of moving some things out of the house," Jace replied guardedly as she set her phone on the counter. She'd made sure the display was facing him. "I heard from Dominic that he was also asked these questions, so I'm trying not to take offense."

"Your brother-in-law still speaks with you? Helps you out at the shop?" Brook asked right as the front entrance opened and revealed an older man in his sixties. "Even after your separation?"

"Chandler is a good guy. He's trying not to choose sides." Jace had lowered his voice so that his customer couldn't overhear their conversation. "Look, everyone knows that Allen gave you access to his security footage. A lot of us can't afford that type of equipment, and I'm one of those shop owners. As for remembering a face from years ago, that's doubtful, but feel free to speak with Chandler. He's been helping out at the shop for years."

Brook retrieved her phone that Jace had barely glanced at now that the customer was mere feet from the counter. Since the man's focus was solely on the large tackle box, she could only assume that he was the one on the phone earlier. No wonder he'd been able to arrive so quickly. She recognized him from the bar.

"Hi, Mitch. I got everything ready for you, and you're going to love the..."

Brook cleared the display on her phone before sliding it back into the pocket of her jacket. She'd already known the name of Jace's brother-in-law, but she'd learned long ago that engaging a witness sometimes led them to be more forthcoming with information.

"Ma'am? Are you that federal agent who has been investigating that girl's murder?" Mitch asked as he kept switching his focus between her face and the pocket where she'd stored her phone. Before she could reply, he pointed toward her jacket. "May I see that picture again?"

Mitch's focus hadn't been on his tackle box, but instead on her phone. She didn't hesitate to retrieve her it and pull up Helen Beckham's photograph.

"I'm Brook Sloane, a consultant with the FBI," she corrected as she handed over her phone. Mitch had pulled out a set of reading glasses from underneath his jacket and slipped them onto the bridge of his nose. "And you are?"

"Mitch Duncan." He studied the photograph before shaking his head. "Sorry. I thought I recognized her."

"No problem, Mr. Duncan," Brook said as she retrieved her phone. "I appreciate you taking a look anyway."

Brook bid both men goodbye as she began to walk toward the exit. Something about Mitch's interest in Helen Beckham's picture had captured her attention, and she hesitated to reach for the doorknob.

The unsub preferred young brunettes in their twenties, and he was selecting them for a specific reason known only to him...for now. Even more specifically, their physical features had caught his attention while he'd been hiking the trails. It was as if he couldn't stop himself once he caught sight of them.

While the deaths of those women might have been played out over and over in the unsub's mind down to the last detail, their abductions had been spontaneous.

Which was why the team hadn't been able to find anything in Carissa Norman's past that would give them answers to the identity of the unsub. Brook was a big advocate that most if not all the answers rested with the first victim.

In this case, there were no connections between the unsub and the victims.

Yes, the unsub had planned out their demise in his head, but he hadn't intended to act on those fantasies. Crossing paths with them on the trails must have triggered his need for answers to something very personal and extremely traumatic.

"Mr. Duncan?"

Brook had turned back to find Jace handing over the small bag of lures that Mitch had purchased. The tackle box was already in the man's left hand.

"Yes, ma'am?"

"Who did you think the young woman was in the picture?"

"A gal who used to live in Moonshine Valley," Mitch said offhandedly as he lifted the bag off the counter. "Her family moved away years ago, though. Oh, what was her name...Tricia. That's right. Tricia Zetter."

Chapter Eighteen

Sylvie Deering

October 2023

Tuesday — 7:12am

A loud ding indicated that the elevator had arrived at its intended destination. The doors swooshed open, but Sylvie didn't immediately take a step forward. She should have probably made the drive back to the prison to visit her father, but she'd found herself pulling into the parking garage of work instead. She was avoiding the entire situation, and it wasn't lost on her that death would eventually make that all but impossible.

Nigel Hubert Deering was dying from pancreatic cancer.

Her father, who used to take her with him into work on Fridays so that she could spend the day with him. The kind man who used to always make sure there was a chocolate croissant waiting for her. He'd never once gotten angry with her over the smears that she'd left on important documents. How could such an amazing human being with a great capacity for empathy and understanding destroy so many lives?

Sylvie struggled to recall when greed had begun to stain his soul like her chocolate-covered fingers had done to those pristine spreadsheets. No particular memory came to mind. Her father's deep passion for helping people had simply faded away, much like his body would in the coming months.

Karma had finally come around, and Sylvie couldn't help but experience a sense of bitter satisfaction. Her father's actions had caused so much pain and destruction. Not only to other individuals, but to her. He'd shattered everything she held dear, yet such a death sentence brought a wave of guilt over such a vicious emotion.

Was she any better than her father?

The elevator doors had remained open as long as possible, and Sylvie had to reach out to prevent them from closing shut. She stepped out into the small entryway before closing the distance to the glass doors. The biometric scanner that Bit had programmed scanned her iris before disengaging the lock. Given the firm's clientele, Brook had taken additional precautions besides choosing a building that leased to a national bank.

Such security provisions mostly had to do with Jacob Walsh.

Sylvie opened the glass door and crossed over the threshold until she stepped onto the marble tile. As the door closed behind her, the strong aroma of rich tea leaves being steeped to perfection wafted in the air. Since Arden wasn't at his desk in the front reception area, she figured he was still in the kitchen preparing her favorite beverage.

The modern décor of the offices was basically a mixture of elegant glass panels and classic black furniture. Brook never had to explain to the team why she'd taken the office that faced the main entrance. She preferred to confront whatever and whoever might be headed her way. Sylvie couldn't blame her given such a traumatic past and threatening present.

"Good morning, Sylvie."

She hadn't even made it down the hallway to where her office was located when Arden exited the kitchen with two steaming teacups in hand. She wasn't sure why such a gesture brought tears to her eyes, but she quickly ducked into her office so that he wouldn't witness her moment of weakness. The man had a knack for knowing exactly what a person needed at just the right time.

"Good morning, Arden," Sylvie replied after clearing her throat. She also managed to wipe the corner of her eye as she opened the bottom drawer of her desk. Once she'd collected her phone from her purse, she then stored the designer handbag into its usual spot. "Do I want to know why you made two cups of tea? Not that I'm complaining or anything. It's just what I needed this morning."

"Brook mentioned that you had returned to the city to tend to a personal matter," Arden revealed as he carefully handed her one of the teacups. The sides of his salt and pepper mustache were curled down in concern, though he shied away from the topic of her father. "The lot of you are all alike, though. Can't stay away from work, especially during an active case. I figured you'd be in bright and early given the information that Brook had uncovered last night."

"This coming from the man who couldn't stand retirement?" Sylvie asked with a small smile. She then winced upon sensing the tightness around her hairline. She hadn't realized how taunt she'd pulled back her hair to secure in a bun at the base of her neck. "I hadn't planned on coming in this morning, but I got to thinking about the case while I was brushing my teeth. Brook found a lead?"

"One Tricia Zetter." Arden gestured toward the door of her office. "I have everything up on the 4k monitor in the conference room for you. You'll find that Tricia Zetter lived in Moonshine Valley until she was eighteen years old. That was in 2018. She then joined the military, and her parents moved south shortly thereafter."

"2018. The year that Carissa Norman was murdered," Sylvie murmured as she followed Arden out of her office, down the short hallway, and into the conference room. Sure enough, the 4k monitor was lit up with all the relevant information...including Tricia Zetter's picture. "Wow. Tricia Zetter does look an awful lot like Carissa Norman. It looks as if we discovered the unsub's catalyst."

Sylvie set her teacup down on the table.

"I'll be right back. I need my tablet and my leather notebook."

Sylvie retraced her steps as she kept ahold of her phone. It was good to be back in her element. It was as if she hadn't been on solid ground in days, and work was her tether to sanity.

No wonder Brook was a workaholic.

Sylvie's thoughts had finally cleared upon being reminded that life was fleeting. Those women hadn't expected to be abducted, tortured, and killed on a day that they'd simply wanted to enjoy nature. The job that Sylvie had been hired to do came with risks, and there was no guarantee that she would outlive her father.

Truthfully, such a thought was rather morbid.

Yet it was a reminder that forgiveness had an expiration date.

Sylvie remained beside her desk as she placed a call to her father's lawyer. Once she had him on the line, she gave her agreement to be the one who provided a location for her father after his compassionate release request was granted by the federal prison. A list of requirements would be sent to her, and she would be given time to prepare for his arrival. First and foremost, she needed to contact hospice.

"I'll reach out to them this afternoon," Sylvie said as she picked up her leatherbound notebook. It had become habit to write down certain key facts regarding a case on paper. Such a routine made it possible for her to make connections that she otherwise couldn't when staring at a computer screen. She would do the same when preparing for her father's arrival at her apartment. "Please keep me apprised of any pertinent dates regarding the motion you'll be filing in the coming days."

Sylvie didn't leave her office until she'd completed her phone call. She'd eventually break the news to the team of her upcoming plans. Given such a huge break in the case regarding Tricia Zetter, there was a good chance the investigation would be over and done with before her father's motion was granted. Sylvie figured the list of what needed to be accomplished was quite vast.

"Alright, Arden," Sylvie said as she walked back into the conference room. "What has Bit discovered about Tricia Zetter? I'm assuming that Brook has already spoken to her?"

"Unfortunately, no." Arden waited for Sylvie to take a seat and enjoy a sip of her tea before continuing. "Tricia Zetter joined the Navy five years ago, and she is currently on deployment."

Sylvie didn't have to be told that Brook was in the midst of scheduling arrangements to connect with Zetter. A video conference would be set up at a specific date and time. In the meantime, Brook or Theo would have undoubtedly reached out to the family members.

"What do we have on Tricia Zetter so far?"

"Born and raised in Moonshine Valley. Typical childhood," Arden said as he glanced at the screen. "Nothing stands out, and her record is squeaky clean. No arrests, no traffic violations. She graduated high school with honors and joined the Navy shortly thereafter. She's been serving as a medic on a naval vessel for the past two years, and her commanding officer has nothing but high praise for her."

"That's surprisingly clean for someone who could be the catalyst for a serial killer." Sylvie savored her tea as she read over the highlighted sections displayed on the monitor. There was no indication of past restraining orders, no steady boyfriends during high school, and no known past grudges. "It's as if she lived—lives—a completely unremarkable life."

"Shall we join in the morning meeting?"

Sylvie nodded, appreciating that Arden had waited until he'd caught her up before initiating the video conference. He hadn't been joining in on the morning meetings regarding this case due to Brook needing him to oversee some projects here in the city. Arden had also been assisting Brook on her class at the college, as well as collecting potential cold cases that needed review.

"Sylvie, we talked about this," Brook said immediately after catching sight of Sylvie sitting with Arden. Brook currently stood in front of the table with a cup of coffee in her right hand and a frown on her face. "What are you doing in the office?"

"Saving my sanity," Sylvie quipped, garnering a smile from Bit. He'd switched out his grey knitted hat for a mustard-colored one. She grimaced, because she'd told him time and again that the bright hue washed out his already pale features. "In all seriousness, everything is okay. I'll explain more later, but suffice it to say that I need something to keep me busy for a few days while the lawyers file some motions. It's pointless for me to be at home and twiddling my thumbs."

Brook appeared hesitant, but Bit stepped right up to the plate as any best friend would do in this situation.

"I'll have you know that I spilled a bowl of chili on my grey beanie." Bit then pointed to his head. "Hence the reason for the yellow one, because my blue beanie has ketchup on it."

Arden would have definitely asked how Bit had managed to spill chili and condiments on two pieces of fabric that had been on his head, but Sylvie reached over and patted the older man's arm. She shook her head to indicate it wasn't worth his time. Bit had a way of staining his clothes, but never once had he ever gotten so much as a crumb in the numerous keyboards in front of him.

"Arden caught me up on Tricia Zetter." Sylvie didn't waste any time getting right down to business. "It looks as if she didn't have a steady boyfriend throughout high school, but who took her to homecoming and prom? Also, the unsub could be someone who wanted to date her."

"Good idea on the high school dances, but I'm not so sure the unsub has the demeanor to stalk someone." Brook reached out and pulled a chair around the edge of the table so that she could sit facing the portable monitor. "We're looking for someone who is seeking answers. He tortured those women for hours. It's as if he's using them as a substitute for Tricia Zetter, which can only mean that she is the one who has the answers that he seeks."

"You're saying that Tricia has a secret that no one else knows?" Sylvie asked for better clarification.

"In a manner of speaking." Brook's gaze had drifted to the right of the camera, which meant that she was reading over information displayed on the screen. "At least, the unsub believes that Tricia Zetter has answers to whatever it is that he's searching for up in those mountains. There is a chance that she doesn't know anything. He could have made it all up in his head."

"Which puts us back at square one," Sylvie said as she studied Tricia Zetter's photograph. "Well, we'll go through her life with a fine-tooth comb until you get the chance to speak with her. Bit, if you could send me a list of her classmates, I'll start making calls."

"I can help you with that if you'd like," Arden said right before the main line indicated an incoming call. "S&E Investigations. How may I help you today?"

Arden had accepted the call via a specialized earpiece for the office's phone system. He quietly stood and made his way out of the conference room so that he wouldn't disrupt the rest of the morning briefing.

"I've already uploaded the list, including teachers and school staff." Bit was looking at someone off screen, and Sylvie figured out it was Erika based on his next comment. "Thanks, Erika. Tricia Zetter also belonged to an afterschool church bible study, so I'll send you a list of those members, as well."

"Erika, it states that Tricia has two older brothers and a sister. Do you know the family? Did any of them have hiking or climbing experience?" Sylvie asked as she reached for the remote. She began to scroll through the detailed information that had already been gathered on the family. "Maybe we should look more into Tricia Zetter's family dynamics."

"The two brothers do fit the age bracket of the unsub," Brook agreed with a nod.

"I don't know the Zetter family," Erika said as she moved into the camera's frame. She must have been standing near the window, and she gave a slight wave before continuing her response. "I lived a few towns over growing up, and the Zetter family moved from Moonshine Valley before I became a park ranger. I never had any dealings with them, but Riggs went to school with one of Tricia's brothers."

Brook had set her coffee mug down on the table. She was twisting the outer band of her worry ring, but that wasn't unusual. Sylvie was well aware that Brook had reservations about Riggs, and Sylvie couldn't dismiss those concerns, either. There was an edge to the man who had been fostered by a shitty past, and he fit certain criteria in the profile. Still, Sylvie didn't get the sense that he killed those women.

"Bit, is there any connection between those we singled out of the search parties and Tricia Zetter?" Sylvie figured that Brook and the team had already gone over these questions, but repetition had a way of discovering vital data that had otherwise been overlooked. Bit shook his head in response since he'd just taken a bite of a jelly donut. "By the way, where is Theo?"

"I asked Theo and Riggs to canvass the area around the cabin where you discovered the blood stains left behind from Helen Beckham. The unsub has disposed of at least two bodies up in those mountains, which means that he has a burial ground." Brook had dressed in a pair of dark jeans and a black turtleneck. She appeared ready to go hiking herself. "Going off the information that we have available, Helen Beckham was the killer's second victim. While the unsub would have learned from his mistakes during the first murder, there is still the chance that he made a mistake."

"I was thinking about that on the flight home. Why not just burn the cabins? Why go to all the trouble of carrying cleaning supplies and spending hours attempting to remove every trace of a murder when setting fire to those old structures would have been the simplest solution? What if he actually attempted to do so with the location where he tortured Carissa Norman, but all the killer managed to do was call attention to the crime scene?"

"That's it, Sylvie," Brook praised as she stood from her chair upon hearing Sylvie's theory. "Fantastic work. Bit, search the database for structures that burned down around the time of Carissa Norman's abduction. Erika, once Bit has that information, I want you to speak to the park rangers and the firefighters. I know some fires are allowed to burn, so also check with the individuals who were stationed in the monitoring towers during that time span. Find out all you can on those sites. We can make this work for us."

"What do you mean?" Sylvie asked cautiously as Brook's tone had hardened upon her last statement. "How can locating the first crime scene benefit us when there is nothing left but solidified ash?"

"The unsub doesn't know there is nothing left," Brook amended with a small smile of satisfaction. "I was going to propose a way that we could lure the unsub to the site of Helen Beckham's crime scene, but using the place where Carissa Norman was killed would be even better. We can spread the rumor that we've discovered the site, but we're having trouble getting a forensics team up there. Paranoia will have the killer believing there is a chance we could uncover his DNA, regardless of the impracticality of it all."

"And if all goes as planned, the unsub will expose himself during an attempt to reach the site before anyone else," Sylvie said cautiously as she finished off Brook's thought process. "Brook, what if we're wrong? What if the unsub is smarter than that and such a plan drives him to go dormant for the next two to three years?"

"The unsub was going dormant anyway, Sylvie. We can't lose the momentum this plan offers us. Not now," Brook murmured in determination. "Not now when we're so close."

Chapter Nineteen

Brooklyn Sloane

October 2023

Tuesday — 1:17pm

Darlene Hummel's body rested on a pile of leaves that had gathered against a fallen log. Her sightless eyes stared up at the sky as if searching for answers that lay just beyond the thin, wisps of clouds. The color had long since drained from her face, and her lips had faded into a light purple that Brook always signified with death.

"This isn't the work of our unsub," Brook declared confidently, not upset by the fact that Otto had requested her presence at the crime scene. They still needed to color inside the lines on this investigation since the murder had occurred inside a federal jurisdiction. "A forensics team should be able to find evidence that Lance Griffin killed his fiancé. Did you bag his jacket? Gloves? Clothes?"

A search group had discovered Hummel's remains a few hours ago. Protocol had been followed, but Brook had no choice but to put in an appearance since she'd alerted the Charlotte field office that she was working hand in hand with the local sheriff's department. That meant that she'd had to hike close to two hours to reach the crime scene.

"Yes, though not without some pushback from Griffin's lawyer."

"Hummel bled to death by having her throat slit, but those other slices in her skin? All postmortem. Griffin couldn't bring himself to do more than that." Brook scanned the immediate area before meeting the sheriff's gaze. "It's doubtful that you'll ever find the weapon. Griffin probably walked a good half hour away from here before tossing the knife over some cliff. Doesn't mean that those still here shouldn't divvy up some grids and cast a wider search."

It was evident that Otto had picked up on Brook's cues. He called over Park Ranger Hal Eggers, who had been listening very intently to their conversation. Once Otto had given him additional instructions, it didn't take long for Hal to gather those in the search group instructions on how to proceed. Otto advised one of his deputies to remain near the crime scene until a forensics team arrived, which Brook had already requested before lacing up her hiking boots back in her room above the bar.

"My team and I are going to lay some ground work to force the unsub's hand." Brook kept her tone low so that her voice wouldn't carry through the woods. "Before I bring you in, I need some information."

Otto had changed out of his sheriff's uniform into more appropriate clothing for his hike this morning. He'd waited for her in the small parking lot that fed into several trails, and they were then guided to the crime scene by one of the park rangers. He hadn't complained once, even though she was well aware that entering the mountains wasn't his favorite pastime.

Erika had stayed behind with Bit to help navigate the search into Tricia Zetter's past. Brook could have gone through the proper channels and waited a day or two before speaking with Zetter, but she'd taken a shortcut by calling Graham.

He wasn't in the country, either.

Brook had noticed that such a significant detail never stopped Graham from returning her call immediately after receiving a voicemail from her. It was one of the reasons that she hardly ever left messages, because she didn't want to distract him from his mission. This situation was different, and he'd called within ten minutes of her leaving him a detailed message as to why it was imperative that she speak with a navy servicemember who was currently deployed somewhere in far reaching waters.

Without hesitation, Graham had promptly told her what time to expect the video call.

"I take it there's been a break in the case?"

"Yes." Brook shifted so that she could keep an eye on Hal Eggers. "Tricia Zetter. We believe that she is the catalyst for the unsub's behavior, and we're looking into her background now. I'm set to speak with her at seven o'clock tonight."

"Isn't Tricia Zetter the one who joined the military?"

"Navy. She's deployed right now, which is why we can't connect until this evening." Brook needed some answers with regard to other dangling threads. "Ned Proehl. Where are you with his case?"

"Nowhere." Otto shrugged, as if to say he was doing the best he could with the resources at his disposal. "No one has seen or heard from him since last week. Irene has been avoiding me, though. Makes me think that she knows where her nephew is, but she doesn't want to say for fear that he's a suspect in your investigation."

"What do you know about Gabe Raskins?"

"Gabe? Gabe Raskins?" Otto waited for her confirmation before going into more detail. "Wyn's son, as you already know. He's not the model citizen, but he's gotten back on the right track after nailing down a job."

"I heard that Raskins is a rafting guide, but how well does he know these mountains?" Brook asked, knowing no amount of online research would give her the answers she sought in regard to Wyn's son. "Well enough to know where structures and dwellings have all but been abandoned?"

"Maybe," Otto hedged in his reply. "From my understanding, Wyn wasn't around a lot when Gabe was a kid. Hell, I'm not sure that Wyn even knew he was Gabe's father until the boy was a couple of years old. Gabe was with his mother most of the time, and she was too busy scoring drugs to be any kind of role model. I was still in the service, but I heard that Wyn got his act together after receiving a call from social services. Gabe would have been around ten years old at the time. His mother had been admitted to the hospital with an overdose. Heroin. Wyn started a relationship with the boy, but it was hit and miss over the years."

"Is Gabe Raskins into that life?" Brook asked before being more specific. "Heroin? Cocaine?"

"I know that he used to run with that crowd, but I've never seen him personally strung out. Now? He owns a small place across town, shows up to work on time, and keeps to himself. I don't see him as your unsub."

Brook could have continued to list off the individuals on the suspect list, but they'd be stuck on the mountain the rest of the day. She didn't have the time, and Otto had his own investigation to wrap up.

"There's a good possibility that we discovered the cabin where Carissa Norman was killed, but it will be a day or two before a forensics team can process what remains of the scene."

"Surely there are more forensic techs who can—"

"There's not another team available right now, especially since they need to process the one here."

Otto slowly nodded his understanding, and he wisely didn't follow up with any questions when he caught sight of someone nearby. The sheriff's crime scene was the perfect justification needed to set things in motion. It wasn't Brook's preference to lure an unsub out into the open with even the best laid plans. There were simply too many ways for such a situation to go wrong. Unfortunately, based on the previous pattern of the unsub's crimes, he was about to go dormant for the next few years.

"I was going to divert Riggs and Theo to what's left of the structure, but I can't take the chance that they would need to spend the night without the proper equipment and supplies," Brook said as she observed some of the members of the search party come within earshot. "I'm closer, but I'm going to need someone to escort me there and then back down to town before sunset. Mind if I borrow one of the park rangers?"

Otto didn't immediately respond to Brook's request. He was studying her intently, and it was obvious that he wanted more information. She couldn't give him specific details right now, and she wouldn't jeopardize their only chance at apprehending their suspect.

"Of course." Otto scanned the immediate area before calling out a name. "Hal, your shift ends at seventeen hundred hours, right?"

"That's right," Hal responded once he'd gotten close enough. Since Brook wasn't his favorite person right now, she noticed that he kept his focus on Otto. "I'll help with the grid search until about three o'clock, but you and I both know that we're not going to find a weapon. We could cover miles and miles of this terrain, and we'd never recover the knife that asshole used on her. Shame, too."

Brook would have rather stuck with the guide who had originally escorted her and Otto this morning, but she understood why the sheriff wanted to keep Emilio Acosta at the crime scene. Emilio's original shift should have started at noon and ended at nine o'clock this evening. He'd clocked in some overtime by meeting them a couple of hours before the start of his shift.

"Would you escort Ms. Sloane to..."

Otto let his sentence trail off as he waited for Brook to pull out a set of coordinates that Bit had written down on a piece of paper. There was also some other information attached that should make it easier for a park ranger to locate the site without too much trouble. Specific trail intersections had been added, and it didn't take long for Hal to give an estimated time of arrival.

"We can reach this location in about an hour."

Hal met her gaze, and she waited for him to voice his opinion. He'd been vocal up to this point, never shying away from asserting his opinion into a conversation. She decided to take matters into her own hands now that their strategy had been set in motion.

"We believe that structure is the location where Carissa Norman was killed, but it was burned down about five years ago." Brook paused for effect, garnering the attention of not only Otto and Hal, but also of the deputy standing guard about thirty feet in front Darlene Hummel's remains. Far enough away not to contaminate the crime scene, but close enough to make sure nothing was disturbed before a forensics team could process the area. "Coincidentally, right after Carissa Norman's disappearance."

"What do you expect to find if the place burned down?" Hal asked with a frown. He tucked the piece of paper into the pocket of his jacket. "When we need to veer off the main trail, there are parts of the terrain that can be tricky to hike. Are you sure it's worth a trip out there if there's going to be nothing but ash?"

"A lot of people don't realize that trace evidence, such as DNA, hair, fibers, and even footprints could have been left behind by the unsub. Should we discover that Carissa Norman was the first victim as we suspect, then it stands to reason mistakes were made during her murder. It would certainly explain why the structure was burned to the ground, wouldn't it?"

Hal considered her explanation before nodding his agreement.

"We should get started then," Hal said before looking over his right shoulder. "We can use that trail for about a half mile before we need to cut through some dense vegetation."

Otto seemed to want to add something to the conversation, but he compressed his lips together. It was obvious that he didn't approve of her choices, but the unsub had probably already returned to his regular life by now. The only reason that he was being constantly reminded of those momentary lapses in judgement was due to pressure from law enforcement.

What would the unsub do when a little more pressure was applied to his conscience?

Brook was hoping for desperation to set into the unsub's frame of mind, knowing full well that it could lead to a mistake that would ultimately spearhead an arrest. It was a chance that she and the team were willing to take, but the seeds of doubt needed to be planted first. She just so happened to be the one with the shovel.

Chapter Twenty

Bobby "Bit" Nowacki

October 2023

Tuesday — 6:47pm

Would you like to meet at a coffee shop one evening when you get back into town?

Bit stared at the invitation on the laptop screen with apprehension. He hadn't had time to log into the online game that he'd created, and now he wished that he hadn't pulled up the messaging board. The only reason he'd opened his personal tabs was to reply to an email that his sister had sent regarding Halloween. They always enjoyed a scary movie marathon, but he wasn't so sure that he'd be back home for the holiday. Once he'd sent his response to his sister, his gaze had been drawn to the notification from Zoey Collins.

He couldn't bring himself to type a response.

"Are you ready, Bit? We should walk over to the diner to pick up those pizzas and bait the hook." Erika stood near the doorway, clearly anxious to take a more active role in the investigation. "I went downstairs to see if any members of the press were at the bar, but a lot of them are still over at the diner eating dinner. This is the perfect chance for us to talk in front of them and have them believe they got the inside scoop."

"Yeah," Bit mumbled as he quickly logged out of several applications, including the one with Zoey's invitation. He wasn't the type of man who got coffee with a woman. He wasn't even the type of man who dated, which was why he'd gotten so comfortable around Sylvie. "I'm coming. Hey, Boss? We should be back in twenty minutes, but just in case we're not, you're all set up for the video conference with Tricia Zetter. Just accept the video call when prompted, okay?"

"I won't touch anything else but the enter button, Bit." Brook leaned back and stretched out her legs. She'd just gotten back from what remained of the burned structure where they believed Carissa Norman had been murdered, and Brook's cheeks and nose were still red from the cool, crisp weather. "Do the two of you need to go over what needs to be said in front of the members of the press?"

"No, Boss. We've got it." Bit adjusted his knit hat so that the soft fabric covered his ears. "Theo and Riggs returned to town while you and Eggers were hiking this afternoon. The two of them gathered enough food, supplies, and equipment to spend the night near the area of interest. No one noticed a thing since they went out the back exit."

"Do you think this plan will work?" Erika asked as she smoothed the front of her uniform shirt.

Bit noticed that Brook winced a little upon hearing the question. This wasn't how she preferred to run an investigation, but he understood the reasoning behind her decision to try and lure the unsub out of hiding. They'd discussed it in-depth before the sheriff had called and requested her presence at the crime scene of Darlene Hummel.

"It's our best shot," Bit said confidently as he walked around Brook's chair. "We won't be long, Boss."

Bit brushed past Erika, but he waited for her to close the door. It wouldn't do to have anyone overhear Brook's conversation with Tricia Zetter, especially Wyn. His son was still a suspect. A lot of the people who hung out at the bar were suspects, and Bit noticed right away that a lot of the members of today's search party had claimed several tables. They had to be well into their second round of drinks.

There was one individual who wasn't at the bar, and that person just so happened to be Gabe Raskins. If he was their unsub, would he make the decision to return to the scene of the crime? Only those who had been up on the mountain today had overheard Brook request a guide to what remained of the burned structure where they suspected Carissa Norman had been killed. Bit had the list of those who'd joined in on yesterday and this morning's search parties, and Gabe's name hadn't been listed on the spreadsheet that Erika had retrieved from Hal Eggers.

The purpose of Bit and Erika speaking somewhat freely in front of the members of the press was so that they would print the scoop for tomorrow's headline or maybe even cover the story on tonight's local news channel. It was then that the unsub should make an attempt to clean up what trace evidence had allegedly been left behind. With any luck, Theo and Riggs would make an arrest and escort the killer back to town.

"You aren't wearing a jacket," Erika pointed out as they reached the front door of the bar. "I'll wait for you if you want to go back upstairs to grab it."

"We're only walking across the street." Bit opened the door and ended up gritting his teeth at the cold temperature. Why was the October weather so much crisper here than in D.C.? He managed to put on a brave face as he motioned Erika ahead of him. "Did you notice the news vans? There were two this morning, but another one must have gotten tired waiting for the sheriff to return to the B&B."

Sheriff Otto Jackson had kept in touch with Brook since she'd arrived back into town. In turn, she'd given the team an update on the remains that had been discovered this morning. Darlene Hummel had been murdered, and it was looking more and more like her fiancé was guilty of said crime. The sheriff currently had Lance Griffin at the station being questioned with the man's lawyer present. One would think that the media would be parked out front of the police station forty-five minutes from Moonshine Valley. As it stood, word must have leaked that the police believed Darlene Hummel was not the victim of the serial killer.

"The usual volunteers should all be back to their normal routines," Erika said as she tugged on the zipper of her jacket. Bit was doing everything in his power not to shiver. "Maybe once the press gets wind of what we have to say, one of the reporters might go live for the ten o'clock news. If no one bites, then I assume we move on from the volunteers, right?"

Brook had gone over and over the possibilities of what could happen once their plan was set in motion, which was why she'd requested that Theo and Riggs camp out near the remains of the burnt structure. Brook had mentioned that there was hardly anything left of the log cabin, but it was doubtful that the unsub would be able to stop himself from going back to the scene of the crime. At least, that was the reaction they were hoping for later tonight or tomorrow morning.

"Boss wouldn't be making these types of preparations if she wasn't convinced the unsub was one of the volunteers," Bit managed to say without chattering. "Did you know that she had the best closing rate in the Bureau? Her profiles are becoming legendary, and she was even asked to teach a course at one of the universities."

Bit shot Erika a sideways look of concern as they stepped up onto the curb. He reached for the handle on the diner's door. It took all his strength not to tug on the handle to seek the warmth inside, but he had to ask Erika something first.

"Do you still think that there is a chance that Allen Brixton abducted, tortured, and murdered those women?"

"No." Erika cleared her throat and reached for the handle. She pushed his hand aside and opened the door. "Theo confirmed Allen's alibi for when Luna Breen was killed, so we don't need to worry about him, right? He was with my sister in Vegas. Let's just get this over with so that we can go back to the bar."

Bit wasn't a man who got in someone else's personal space, but he couldn't let their conversation slide—not when Theo was camping out in the mountains with only Riggs, another local, as backup.

"Dominic Ryder." Bit had taken a quick step across the threshold and made sure that Erika couldn't advance toward the counter. He would have also liked to relish the warmth that was radiating from the massive fireplace on the other side of the room, but he kept his focus on his current coconspirator. "You think that Dominic might be the unsub."

"How did you..."

Erika let her voice trail off before biting the inside of her cheek. She broke off their stare. Bit had learned a lot from Sylvie and Theo over the past couple of years. Brook, especially. He'd studied the way they would monitor a room, how they observed body language, and especially the manner in which they kept close tabs on those outsiders involved with an investigation.

Upon exiting the bar, Erika's gaze had swept over the patrons enjoying their evening. There was only one table that had truly captured her interest, and Bit had noticed the way Dominic Ryder had acknowledged her presence. At first, Bit had thought it had been mere courtesy, but he now realized that it was much more than that.

"You're personally involved with Dominic Ryder," Bit whispered in incredulity as he adjusted his knitted hat in disbelief. "And you didn't say anything. This entire time, you've been working this investigation with us, and you didn't say a word that you were involved with a potential suspect. A prime suspect who just so happens to be part of the press."

Bit had gone above and beyond in his online search of everyone involved with the investigation, and there had never been any kind of link between Erika and Dominic. He trusted his programs explicitly, so that meant either the relationship was brand new or they had purposefully kept it secret from everyone.

"Not that it's any of your business, but we had a one night stand a couple months back." Erika tugged at the collar of her jacket with a mixture of annoyance and agitation. "I didn't think it was relevant to the investigation."

"Not relevant?" Bit wasn't usually one to come down on someone else. He always made an attempt to try and view things from another's perspective. Given the fact that this was a murder investigation, he'd come up blank. "The man you slept with is a potential suspect in a murder investigation, and you didn't think it was relevant to the case? Did you say anything to Dominic about what we're doing this evening?"

"No, but everyone else—including members of the press—will hear about it if you don't turn around right now. We're causing a scene."

Bit glanced over his shoulder and noticed the stares of a few people, but they were mostly locals. He'd seen them often when picking up orders or during his walk down to the bakery. The reporters and their crew were too busy looking at their phones, so it was relatively easy to tell them apart.

"Let's get this over with," Bit muttered with apprehension. Brook and the others needed to be alerted that the case might have been compromised, regardless of Erika's denial. The performance that he and Erika were about to give could be for naught if she'd inadvertently let something slip in a conversation with Dominic Ryder. "Did I mention that I have a newfound respect for actors?"

"We're technically not acting," Erika whispered as they continued their way to the counter. "We're just discussing details of the case."

Bit acknowledged her rational view of their current situation, but that didn't mean his stomach agreed with it. He rested a hand over his abdomen in an attempt to quell his nerves.

"Hi, Bit," Irene called out from behind the wooden countertop. She had a hand towel thrown over her right shoulder, and she was setting a soft drink down in front of someone. "Erika, it's good to see you. I figured you were working late tonight after hearing about the anchovies. Your order should be up in a few minutes. Can I get you two some drinks while you wait?"

"I'd love a large iced tea to go, please," Erika replied before gesturing toward the crowded tables and stools. "Business is good tonight."

"I heard Wyn's place is packed, as well." Irene turned so that she could pull one of the disposable cups off the top stack. "Care to share any updates on the case? Everyone is a bit on edge after hearing that another hiker was found dead, and I can't blame them. Is it true that

Hiker's Haven is the connection? By the way, Kirk had to take Mauve into the hospital about an hour ago. Poor thing."

"We're not sure about the connection to Hiker's Haven," Erika said after a brief pause. She glanced at Bit as if to say that he should have been the one to follow up Irene's question with an answer, but he was too interested in the lighted display of the diner owner's phone. She'd left it near the coffee pot. "We should know more in the coming days, though. The sheriff doesn't think that Darlene Hummel is a part of our investigation. We discovered another site where we believe another woman was murdered around five years ago. Ms. Sloane checked it out today with Hal, and she discovered something that could help identify the killer. She requested a forensics team to process the remains of the structure, but they were diverted to the body discovered by the search party this morning. Unfortunately, it might take them a day or two to reach the other site."

Irene must have silenced her phone. She was so engrossed in what Erika had to say regarding the investigation that she hadn't even noticed that someone was calling her. What Bit found most interesting was that the call was from a blocked number. The name wasn't revealed, which just so happened to occur when the caller used a burner.

Was Irene's nephew trying to get in touch with her?

"You two are working the investigation, right?" The question had originated from the male subject who had been given the soft drink. His keen interest was telling, but it was the way that he'd nudged the woman beside him that gave away his occupation. "Are you hearing this?"

The woman was nodding vigorously as she used his arm for leverage to step off the stool. She then tapped his shoulder, which Bit figured was an indication for the man to go out to the van and retrieve his camera.

"Erika, we're here to grab the pizzas," Bit murmured as he rested a hand on the counter. "We shouldn't talk about the case."

"It's Irene," Erika said with feigned irritation, just like they'd rehearsed. "It's not like everyone doesn't already know about the hiker who went missing, Bit. Moonshine Valley isn't like the other tourist towns. Everyone knows everything the second it happens around here. Speaking of which, I heard you were adding almond-crusted walleye to the menu. Is that true?"

While Irene responded to Erika's question, Bit casually kept an eye on the owner's cell phone. A notification had flashed on the display. Irene had just received a voicemail, but it didn't matter. Bit had memorized the number and would run a trace on it the moment he had access to his computer.

"Excuse me," the reporter said after coming to a stop next to Erika. "Did you say that the lead investigator has dispatched a forensics team to an area suspected of being another crime scene? You wouldn't happen to know the coordinates for such a site, would you?"

"Only a local would be able to—"

"We're not at liberty to say," Bit stressed loudly as he caught Erika's gaze. He shook his head for effect. "We really should be getting back."

Erika gave the reporter a small shrug in the form of an apology before flashing a smile at Irene. The owner had collected the five large pizzas that the chef had slipped through the small window and was walking their way. Bit had purposefully ordered a lot of food so that the locals believed everyone on the team had returned from their trek in the mountains. He reached out and took the stack of boxes from Irene.

"Can you at least tell me what evidence the lead investigator believes was left at this newly discovered crime scene?" the reporter asked right as her cameraman had returned, causing the others to make a beeline for the door. Their reactions were exactly what Brook had been counting on, and Erika had done an excellent job of selling the so-called facts. "How long will it take to get a forensics team—"

"What can you tell us about Darlene Hummel? Is there a connection between—"

"Doug, are we rolling? I want to—"

The questions kept being fired at them at a rapid pace, but Bit and Erika made it appear as if they were uncomfortable with all the attention. They managed to sidestep the cameraman, who currently had a news camera on his shoulder, before quickly walking toward the exit.

Bit continued to repeat the phone number that he'd seen on Irene's phone. He couldn't remember things the way Sylvie could, and it didn't help that his thoughts kept focusing on Erika's relationship with Dominic. She might not believe that she'd let pertinent information regarding the case slip out in front of him, but such a revelation was just another thread that they would need to watch closely over the next twenty-four hours.

A sudden, blinding light from a camera almost caused Bit to misjudge the distance to the curb, but he managed to stay upright and not drop the pizzas. Questions were still being hurled at them even as they finally managed to cross the street. The reporters seemed to be feeding off one another. By some chance that the unsub hadn't heard about the so-called delay of getting a forensics team back up the mountain, there was little doubt that he would soon hear about it on the local news.

In the meantime, Bit would trace the number that he was still repeating over and over in his mind. If Irene's nephew had been calling her, there was a good chance that she would reveal what she'd just heard about the investigation. Such news might finally prompt Ned

Proehl out of hiding, but there was a good chance that Bit could locate him first.

Chapter Twenty-One

Sylvie Deering

October 2023

Tuesday — 8:21pm

Wisps of steam rose into the air from the hot water that had been poured over the mesh tea infuser. The clear water began to turn murky until a deep amber color began to materialize, and with it the familiar hint of caramel. The black tea leaves continued to steep until Sylvie was able to remove the infuser and place the steel ball into the kitchen sink.

She'd given up using the machine that Arden seemed to have tamed in the months that he'd worked for S&E Investigations. Apparently, the only one who could get the finicky appliance to work properly was a sixty-seven-year-old man who still wrote everything down longhand and refused to rely on technology.

As she added a touch of honey to her tea, the tension that had solidified in her shoulders began to ease. It helped that her father's lawyer had returned her call to notify her that a motion had been filed this afternoon to request a compassionate release. If the judge saw fit to grant such a motion, Sylvie would then reach out to hospice and begin the process of preparing her spare bedroom for her father's arrival.

Given that there was nothing to do in the meantime, Sylvie would pour her concentration into the case. Anything was better than sitting at home and staring at the four walls of her living room while second-guessing her recent decisions. Every time that she thought she'd made peace with her current situation, a sliver of doubt would creep back in and overwhelm her with a sense of futility.

Sylvie set the spoon next to the tea infuser, deciding to clean up the kitchen later. It was going to be a long night anyway, and she figured she'd drink a couple more cups of tea before she left for home. Given that Brook had made a decision that could force the unsub's hand, it was best to be accessible.

A unique ringtone reverberating through the offices caused Sylvie to quickly and carefully make her way back to the conference room. Brook or Bit had initiated a video conference, and Sylvie managed to accept the incoming call without spilling a drop of her tea.

"How did the interview go with Tricia Zetter?"

"Not as fruitful as I'd hoped," Brook said as she leaned back in her chair with slight irritation. Her long, black hair was draped over her right shoulder, blending in with the black fabric of her turtleneck. It was the fact that she'd used a hair tie to keep them there that told of her annoyance, though she wasn't usually one to give away tells. "The video call was disconnected, and Bit is in the process of trying to establish another connection."

"There's a storm in the Pacific that is causing some connectivity issues," Bit explained from behind one of his laptops. There was quite the stack of pizza boxes on the table, but there was no sign of anyone else in the room. She was well aware that Theo and Riggs were camping out near the site believed to be where Carissa Norman had been murdered, but Sylvie figured that the sheriff or Erika would have remained behind. "It could be another half hour before Boss can speak with Tricia Zetter again."

"On the bright side, Bit was able to track down Ned Proehl." Brook stood from the chair and leaned back slightly to stretch her back muscles. "He's holed up in some seedy motel across state line. I've alerted Otto, and he reached out to the local police in that area. Since Proehl violated his parole, he can be taken into custody."

Sylvie figured that was one less player off the board. She picked up her tea and took a sip, thinking over the possible consequences of leaking false information to the press. She agreed that the unsub was more than likely to go dormant unless given a slight shove, but it would have been more beneficial had the setup not been two hours away from civilization.

"Have you touched base with Theo and Riggs?" Sylvie asked as she pushed aside her tablet to make room for her cup on the conference room table. "Considering the strenuous hike that it would take to reach their destination, all should be quiet up there."

"They've been on time with their hourly check-ins." Brook began to stretch her right arm across her chest. "I've been thinking about the crime scenes, and I don't believe that the unsub would have carried his victims' bodies too far from the structures. He wouldn't have one burial ground, because he's not killing them for pleasure. He doesn't want a reminder of his transgressions."

"I take it that you'll send a team to each suspected crime scene?"

"Yes." Brook rotated her right shoulder now that she'd stretched out her muscles. Her motions caused Sylvie to do the same. "The topics that I did manage to bring up to Tricia Zetter mostly included her friends in high school. I was hoping to narrow down the male subjects who fit the profile. Did she know something about one of them that could hurt their future? Had anyone made threats to her back in high school? Was she a part of something that could affect someone else's future? None of her responses gave an indication as to the identity of the unsub."

"Bit, did you have time to comb through Zetter's social media? Did anything stand out in her private messages? She joined the military in 2018, right?"

"Nothing stood out, Little T." Bit peered over his screen. "I'm looking for accounts on other applications now."

"I noticed that Tricia's list of social media friends from back then was uploaded into the file, so I'll start to comb through some of their profiles. Maybe there's mention of a trip or activity she and her friends were all involved with during that time...some secret that they all believe one another knows about. Whatever answers the unsub might be seeking, there could be a chance that Tricia doesn't even know about it."

"One of the local stations aired the information they overhead between Bit, Erika, and Irene." Brook had stepped out from between the chair and table. "Otto drove over to the hospital to check on Mauve after questioning Griffin, who basically remained silent at the directive of his lawyer. No arrest can be made until the lab returns with the forensics evidence from the man's jacket. There's no way that Griffin didn't get Hummel's blood on him when he slit her throat. Anyway, while Otto was at the hospital, he mentioned the delay of the forensics team to Kirk. Since he is the one who will be returning to Hiker's

Haven tonight, I'm sure he'll spread the word to any employees or guests. By tomorrow morning, the entire town should have the details."

"Until then, we wait," Sylvie murmured as she reached for the remote. "I'll be in the office for another few hours. Let me know if you connect with Tricia Zetter again."

Sylvie could sense Brook's scrutiny, but she merely nodded her agreement.

"I'm going downstairs to see if I can get Wyn to brew up another carafe of coffee. The diner will be closing soon, and I don't want to venture outside. It's going to be a long night."

Sylvie waited to speak until after Brook had exited the room and closed the door behind her.

"You thought Boss was going to send you home," Bit said with a smirk. Considering that Sylvie could still hear the click of the keys on his keyboard, it was obvious that he never stopped concentrating on the task in front of him. "You lucked out, because we no longer have a liaison with the park rangers. Boss mentioned something about bringing Eggers on board."

"What are you talking about, Bit?" Maybe Sylvie was more exhausted than she thought, because his words had made no sense. "Did something happen to Erika?"

"You could say that," Bit mumbled as he finally pressed one more key with a flourish before he gave Sylvie his complete attention. "Erika had a one-night stand with Dominic Ryder a few months ago. She didn't share that upon knowing Dominic's name had been added to the suspect list. You can imagine how that went over. Boss has spent the last twelve hours—knowing her, a lot longer than that—planning this setup all the way down to the use of the press, so she didn't hold anything back."

Sylvie winced at the mere thought of such a confrontation between Brook and Erika. Honesty was of utmost importance to Brook, and there was no compromise to be had should that trust be violated during an investigation. It didn't matter that Erika most likely thought her personal life should remain private. It certainly wasn't Sylvie's place to pass personal judgement, but it was in Brook's purview to take action against such a relevant omission that could affect the outcome of a murder investigation.

"Zoey asked me out for coffee."

"You don't drink coffee."

"I didn't tell her that," Bit said in irritation before readjusting his hat. Sylvie hid a smile at the nervous gesture. "I will, though."

"If visiting my father has taught me anything, it's that life is too short not to be happy." Sylvie twisted her teacup around a few times in contemplation. "Tell Zoey that you want to meet over at the pub across the street from our offices. You love their Jägerbombs. Plus, it's a place that you're comfortable with, which means that you'll be at ease during the date."

"It's not a date, Little T," Bit denied as his right knee began to jostle up and down. Sylvie could tell just how fast from the way his entire body was twitching in the chair. "We're just meeting each other in person. I mean, we've technically been communicating with each other for the past couple of months. It's not like we're strangers."

Bit wasn't one to act spontaneous. He preferred to stick to his routine, and he wasn't the type of person to take risks, especially when it came to his personal life. He just needed a little push in the right direction.

"Whatever you want to call this meet-and-greet, just have fun. There's nothing wrong with making more friends. This job doesn't really afford us to enjoy a personal life on a regular basis, and we have to take advantage of the times that it does."

A notification that Bit had set up for a program began to chime, and it was also a reminder that they had a lot of work ahead of them. Sylvie called out that she would talk to him later before pressing a button on the remote. The video closed down, leaving some of the documents that she'd been reviewing on the screen.

She set the remote on the table before removing her black-rimmed glasses. There were smudge marks on the lenses, so she used the bottom edge of her blue tank top that she'd worn underneath a matching cardigan sweater to wipe off the fingerprint marks. Once her lenses were free of blemishes, she slipped on her frames.

Needing something else besides clear eyesight and a cup of tea, Sylvie connected her phone to the office's Bluetooth system. Once she had her pop music playing in the background, she got to work closing down the various documents that she had displayed on the screen. Instead, she needed something else to clear her thoughts when it came to the missing persons files, the statements by friends and families, and also the various coordinates that she'd tried to make sense of this past week.

The unsub was definitely someone familiar with Moonshine Valley and the surrounding towns, as well as Hiker's Havens. All three women had stayed at the bed and breakfast, they had all ventured into town, and they had all set out to hike trails in the Smoky Mountains. There was not one specific trail, there had been no particular kill site, and there was basically no trace evidence to tie in one unsub.

The only outlier had been the gentleman who mistook Helen Beckham's picture for that of Tricia Zetter. Tricia was who they needed to concentrate on, but they'd only been aware of such possible connection for a little over twelve hours.

Sylvie spent the next five minutes scrolling through Tricia Zetter's social media pages. The brunette posted a lot of photographs with other service members who were all clearly good friends. It took Sylvie an additional ten minutes to access pictures and posts dated many years ago. By the time Sylvie had reached ones dating back to Tricia's high school years, something identifiable began to make itself known—Tricia Zetter and her sister could have passed for twins.

Only there was a good fifteen-year difference between the sisters.

The two brothers had been born in between Ava and Tricia Zetter.

The first thing that Sylvie confirmed was Ava Zetter's status. The woman was still alive, married with two children, and living near Houston. Those facts alone would have discounted Ava as being a person of interest in the case, but Sylvie couldn't shake the feeling that maybe they were focused on the wrong sister.

Sylvie accessed Ava Zetter's photographs on her social media site and began the tedious effort of going back twenty years. One post in particular was dated May 2003 and featured six individuals who had gone hiking one summer after graduation.

Six friends who had been excited to share their last summer together before starting a new chapter in their lives. Six hikers who set off to spend a week climbing the mountains and exploring the great beyond.

Unfortunately, only five had returned to Moonshine Valley.

Chapter Twenty-Two

Brooklyn Sloane

October 2023

Tuesday — 8:54pm

The only information that had appeared in Agent Russell Houser's text message was a date, time, and address. It just so happened to be the address of Sarah Evanston's mother. The federal agent had come through and convinced Sarah to meet with Brook. The fact that he hadn't added any additional details told of his disproval of such a meeting.

Agent Houser had a very valid point.

What woman in her right mind would want to meet with the sister of the man who'd tried to kill her? The monster who had succeeded in disfiguring her to the point that she would probably never feel comfortable being seen out in public? From Brook's understanding, Sarah still had many surgeries to undergo in an effort to look somewhat human, though she would never compare to the woman who had spent her entire career in front of a camera.

"Boss? Do you want me to go downstairs for you?"

"No, Bit," Brook said as she stood up from her chair. She needed to stretch her legs, anyway. "I probably should have stayed downstairs to wait for Wyn to brew the coffee, but there were just too many people down there."

"You mean reporters?"

"Yes." Brook slid her phone in the back pocket of her jeans. She still had on her hiking boots, because they were surprisingly comfortable. "And locals. Trust me, the reporters hit the jackpot down there. They'll know everything there is to know about Hiker's Haven, Kirk Sampson, and Mauve Benson before the night is through. It won't matter that we've already cleared Kirk with an alibi."

"Not the way we'd hoped for things to go, but there should still be a good chance that the unsub tries to clean up the first crime scene, right?"

"Given the profile, I'm confident that the cabin that burned down a week after Carissa Norman went missing was the location of her death. Still, there is a margin for error that we need to take into account. It's the reason that I don't typically agree with setups like this one." By this time, Brook had walked to the door. "It could backfire, and we're right back to square one. I'll be back with a full carafe in hand. Anything I can get you while I'm downstairs?"

"A bowl of peanuts."

"I can make that happen," Brook said as she wrapped her hand around the doorknob.

The satellite phone rang before she could walk out into the hallway, though the noise level of the bar was quite deafening with the numerous conversations attempting to be heard over the music blaring from the jukebox. She waited until Bit gave her a thumbs up that Theo's check-in was no different than his last.

Brook carefully made her way down the wooden steps. The carafe full of coffee that Wyn had made for her had been set at the end of the bar. She only had to take a few steps from the staircase to reach it, but there wasn't one bowl of peanuts in sight that hadn't been half eaten.

Wyn was mixing what looked to be a rum and Coke. He would hook her up with a bowl of fresh peanuts, only she was running on a short supply patience. A reporter was already instructing her cameraman to grab his camera, which he'd set in a chair. They'd definitely taken the bait, but she didn't have anything to add.

"Brook!"

She sought out the individual who had called her name. Dominic had stood from his chair to make his way over to the bar, but the direction he would have taken to reach her would have meant crossing paths with two of the reporters. She quickly held up a hand for him to remain near his table.

Truthfully, she'd rather not speak with him at the moment.

Brook hadn't been pleased to discover that Erika and Dominic had kept their previous one-night stand under wraps. Dominic wouldn't have given it a second thought, but Erika had seen the blogger's name on their list of suspects. No one was ever removed unless a solid alibi was established during said timeline.

Taking the long way around, Brook kept close to the wall so that she could avoid the numerous members of the press. She wasn't sure where they were all staying tonight. Hiker's Haven wasn't a viable option. Mauve was still in the hospital, and it was doubtful that Kirk would rent out rooms to the press. Their current guests wouldn't want to be under that type of scrutiny. Given the distance to the next town over, the reporters and those individuals operating the cameras should be vacating the bar soon enough.

"Excuse me," Brook murmured as she attempted to brush past someone. When the male subject didn't move right away, she took a step back to maintain some personal space. "I apologize. I'm just trying to—"

"Is it true?"

Brook tensed upon hearing the tension in the man's voice. His tone was thick with emotion, and it was also low enough that his question hadn't garnered the attention of the patrons. She studied his face, noticing enough similarities between him and Carissa Norman to make the connection.

Carissa's father must have recognized Brook from the press briefing that she and Otto had given the other morning. She wasn't sure why Mr. Norman hadn't returned her call, but they couldn't very well discuss such a delicate topic in front of members of the press.

"Mr. Norman, I've attempted to call you and your wife several times," Brook replied in the same level of tenor. The last thing she needed at the moment was to have a member of the press recognize him. "Why don't we go upstairs and speak privately? I'm sure you've noticed that this place is crawling with reporters, and—"

"Is it true?" Gus Norman asked with anguish. "Was my daughter a victim of a serial killer?"

"I believe that to be the case, but we have no evidence to support that theory at the moment," Brook responded, believing the only way to get Mr. Norman to see reason was to answer him honestly. "I would really like to discuss your daughter's disappearance in private, Mr. Norman. My team and I have rented some rooms on the second level. Why don't we—"

"Brook? Could we please talk in private?" Dominic asked as impatience had gotten the best of him. "Erika left here all upset, and she wouldn't even stop to talk to me. Well, she did, but only long enough to say it was all my fault that she was no longer a liaison between your firm and the park rangers. I know that you have an issue with my profession, but I wanted to explain that—"

"Not now, Dominic."

"Erika didn't do anything wrong, though." Dominic shifted apprehensively from side to side. "What took place between us was—"

"Dominic, now is not the time." Brook had turned toward him and steeled her tone to the point where he couldn't misinterpret her words. The last thing that she needed was for Dominic to identify Gus Norman. "Please return to your table, and I'll be over there to discuss the situation in a few moments."

Dominic appeared to want to debate the issue. Fortunately, he made the right decision and turned around without saying another word. As Jace and another friend waited for Dominic to return to their table, Brook focused on Gus Norman.

"Please, Mr. Norman, let's go upstairs and speak about this in private. We'll talk over some coffee, and I'll explain why my team and I believe your daughter's disappearance is related to our case," Brook said softly so that only he could hear her. "A colleague of mine is inside the third room. Go on up, and I'll grab another mug."

Gus Norman could only nod, and it was evident that not a day had passed in five years that this man hadn't grieved for his daughter. His anguish reminded Brook of the families who had lost their daughters to Jacob's sick and twisted conduct. The press had covered the cause of death in Luna Breen's case, which meant that Gus now understood the agony that his daughter had almost certainly suffered in the hours before her death.

Brook pulled out her cell phone and quickly dialed Bit. He answered on the first ring.

"Gus Norman showed up at the bar. I just sent him upstairs, so shut off the monitor and close my laptop."

"Will do, Boss."

"I need to speak with Dominic, but I won't be too long." Brook had to press her finger against her left ear so that she could finish her conversation. "It would be best not to discuss what is taking place tonight with Theo and Riggs."

"I hear you, Boss. I'll make sure...hey, Little T is calling in. Let me take this before Mr. Norman knocks on the door."

"Thanks, Bit."

Brook disconnected the call and slid her cell phone into the back pocket of her jeans. It hadn't escaped her notice that Dominic had been monitoring her every move. Seeing as she didn't want him barging in the room upstairs, it was best that she handle the situation now.

"Who was that?" Dominic asked with curiosity as she advanced toward him.

"Dominic, my team and I are very busy at the moment," Brook replied, purposefully ignoring his question. She brushed passed him. There was no need for the other two men to hear what she had to say, and she continued to walk for maybe ten feet until there was nowhere else to go. "As for Erika, there is more to the situation than what you've theorized, and I don't have to give my reasons as to why I removed Ms. Ashton from this case."

"You don't need to give your reasons, because it's obvious that you don't trust me." Dominic had his back to the heart of the bar, so he couldn't see the reactions that he'd garnered from his raised voice. "You believe that Erika was going to feed me information or some shit like that, right? She wouldn't do that, and I respect Riggs' position enough not to ask."

"Are you done?"

Dominic must have expected more of a response from Brook due to the way he raised an eyebrow and raised a hand in exasperation. By this point, the reporters weren't sure where to put their focus. Gus Norman had stopped at the bottom of the staircase on the other side of the bar, but he made no attempt to ascend them. He was undoubtedly curious about Dominic and how he fit into the murder investigation. Well, he wasn't the only one, but those remaining members of the press also wanted to know the same of Mr. Norman.

"Look, I didn't mean to make things worse," Dominic said ruefully after clearing his throat. He'd also lowered his voice after realizing the attention that he'd drawn to them. Movement above the banister upstairs revealed that Bit had opened the door. He could now be seen standing next to the wooden railing. "I'm sorry if I..."

Dominic continued to issue an apology, but someone else had caught Brook's attention when she'd taken her gaze off Bit. A male subject sitting at the table within her line of sight had crossed his ankle over his knee, revealing the tread on the bottom of his hiking boot. It just so happened to have a small rock lodged in the edge of the worn tread line.

"...should ask Riggs. Where is he tonight, anyway?"

Brook raised her gaze from the rock to meet the leveled stare of the unsub.

Chapter Twenty-Three

Brooklyn Sloane

October 2023

Tuesday — 9:17pm

Jace Mathers.

Not only had Jace been involved with the search of each victim, but he also matched specific characteristics listed in the profile. She recalled being in the bait shop to ask if he'd recognized Helen Beckham. He'd barely even glanced at the photograph, and she hadn't given it much thought at the time.

Brook never let on that she suspected Jace. She needed to substantiate her belief of his guilt, because many individuals probably had a small rock stuck in the treads of their hiking boots. On the other hand, she had never mentioned that miniscule fact during the briefing that he'd attended last week.

The vibration of Brook's phone had reaching into her back pocket.

"Riggs and Theo are investigating a lead," Brook replied as she turned her attention from Jace to Dominic. She motioned toward his table so that she could speak loud enough for the other two men to hear, but low enough not to carry to the other tables. "You say that you're trustworthy, Dominic. This will be your chance to prove it. You see, Riggs recognized a description of a walking stick that I believe the unsub had in his possession during the murders. It has come to our attention that Helen Beckham spoke to her killer the day before she was abducted from the trail. But I trust that you'll keep that information to yourself."

By this time, Dominic was standing right behind his chair.

Jace, on the other hand, had tightened his fingers around his knee to the point that his knuckles were white. Although Brook's experiment had resulted in the reaction she'd intentionally sought, she still didn't have enough confirmation to make an arrest. She certainly wouldn't do so in a room full of spectators. There was no telling how Jace would react, and she wouldn't put others' lives in danger.

"If you'll excuse me, I have a lot of work to do."

Jace stood quickly and blocked her path. His breathing had turned shallow. She also noticed that a small sheen of perspiration had coated his forehead. His fight, flight, freeze, and fawn responses were all at war with one another, and his body had yet to choose a reaction.

"Jace, I wanted to let you know that I was able to get you a discount on a security system that you'll be able to monitor yourself without the monthly fee," Brook said to help level out the adrenaline rushing through his veins. She'd much prefer the third option of the well-known stress response. No one was likely to get hurt, and she would have time to confirm her suspicions. "I'll give the information to Riggs, and he can forward it to you at a more convenient time."

Jace didn't reply nor did he move out of her way.

The conversations around them had become hushed to the point that the music seemed louder, and Brook could sense that Jace wasn't comfortable with the attention. She took matters into her own hands when her cell phone vibrated once more. She quickly scanned Bit's message, her remaining reservations fading away to be replaced with the options laid out in front of her.

Ava Zetter had been climbing with Jace's brother on that fateful day.

A previous conversation with Jace came to the forefront, and Brook recalled that he'd spoken in present tense when referring to his brother. At the time, she'd merely thought it was a slip of the tongue. It had been much more than that, but hindsight was twenty-twenty.

"I have to return a phone call," Brook murmured, feigning her distraction. There was a much better place and time to make an arrest. She glanced up from her phone and flashed a brief smile. "Enjoy the rest of your evening."

Brook stepped around Jace, not giving him time to say something in return. One of the reporters began to shout question after question, especially regarding Gus Norman. The press had done their due diligence, and one of the cameramen was already filming the man's response.

Brook motioned for Bit to extract Carissa's father from what was sure to be an unpleasant altercation with the media. Such overstimulation could create a perilous situation, because it was only a matter of time before her previous statement regarding Riggs' familiarity with said walking stick undoubtedly caused paranoia in Jace's already unstable state of mind.

"Do you know where he is?"

Jace had all but yelled out his question, causing Brook to slowly turn around. He was still standing near the table, although Dominic didn't seem to know what was taking place. Everyone's attention quickly shifted from Gus Norman to the man causing a scene.

"Who? Riggs?" Brook asked, once again doing her best to divert Jace's attention away from the very seed that she'd planted moments ago. She slowly slid her cell phone into her pocket so that her hands would be free to reach for her firearm if the situation deteriorated from here. "Riggs and Theo are tracking down a lead, though I doubt it will amount to much. They should be back soon."

Brook figured between her comments and the fact that Jace had to have heard about the site that they had discovered and believed was the place where Carissa Norman had been killed, there was no turning back. If Dominic hadn't called her over to the table, Jace most likely would have tried to hike the mountain well before morning, and long before a forensics team could reach the burnt remnants of the old structure.

Only Brook didn't believe in regrets or dwelling on what-ifs, and she sure as hell wouldn't start now. The only thing left to do was mitigate the damage and wait for the appropriate time to make an official arrest.

"I was talking about my brother," Jace asked in a different tenor. One that Brook imagined that he'd used when torturing his victims. "Chris. You know where he is, don't you?"

"Jace? What are you—"

"How could you not see it, Dominic?" Jace asked in true disbelief as he began to back away. Now that he was facing her, there was limited space between him and the exit. Brook was fine with Jace leaving a bar full of patrons. She even took a step forward to force him in that direction, preferring that there be no one in harm's way. "Chris isn't dead. My brother didn't die that day, and Ava knows the truth. I think Ava is keeping him up in those mountains somewhere. Ava knows where Chris is, and she's not telling me. Don't you remember?

Everyone knew that Ava didn't want my brother to leave town. He was supposed to go off to college, get a business degree, and then expand the family business. He was going to make us a household name. Ava didn't want to be without him, though. She did something to Chris. Tricked him into staying up there. I need to find him. I need to tell him that she's a liar."

By this time, the other friend who had been sitting at the table pushed back his chair. The man's concerned gaze kept flickering from Jace to Brook to all the individuals recording every second of Jace's mental breakdown.

"Dominic," Brook warned, slowly holding up her hand in warning. "Don't engage."

It was as if hearing his friend's name caused Jace to snap out of his delusion. He began to look over the gathering crowd in alarm, especially those who had professional news cameras aimed in his direction. No wonder so many years passed between victims. And it also wasn't so difficult to understand why the man's marriage had fallen apart in recent years.

Brook had done the math in her head and connected the exact moment that Jace had begun to experience delusions regarding his brother. Five years ago, two events had taken place—Jace's father had passed away, and Tricia Zetter had left town. The two combined events must have triggered some type of psychological response where Jace believed that his brother was still alive, and the young woman who had been with Chris Mathers at the time of his death had all the answers.

All sense of reality must have been suspended when Jace had spotted Carissa Norman, Helen Beckham, and Luna Breen. Brook figured their deaths triggered him back to the present, and he was left with the fallout of his actions. He'd had no choice but to cover up his crimes.

"I didn't mean to..." Jace's voice trailed off as he began to shake his head. He was no longer confrontational. He was desperate. Unfortunately, the door swung open to reveal two women. It was too late to warn them. Jace had already pulled the knife out of the sheath attached to his belt, giving Brook no choice but draw her firearm from its holster. "I'll slit her throat. I swear, I'll kill her right now if you don't let me walk out that door."

Jace's arm had tightened around the woman's neck. She let out a whimper, which could be heard throughout the bar. Someone had cut the music. Regrettably, the gasps and low murmurs only seemed to agitate him even more.

"And go where, Jace?" Brook asked calmly as she kept her weapon trained on him. She took a step to the right. Her objective had changed, and she couldn't allow Jace to leave with a hostage. "There's nowhere for you to go."

"My wife—" Jace's voice cracked as he attempted to hold himself together. Brook took another step, forcing Jace to keep his back to the far wall while moving farther away from the door. "She didn't deserve a husband like me. You need to tell her something for me. You need to tell her that I didn't mean to hurt them. I couldn't help myself."

"I know, Jace," Brook replied gently as she shifted some more. "Bit, please see to it that everyone leaves the bar."

Brook was pleased to know that Bit had positioned himself directly across from Jace. She'd trusted that Bit would know exactly what she needed, as they had trained for situations like this many times over the past two years. Bit might not ever feel at ease in the field, but he could definitely handle his own.

There were some individuals in the bar who couldn't get out of the place fast enough, and then were some who wanted to remain behind.

Reporters, those working the cameras, and Jace's close friends to name a few.

"Jace, you've already said that you didn't mean to hurt those women." Brook gradually relaxed her stance to show him that she wasn't going to be an additional threat. She even raised her weapon before slowly lowering it down to her side. She directed her next question to the young woman. "What's your name?"

"C-Cindy," she managed to say as she gripped Jace's forearm in desperation.

"Don't talk," Jace instructed as he tightened his grip around Cindy's neck. "I know what you're doing, and you need to stop. Just let me walk out that door."

"I can't do that, Jace. It's my job to make sure that everyone in here is safe." Brook loathed that some of this altercation would most likely be aired on the eleven o'clock news. She couldn't turn around, so she had no idea who was left with them inside the bar other than Dominic. He was in her line of vision, although their other friend had quickly left the second that he'd been given a chance. There was a way to use those who were left to her advantage, though. "Jace, you really don't want your wife or your brother-in-law to see the news tonight. They need to hear from you what happened and why. They deserve to hear it from you."

Brook's words seemed to cause Jace to pause, and he glanced toward Dominic.

"Isn't that right, Dominic?" Brook asked, pushing the man to engage with his friend now that the situation had escalated to the point of no return.

"Yeah. I mean, yes."

"Let Cindy go, Jace. Let her go, and I promise to get you the help that you need," Brook said softly as she could hear Bit still attempting to clear the area. She lifted her weapon to slide it inside her holster, all the while keeping a firm grip on the butt. "I'll holster my firearm, but in turn, I need you to release Cindy and slowly place the knife on the floor. You can do it, Jace."

Jace began to shake his head, but Brook held up her left hand to stop him from disputing her claim. He was emotional, unstable, and there was no telling what he might do if given time to try and process that life as he knew it was over.

"Jace, I'll have Bit call your wife. She'll drive down here, and I will make sure that there is time for the two of you to talk. She'll hear what you have to say, and she'll understand."

"My brother..."

"Is gone, and you know deep in heart that Chris died doing something that he loved," Brook said as she motioned for Cindy to step forward. The young woman was too terrified to try, so Brook had no choice but to get Jace to loosen his grip. "I spoke to Ava myself, Jace. She shared with me that losing Chris that fateful day still haunts her. She never got over losing him. And I know that you sometimes get confused, but don't you think that Chris would have figured out a way to come home if he'd somehow managed to survive that fall? There was no deception, Jace. Put down the knife, and I can get you the help that you need."

Jace wiped the tears that had fallen with the back of his hand while slowly nodding his agreement. The moment his arm hung to his side, Cindy let out a cry and ran for the exit. Brook never once shifted her focus from Jace.

"I didn't mean to hurt them," Jace whispered as he followed the motions of her left hand. She was slowly gesturing for him to lower the knife, not wanting to step too close and get caught off guard. Maintaining the upper hand was critical. "I don't know what happened. I can't explain it. I blinked, and those women had turned into Ava. She was with Chris that day. She kept trying to say that he—"

"Jace, your wife should be here soon," Brook said before he could convince himself all over again that Ava had done something terrible to his brother. "You don't want your wife to see you holding a knife, so I'm going to need you to place it on the floor. Go ahead. I'll sit with you until she joins us, okay?"

Jace nodded, though Brook could sense that he was overcome with extreme emotion. Such a mental break could go one of two ways, and she didn't want there to be any more destruction. The moment the blade of the knife clanked against the hardwood floor, Brook kept a hand on her firearm as she stepped forward to collect his weapon.

"Boss, he's going to—"

Gus Norman was a father who had nothing left to lose. Brook had hoped that he'd listened to Bit and vacated the area, but she couldn't blame him for wanting to witness the downfall of the man who had killed his daughter.

Gus had stayed close enough to the wall that Brook couldn't prevent him from reaching the knife first. She had no choice but to draw her weapon once more and call out a warning, but it was too late. Gus had already lunged forward with a force that was almost inhuman. His eyes were wide, his face had contorted in fury, and the momentum fueled by five years of grief-ridden rage helped drive the blade of the knife directly into the right side of Jace's torso.

Brook didn't hesitate, and she rushed forward before Gus had even taken a step back. She'd instinctively snatched a jacket that had been hanging from the back of a chair, ordering Dominic to call 911. Given that the media had almost certainly gone live on the air the second that Jace had taken a hostage, she figured the sheriff was already on his way to Moonshine Valley. Paramedics were needed, though she doubted they would arrive in time to save Jace's life.

Gus had stabbed the man directly in the liver.

"He killed my daughter," Gus sobbed as Bit all but dragged the man far enough away to allow Brook to kneel beside Jace. "He killed my baby girl. He killed..."

"Jace, stay with me," Brook ordered as she pressed the jacket against the wound. He instinctively grabbed her wrist while she confirmed that the knife was off to the side. It must have fallen from Gus' hand at some point before he'd taken a step back. "Look at me, Jace. Your wife is on the way. You want to talk to her, right?"

Jace tried to nod, but the slight movement had caused blood to sputter from his lips. She didn't let on that anything was wrong as she continued to talk to him. The tip of the knife must have punctured his lungs, as well as his liver. Unfortunately, nothing she said at this point would keep Jace alive long enough to reveal the burial sites of Carissa Norman and Helen Beckham. Brook had hoped to give their families some form of closure, but Carissa's father had taken the matter out of Brook's hands.

Gus Norman had chosen to go about attaining such accord in a different way. He hadn't thought about the price or the consequences. Grief had become his blinders. He'd acted on a father's instinct. Some would commend his actions while others would condemn them.

Jace's grip around her wrist loosened, and Brook slowly released the pressure on his wound. She ceased speaking as she leaned back on the heels of her boots. As he took his last breath, the echoes of his sins remained and would forever be heard.

Chapter Twenty-Four

Brooklyn Sloane

October 2023

Saturday — 9:28am

Vermont could only be described as a breathtaking mosaic of vibrant reds, oranges, and yellows. It was as if a beautiful painting had either come to life or had somehow pulled its painter into a world of warm serenity. The air carried a hint of earthiness, mostly due to the tinge of wood smoke rising from some of the chimneys in the quaint suburb. The two-story house nestled in among the other New England styled homes was adorned with a warm palette of earthy tones. Carved pumpkins had been placed on each step in preparation for the holiday, an aged wooden swing swayed gently back and forth in the light breeze, and a peaked roof with dark shingles protected those within.

Brook could understand why Sarah Evanston would choose to return to her childhood home, but nothing could protect her from Jacob Walsh. The former reporter had inadvertently hung a red neon sign above her mother's house. According to Agent Houser, nothing he'd said to Sarah had any impact on her decision to leave the witness protection program.

Brook was hoping to remedy that this morning.

Since she'd flown straight from North Carolina to Vermont, she'd made sure to have one of her business suits dry-cleaned at Moonshine Valley's tailor. She needed to address Sarah as a professional rather than just Jacob's sister. To do that, Brook had dressed as she would upon meeting a potential client.

It had taken a total of three days to wrap up the Mather investigation. Theo and Bit were still in Moonshine Valley to finish up some paperwork in tandem with the park rangers and the sheriff's office. Theo and Riggs had guided a federal forensics team to the third location. The investigation would be seen through to the end, regardless that Jace Mather's was dead. Should trace evidence be found that could tie the burnt structure to Carissa Norman, the results could help Gus Norman during his trial.

Brook had treated Otto to dinner last night, and the two of them also had a long discussion with Irene. Otto had offered to speak to the parole board on behalf of Ned and explain that he'd only crossed state lines and missed his parole check-ins due to fear. It was doubtful such testimony would reduce the additional time in prison, but no one ever really knew which way a judge would rule on those types of charges.

It seemed that a lot of situations hinged on what someone said nowadays, and today was no exception.

Brook had taken time to survey the immediate surroundings as she walked up the porch steps. The neighborhood was relatively quiet, and there didn't seem to be a lot of through traffic. As such, it would be more difficult for someone to monitor the occupants' activities.

Brook pressed the doorbell. It was the old-fashioned one without anything fancy. No hidden camera, no alarm system. There was a slight pause before she heard the muffled chime through the side window. She'd almost expected barking, but the following silence told her otherwise. A few moments later, a shadow could be seen through the thin stained-glass window in the center of the door.

"Ms. Evanston?"

Jemma Evanston seemed to have aged ten years in the past seventeen months. She'd stopped coloring her hair, and she'd lost a tremendous amount of weight. Brook had met Sarah's mother at the hospital when her daughter had been undergoing surgery to save her life. Unfortunately, mother and daughter had to say goodbye to each other while Sarah had still been in recovery.

"Hello, Ms. Sloane." The woman's cold tone wasn't unexpected, and Brook recalled how Theo had diffused a rather emotional situation in the waiting room while they'd stayed to hear whether or not Sarah would pull through. Brook had left the hospital soon afterward. "Please, come in."

Brook crossed over the threshold in silence. There was nothing she could say to the woman that would change the past. Her daughter had been brutally attacked, physically and emotionally damaged, and would never again be in front of a camera. Her career as a reporter had been cut short, and no amount of surgery would be able to fully restore her face to its former appearance.

Jacob preferred to slice away every bit of his victim's identity, and he wouldn't stop until Sarah Evanston was six feet underground.

Brook could only imagine the pain that Jemma had suffered by his actions, as well. She'd observed her daughter's injuries for only a brief moment, unable to be there for her during the subsequent surgeries and post-op care. Jemma had to say goodbye to her only child, knowing that was the only way to keep her safe.

Brook hadn't come to only speak with Sarah.

Brook was counting on Jemma's love for her daughter to convince Sarah to reenter the witness protection program.

"Sarah is having coffee in the four-season room. Straight through and to the left."

Without another word, Jemma walked away.

Sarah's mother had chosen to go through the living room and through an archway that most likely led to the kitchen. Brook had noted the aroma of coffee, but there was no hint of breakfast. She found it odd that Jemma would allow her daughter to speak with Brook without supervision. The woman had to know the reason for Brook's visit.

She didn't waste time, knowing that every second that Sarah wasn't in the witness protection program was simply more time for Jacob to figure out a way to finish what he'd started seventeen months ago. No prison cell would prevent him from succeeding, either...unless Brook could tip the scales in Sarah's favor.

"Hello, Sarah."

Brook mindfully stepped down into the four-seasons room. It must have been an addition to the house at some point in recent years, and the large windows overlooked a beautifully landscaped backyard with large sugar maple trees, numerous bird feeders, and at least two bird baths. Leaves had fallen from the trees and were being rustled here and there by the slight breeze.

"Say what you've come to say, and then you can see yourself out."

Brook crossed the hardwood floor, doing her best to soften the clicking sounds of her high heels. She'd gone over the different ways to approach their conversation, and the direction had depended on Sarah initial response.

"Sarah, you wanted to see me. Otherwise, I wouldn't be here." Brook set her purse on the floor next to the leg of the wicker chair. She finally met Sarah's gaze. The impact of the woman's physical appearance was like a blow to Brook's stomach, but she never gave way to that fact. She remained composed, and she would not allow Sarah to use her appearance to influence their discussion. "We both have things to say to one another. You might not believe that we are on a deadline, but we are, so I suggest we don't waste the time that we have been given."

Sarah Evanston's face was disfigured to the point of being unrecognizable. The deformities were so hideous that she hardly resembled a human visage anymore. The deep scars mapped out the history of her suffering, while the blemishes revealed the harsh attempts by surgeons to push through and patch up what flesh had been salvageable. Her disfigurement was so extreme that it was almost impossible for anyone to bear witness to such an atrocity.

"Not even a wince?" Sarah asked derisively, not even able to lift her lip to match her disdain. "You really are a coldhearted bitch, aren't you?"

Brook continued to meet Sarah's stare, refusing to rise to the bait.

"I guess I only have one question for you," Sarah said as she gripped a coffee mug in between her hands. Brook had noticed the scars of the defensive wounds that she'd incurred while trying to fight off Jacob's attack. "I honestly haven't stopped thinking about it since your interview aired on national television. Nice touch, by the way, attempting to garner the sympathy of the people."

Brook could have reminded Sarah that she'd been warned many times that Jacob Walsh was dangerous. The former reporter had been covering an investigation that had nothing to do with Brook's brother, but Sarah had basically taunted him several times by comparing Jacob's handywork to that of another killer. She'd done so knowing the risks, but she'd thought...well, she'd thought that her life was perfect.

Jacob's one pet peeve.

"What question do you have for me, Sarah?"

"Why didn't you do something?" Sarah asked, her voice thick with emotion. "You let your brother murder your best friend, your college roommate, your neighbor, and countless others. All you had to do was saying something."

Brook leaned forward and quietly removed the coffee cup from Sarah's hands. She set the hot beverage down on a side table. While she'd gone over and over the opportunities that she'd been presented with during her teenage years to expose her brother, she could also recall being plagued with many doubts.

She always came back to the same question—how could two siblings who were raised in the same household, in the same town, and by the same parents turn out so different?

"Who was your best friend in high school?" Brook asked as she settled back into her chair. "What was her name?"

"I don't know how that has anything to do with—"

"What was your best friend's name when you were in high school?"

"Rachel."

"Did Rachel have a brother?"

"Yes."

"Did you know him well?"

"Yes, but—"

"Would you have believed Rachel had she told you that her brother was the one who abducted a girl from your school and slashed the flesh off her face?"

Sarah's eyes filled with tears, but they were more for herself than Pamela Murray, the young girl who Brook had been referencing from her own childhood. It was so easy for people to look back and place blame on everyone but the person responsible. Brook was one of those individuals, because there would never be a single day that passed by that she didn't hold herself accountable for the deaths of Jacob's victims. It was the reason that she'd dedicated her life to stopping him, and she couldn't do that without Sarah's help.

"Sarah, I need you to listen to me. I know that you want more than anything for your life to return to some semblance of normalcy. You want to be near your mother when you undergo more corrective surgery, and you want to sleep in a place that you once felt secure," Brook said as she leaned forward. She'd heard the faintest sound of footsteps outside the four-seasons room. Brook needed Jemma Evanston's help, and this was the perfect opportunity to turn an adversary into an ally. "I spoke with Agent Houser, and he's been in touch with the U.S. Marshal Service. They are willing to allow your mother to join the program with you."

"That's not true," Sarah countered with a shake of her head. "My handler explained that witness protection doesn't work that way unless—"

"They've made an exception," Brook stated matter-of-factly, not bothering to go into the details. She'd had to use a few of those coveted favors that she'd stored up over the years, but it was Sarah's only chance at a life. "You and your mother will be given new identities, and the two of you can start over somewhere else."

"There is nowhere for me to go," Sarah said in anguish, curling her fingers into the palms of her hands. "Look at me! Look at this face, and you tell me that I'll be able to blend in somewhere. Agent Houser and my handler have already tried to convince me that I made the wrong decision, but they don't get it. It doesn't even matter if I leave the state let alone the country. If your brother wants to find me, all he has to do is search social media for a disfigured woman who looks like a monstrous freak. I can't even walk into the front entrance of a hospital without hearing the whispers and the—"

"Do you want the same for your mother?"

Brook's question brought Sarah up short. It had also prompted a quick inhalation from Jemma, who had finally brought herself to join them. She was now standing in the doorway, her frail frame in full view.

"Jacob will not stop until he finishes what he started, Sarah. If he finds you here, do you really believe that he will allow your mother to live?" Brook wasn't going to get into specifics, because Jacob would never intentionally take the life of someone like Jemma Evanston. Fear was a powerful motivator, though. "You talk of blame, but what about you? The day that you exited the witness protection program, the second that you entered this house, you put your mother in danger."

"Sarah, honey," Jemma murmured as she joined her daughter on the small wicker couch. "You know that I love you. You're my baby girl, and I will go with you wherever they send us."

"But it won't matter," Sarah whispered in distress as she held her mother's hands. "Look at me, Mom."

Brook reached into her purse and pulled out some information that Bit had been kind enough to put together. There were only a handful of surgeons who had successfully performed a face transplant. With any luck, Jacob would still believe that Sarah was undergoing corrective surgery. He would have already searched out plastic surgeons who specialized in reconstructive surgery, and there was a good chance that

Sarah would already be living a brand-new life as someone else before the thought of a face transplant crossed his mind.

It was long shot, but it was one that Brook was willing to take.

"I'm not saying that there aren't risks," Brook said after having explained Sarah's options. "There are many, but you have alternatives than merely waiting around for Jacob to figure out a way to escape prison. As much as I will do everything in my power to keep my brother behind bars, I also know him well enough that no amount of security will prevail. It's not a matter of if, but when."

Brook reached down for her purse, and she noticed that Jemma's gaze was drawn to the holster at her waist. Maybe now that she had a chance to be with her daughter, Jemma would finally find a way to move forward, as well. Brook stood after gauging the amount of time she'd been inside the house.

"I need your answer, Sarah." Brook hadn't included Jemma in her request, because she would do whatever was necessary to be with her daughter. "Are you going to wait here for Jacob to come finish what he started, or are you going to start a new life?"

Sarah stared at her mother for a moment before finally nodding her response.

"Good." Brook slipped the strap of her purse over her shoulder. As predicted, the doorbell rang. Both mother and daughter tensed at the sound, but Brook quickly put them at ease...well, as much as possible, given the current circumstances. "You've been assigned a new handler. He's waiting for you outside."

"We need time to pack," Jemma said in confusion as she released Sarah's hands. "It shouldn't take long. We can—"

"Mom." Sarah slowly stood. "It doesn't work that way. We can't take anything. We simply start over."

"But how will we pay—"

"Mrs. Evanston, your handler will explain everything to you on the way."

Brook didn't bother to add a destination. She had no idea where the handler would take them, and that was for the best. She'd accomplished what she'd set out to do, and time was of the essence.

"Do you have no compassion?" Sarah asked once they'd reached the front door. She'd stopped and turned around to confront Brook in what she could only assume was genuine curiosity. "None? I've been through this, but my mother's world is about to be turned upside down."

"Your mother lost her world the day that you were attacked," Brook stated pragmatically. "The choice that I've given the two of you today *was* made from compassion, Sarah. I learned a long time ago to compartmentalize. I had to, and not only in order to survive, but to get through each day knowing that I have the power to stop Jacob Walsh. And that power would mean absolutely nothing if I allowed my emotions to get in the way."

Sarah's mother called out to her from the porch. She hesitated briefly before reaching for a decorative scarf. She then placed it over her hair before tying the ends underneath her chin. Pulling the delicate fabric until it covered both sides of her face, she stepped outside. It was then that she looked over her shoulder to give one more parting line.

"You should have killed your brother when you had the chance."

Brook remained on the porch as the handler escorted both women to a black sedan. Once they were both settled in the back seats, he shut the door before walking around to the driver's side door. He lifted a hand in gesture before disappearing behind the tinted windows.

Had this situation been presented to Brook ten years ago, she might have crumbled under Sarah's accusations. Brook would have pleaded for forgiveness, and she would have collapsed under the guilt. Time, experience, and the growth that she'd undergone in the past couple of years had her understanding that blame could be either a wasted emotion or a power motivator.

There was no changing the past, only focusing on the future.

Brook reached into the side pocket of her purse and pulled out her cell phone. She gently pressed the name on the top of her speed dial list and held the phone to her ear. The call was answered on the first ring.

"Why a private villa?"

"It's a sanctuary of tranquility." Graham's rich voice carried across the line, a reminder that there was light in the darkness. One only needed to look beyond the edge of despair. "You'll witness the rhythm of existence in the waves, and you'll experience your heartbeat become one with the ebb and flow of the tides. It's a surreal experience that I'd like to introduce you to, Brooklyn."

Graham had a unique way of viewing life, even during its ugliest days. He'd suffered losses and witnessed atrocities that not even she could imagine, and yet he still managed to view every day as a blessing.

She wanted to see the world through his eyes.

More than anything, she yearned to find solace in the serenity.

"I'm looking forward to it, Graham."

Chapter Twenty-Five

Jacob Walsh

October 2023

Tuesday — 4:03pm

Every minute that passed inside the prison walls seemed longer than the last. Time slowly chipped away at an inmate's insanity, the isolation mimicking a cancer that ate away one's body from the inside out. Despair and darkness were the only constants, and even the most hardened criminals were reduced to mere shadows of their former selves.

Jacob slowly smiled as he was escorted past the degenerates of society.

He wasn't like his current neighbors, and it was only a matter of time before he bid them all goodbye. His first attempt at a breakout had been met with resistance. Though he had planned many escape routes in case of obstacles, it had still come as a shock when his baby sister had finally gotten the upper hand.

It was the first time in their lives that Brook had ever been one step ahead of him, and he could admit that anger had been his first response. Given that he had little else to think about inside his cell, the rage that had consumed him had gradually faded into pride. His sister fought so hard against the belief that they were practically one and the same. He'd feel sorry for her if she hadn't proven her worth at being such an adversary.

Jacob had warned his sister that he would never allow her to be the normal one, and he would make good on his promise. Such a pledge was the reason that he'd put into place so many arrangements.

One of the two guards came to a stop in front of the infirmary. Within seconds, the sound of the locks disengaging could be heard echoing throughout the hallway. By the time that Jacob and the second guard had reached the threshold, the door was wide open, revealing a male subject wearing a dark grey suit.

"Dr. Mizrahi, I presume?"

The surgeon remained silent, his contempt for Jacob evident in his stare.

Samuel Mizrahi merely nodded toward the exam table. One of the guards led Jacob to the small step stool, though there was no need for such assistance. He was tall enough to sit on the table with ease. Once he was settled, he waited patiently for Mizrahi to address the email that had been sent to his office.

Before Jacob had strolled into FBI headquarters and turned himself in, he'd scheduled certain messages to be sent on specific days in the future. There was another one scheduled to be sent three months from now, all from different accounts, of course. If all went as planned today, he'd be able to cancel the rest of the emails.

"I'm here because of my duty to my patient."

"It's good to know that you take your oath seriously, Dr. Mizrahi," Jacob replied as he shifted his weight to be more comfortable for the conversation ahead. "I'll be in good hands then."

"You're assuming that your offer will be approved." Dr. Mizrahi stood a good eight feet away from the exam table. "Federal inmates are not usually allowed to be living donors unless it is for an immediate family member, and only then in rare cases."

"I'm trusting that Senator Cary will see to it that an exception can be made," Jacob replied before lifting both hands to rest against his chest. The metal links of the cuffs made a bit of noise before being silenced by the fabric of his uniform. "I have many amends to make for my previous...shall we call them misdeeds?"

"The chances of you being a match to Jonah Cary are slim at best."

"I have no doubt that my lab reports were attached to the email you received, Dr. Mizrahi." Jacob lowered his forearms and linked his fingers together in confidence. It wasn't like the senator would turn down such an offer. "I'm sure you'll run your own tests to confirm, but you wouldn't be here if you thought you were wasting your time."

"And how exactly did you know that Senator Cary's son needed a liver?"

One didn't just turn themselves over to the federal government without a failsafe. Numerous ones, in fact. What Dr. Mizrahi was looking for were reassurances.

"Does it really matter in the grand scheme of things? I have the ability to save a young boy's life. Run as many tests as you like, Dr. Mizrahi. I have all the time in the world, unlike Jonah Cary."

"You do understand that should you be a match, should this surgery take place, you will be guarded twenty-four-seven in a private room with no windows, no access to unapproved staff, and no means of escape?"

"You've hurt my feelings, Dr. Mizrahi," Jacob replied with a rueful smile. "I'm merely a man who is looking for redemption."

Jacob took it upon himself to swing his legs up onto the exam table. He made himself comfortable, a deep satisfaction settling inside of him. He wouldn't be confined for much longer. He'd spoken the truth about redemption. His salvation laid with finding Sarah Evanston, and he wouldn't rest until he finished what he'd set out to accomplish.

"Dr. Mizrahi?"

A guard had stepped into the infirmary. He waited by the door for the surgeon to look up from the file in his hand, but Jacob decided to move things along. He'd known that the moment the email was sent, such interest in him would send enough shockwaves that the ripples would reach Brook and her firm.

"I do believe that you have a phone call, Dr. Mizrahi." Jacob closed his eyes as he leaned his head against the pillow. He couldn't help but smile once more. "Please say hello to my sister for me."

~ The End ~

Prepare yourself for an exciting clash of intellects as two powerful opponents face off in USA Today Bestselling Author Kennedy Layne's latest gripping thriller within the Touch of Evil series...

Whispers of Sin

Lorelei Jameson, a woman of wealth and mystery, strides purposefully through the doors of S&E Investigations with a mixture of desperation and determination. A year ago, tragedy struck when her younger sister met a horrific end. The cause of death was heinous and unmistakable: a clear, plastic bag had been wrapped around the young woman's head, effectively suffocating her. Now, an eerie sense of déjà vu grips a prominent town as news spreads of another victim succumbing to the same merciless end.

Former FBI consultant Brooklyn Sloane agrees to take the case. However, local authorities bristle at the involvement of a private firm muddling their investigation. Brook and her team are met with even more resistance when she reveals a crucial detail from her profile—the killer is a woman.

Brook and her team find themselves entangled with a master manipulator. Her relentless pursuit of justice will be tested like never before as the boundaries begin to blur between the hunter and the hunted. Who will be left standing when the twisted game of cat and mouse finally comes to a shocking end?

Other Books By Kennedy Layne

Touch of Evil Series

Thirst for Sin

Longing for Sin

Awakening Sin

Possessed by Sin

Corrupted by Sin

Fleeing From Sin

Tainted by Sin

Echoes of Sin

Whispers of Sin

The Graveside Mysteries

Twisted Graves

Delicate Graves

Shadowed Graves

The Widow Taker Trilogy

The Forgotten Widow

The Isolated Widow

The Reclusive Widow

Hex on Me Mysteries

If the Curse Fits

Cursing up the Wrong Tree

The Squeaky Ghost Gets the Curse

The Curse that Bites

Curse Me Under the Mistletoe

Gone Cursing

Paramour Bay Mysteries

Magical Blend

Bewitching Blend

Enchanting Blend

Haunting Blend

Charming Blend

Spellbinding Blend

Cryptic Blend

Broomstick Blend

Spirited Blend

Yuletide Blend

Baffling Blend

Phantom Blend

Batty Blend

Pumpkin Blend

Frosty Blend

Stony Blend

Cocoa Blend

Shamrock Blend

Campfire Blend

Stormy Blend

Sparkling Blend

Hallow Blend

Dandelion Blend

Office Roulette Series

Means

Motive

Opportunity

Keys to Love Series

Unlocking Fear

Unlocking Secrets

Unlocking Lies

Unlocking Shadows

Unlocking Darkness

Surviving Ashes Series

Essential Beginnings

Hidden Flames

Buried Flames

Endless Flames

Rising Flames

CSA Case Files Series

Captured Innocence

Sinful Resurrection

Renewed Faith

Campaign of Desire

Internal Temptation

Radiant Surrender

Redeem My Heart

A Mission of Love

Red Starr Series

Starr's Awakening

Hearths of Fire

Targets Entangled

Igniting Passion

Untold Devotion

Fulfilling Promises

Fated Identity

Red's Salvation

The Safeguard Series

Brutal Obsession

Faithful Addiction

Distant Illusions

Casual Impressions

Honest Intentions

Deadly Premonitions

About the Author

Kennedy Layne is a USA Today bestselling author. She draws inspiration for her romantic thrillers in part from her not-so-secret second life as a wife of a retired Marine Master Sergeant. He doubles as her critique partner, beta reader, and military consultant. Kennedy also has a deep love for cozy mysteries, thrillers, and basically any book that can keep her guessing until the very end. They live in the Midwest with their menagerie of pets. The loyal dogs and mischievous cats appreciate her writing days as much as she does, usually curled up in front of the fireplace.

Email:

kennedylayneauthor@gmail.com

Facebook:

facebook.com/kennedy.layne.94

Twitter:

twitter.com/KennedyL_Author

Website:

www.kennedylayne.com

Newsletter:

www.kennedylayne.com/meet-kennedy.html

Printed in the USA
CPSIA information can be obtained
at www.ICGtesting.com
LVHW022321011024
792691LV00038B/964